IAN SANSOM is the author of *September 1, 1939: A Biography of a Poem, Paper: An Elegy* and the *Mobile Library Mystery* series of novels. He is also a frequent contributor to the *Guardian* and the *London Review of Books*, and a regular broadcaster of BBC Radio 3 and Radio 4. *The Sussex Murder* is the fifth in *The County Guides* series, following *The Norfolk Mystery, Death in Devon, Westmorland Alone* and *Essex Poison*.

Praise for *The County Guides*:

'A delightful, idiosyncratic mystery set in the Thirties . . . There is a touch of Sherlock Holmes and a dash of Lord Peter Wimsey, but the total is put together with a charm that is teasingly precious . . . Beautifully crafted by Sansom, Professor Morely promises to become a little gem of English crime writing; sample him now' *Daily Mail*

'The magnificent Morley is very good company, and Sansom has a lovely way with a mind-bending puzzle' *The Times*

'Sansom is both celebrating and sending up the golden age of detective novels when, in the 1930s, Dorothy L Sayers and Agatha Christie were the queens of crime . . . leaves you looking forward to the next maniacal mystery tour'
MARK SANDERSON, *Evening Standard*

Also by Ian Sansom

September 1, 1939: A Biography of a Poem
Paper: An Elegy
The Truth About Babies
Ring Road
The Enthusiast Almanack
The Enthusiast Field Guide to Poetry

THE MOBILE LIBRARY SERIES
Mr Dixon Disappears
The Delegates' Choice
The Bad Book Affair
The Case of the Missing Books

THE COUNTY GUIDES SERIES
The Norfolk Mystery
Death in Devon
Westmorland Alone
Essex Poison

THE COUNTY GUIDES

THE SUSSEX
MURDER

IAN SANSOM

Fully Illustrated Throughout

4th ESTATE • *London*

4th Estate
An imprint of HarperCollins*Publishers*
1 London Bridge Street
London SE1 9GF

www.4thEstate.co.uk

First published in Great Britain in 2019 by 4th Estate
This paperback edition published in 2020 by 4th Estate

1

Copyright © Ian Sansom 2019

A catalogue record for this book is available from the British Library

ISBN 978-0-00-820738-0

Printed and bound by CPI Group (UK) Ltd, Croydon, CR0 4YY

MIX
Paper from
responsible sources
FSC
www.fsc.org
FSC™ C007454

This book is produced from independently certified FSC™ paper
to ensure responsible forest management

Find out more about HarperCollins and the environment at
www.harpercollins.co.uk/green

For Ciaran

God gives all men all earth to love,
But since man's heart is small,
Ordains for each one spot shall prove
Beloved over all.
Each to his choice, and I rejoice
The lot has fallen to me
In a fair ground – in a fair ground –
Yea, Sussex by the sea!

RUDYARD KIPLING

CHAPTER 1

At about four o'clock, Miss Lizzie Walter, a teacher at the King's Road Primary School, said goodbye to her young pupils. The children clattered out into the dark streets of the town, preparing for the night's revelries – and Miss Lizzie Walter was never seen alive again.

Lizzie lived with her parents, respectable working-class folk, at 11 Saddle Street. Her father was a tradesman, her mother a housewife. She was young, intelligent, hard-working, good-looking. She liked literature, music and art. She was dressed that day in a double-breasted brown tweed coat, but wore no hat.

It is about a twenty-minute walk from King's Road School to Saddle Street and normally Lizzie would have returned home by four thirty, but because of the Bonfire Night preparations her mother and father felt no anxiety regarding her failure to return. Bonfire Night in Lewes is a famous night of revelry. They assumed that she had met friends and gone to join the celebrations.

It was not until six o'clock the following morning, when they discovered her bed had not been slept in, that her parents raised the alarm – and shortly after when I found Lizzie's body floating in the lido at Pells Pool.

We had, at that point, been in Sussex for less than twenty-four hours.

CHAPTER 2

OF ALL OUR TRIPS AND TOURS during those years, our trip
to Sussex was one of the darkest and most difficult: it was
a turning point. We arrived, as always, intent on doing good
and reporting on the good: we were, as so often, on a quest.
We departed less than heroes. None of us could hold our
heads up high.

The County Guides series of guidebooks, as some
readers will doubtless be aware, but others may now well
have forgotten, were intended by their once world-famous
progenitor and my erstwhile employer, Swanton Morley,
as a celebration of all that is good in England, volume after
volume after volume of guides to the English counties, celebrating their variety and uniqueness. *The County Guides*
– in their smart green uniform editions, at one time as familiar as the Bible or the old Odhams *Encyclopaedia* on the
shelves of the aspirant working and middle classes – were
hymns to the noble spirit of Britain. They were intended as
uplifting literature – 'up lit' was the term coined by Morley
in an interview in the short-lived *Progress* magazine in June
1939: 'What this nation needs now is up lit.'

In reality, in every county we travelled to in those

long years together, researching and writing the books, we seemed to encounter the very worst of human nature: downbeat doesn't do it justice. Downcast, downfaced, downthrown and downright.

In Norfolk it was treachery, in Devon it was devilry, in Westmorland tragedy and in Essex farce, but in Sussex we encountered not only murder but mayhem and depravity: it was not just the burning of the crosses and the flaming tar barrels, the torchlit processions, the sheer anarchy of Bonfire Night in Lewes, it was the revelation to ourselves and to each other of our own terrible inadequacies. For ever after, Morley referred to *The County Guides: Sussex* as 'flaming' Sussex. (He had pet names for all the books, in fact: *The County Guides: Essex* was always *Essex Poison* to him, Westmorland was *Westmorland Alone*, Cheshire *Rogue Cheshire*, and etcetera and etcetera).*

---

* Morley's names for our adventures, in roughly the order in which they occurred were: *The Norfolk Mystery, Death in Devon, Westmorland Alone, Essex Poison, The Sussex Murder, Northumberland's Dead, The West Riding Evil, Kent's Secret, Rutland Deceased, The Lincolnshire Riddle, Wiltshire's Ruin, Hampshire Innocents, Rogue Cheshire, Warwickshire's Strangers, Gloucestershire Skeletons, Black Cornwall, The London Crime Co., East Riding Alibis, Berkshire Damned, The Malice of Durham, Bedfordshire's Revenge, The Hertfordshire Revenge, The Lancashire Tragedy, Middlesex Thieves, Nottinghamshire's Fear, Somerset's Night, The Dorset Judgement, Bloody Suffolk, Vanished Huntingdonshire, Buckinghamshire Troubles, Tainted Shropshire, The Challenge of North Riding, Repentant Leicestershire, The Cambridgeshire Killings, The Northamptonshire Sorrows, Derbyshire's Shadow, Oxfordshire Wrongs, Lost Herefordshire, Staffordshire's Danger, False Surrey, The Curse of Cumberland,* and *The Worcestershire Sickness.* My own nickname for our final adventure together is *The End of Jersey and Guernsey.*

Before we arrived in Sussex, Morley, as usual, had drawn up a long list of what to see, with an even longer list of annotations. Having already produced our *County Guides* to Norfolk, Devon, Westmorland and Essex we had begun to develop a kind of routine. We would meet either in London or at Morley's vast and eccentric estate in Norfolk, St George's, where he would brief me and Miriam, his daughter, and we would then embark upon our adventure in his beloved Lagonda, Miriam at the wheel, Morley strapped in behind his typewriter, and me as general factotum.

For our journey to Sussex, Morley's list began with Abbotsford Gardens ('Open to the public on weekdays only, alas, but fabulous aviaries – and monkeys! – and light refreshments!') and included, in addition to all those Sussex places one might reasonably expect to find in any good guidebook and gazetteer, many places that one might reasonably not, such as the Balcombe Viaduct ('A marvel of Victorian engineering!'), the Pavilion in Bexhill ('A marvel of modern engineering!'), the Rising Sun Inn at North Bersted ('The Jubilee Stamp Room: one of the Seven Wonders of the Modern World. A whole room papered from floor to ceiling with postage stamps, said to number in excess of three million'), the Chattri ('War memorial erected by the India Office and the Corporation of Brighton to commemorate the brave Hindu and Sikh soldiers who died in the Great War'), Chick Hill ('Marvellous view to France'), Clapham Wood ('Satanic mists, apparently!'), Climping ('We must visit the Moynes!'), Frant ('Lovely obelisk'), the Heritage Craft School near Chailey ('The salvation home for cripples!'), some Knucker Holes ('Bottomless, some of them, reputedly'), Mick Mills' Race ('Wonderful avenue in St Leonard's Forest where the smuggler Mick Mills raced the devil and won'), Shoreham Beach ('For the railway carriage homes, of course! England's Little Hollywood!') and the Witterings, for no good reason, both East and West.

I'll be honest, I had absolutely no interest in Sussex.

The truth was, I shouldn't even have been in Sussex.

Before we arrived in Sussex, I had decided to resign.

I had at that time worked for Morley for a period of exactly four months. This was late in 1937, after my return from Spain, where I had discovered, to my horror, the horrors of war. Perhaps I should have known better: now at least I knew the worst. Adrift in London, I had answered an advertisement in *The Times* and had found myself apprenticed to the most famous, the most popular – and certainly the most prolific – writer in England. During those four intense, turbulent months, Morley had somehow produced four books – Norfolk, Devon, Westmorland and Essex – in addition to his usual output of articles and opinion pieces on everything from the care of houseplants for the *Lady's Companion*, to the etymology and usage of strange, obscure and pretty much useless words in *John O'London's Weekly*, to endless wearying tales of moral uplift and derring-do for anyone who would have them, including the Catholic *Extension*, the *Christian Observer* and many and various – and thankfully now defunct – earnest freethinking journals.

As his assistant, it was my job not just to sharpen Morley's pencils – though pencil-sharpening, pen-procuring, inkwell-filling, notebook-filing and all manner of other stationery-related activities were indeed a large part of my daily activities – but also to help him and Miriam correct proofs, take photographs, deal with correspondence, pack and prepare for our long journeyings round the country, and to perform all other duties as necessary and as arising, including providing physical protection, offering what would now probably be described as 'emotional' support and encouragement, and of course listening to what one biographer – borrowing a phrase, I believe, from Gilbert and Sullivan – memorably described as Morley's 'elegant outpouring of the lion a-roaring', but which I might describe as his endless, pointless, glorious ramble.

While Morley was working on the proofs for *Essex*, I had been tasked with putting the finishing touches – 'Semi-gloss 'em, Sefton, but semi-gloss only, please, we don't want too much of your smooth and lyrical, thank you' – to a number of articles, including something on 'The Nature and Management of Children', about which I knew precisely nothing; another titled, depressingly, 'Conversations with Vegetables'; and another about the sound of tarmac for an American magazine that called itself *Common Sense* but which displayed no sign whatsoever of possessing such and which paid Morley vast sums for articles on subjects so strange that Miriam liked to joke that the magazine might usefully change its name to *Complete and Utter Nonsense*. ('The Sound of Tarmac', for example, was intended as a companion piece to two inexplicably popular articles we'd produced for the magazine, one on the quality of modern British kerbstones and another on regional, national and international variations in the size of flagstones. The Yanks couldn't get enough of this sort of stuff.) My most recent work, gussying up one of Morley's quick opinion pieces – eight hundred words for a magazine with the unfortunate title of the *Cripple*, a publication aimed at war veterans and the disabled, in praise of Samuel Smiles's *Self-Help*, all about the importance of self-discipline in overcoming difficulties and achieving happiness – had left me feeling not so much self-helped as self-disgusted, as if I had drunk water from a sewer or a poisoned well.

Four months in, I was physically exhausted, I was enervated.

And I was envious.

At college I had naively believed that I was the master of my own destiny; in Spain, I had realised that none of us truly determines our fate; and now I was beginning to think that my entire life was a matter of complete insignificance. The real problem was that the longer I worked for Morley – a true literary lion, a working-class hero, an international figure who was big in Japan and who counted the Queen of Italy among his fans, and indeed frequent correspondents, a man who had pulled himself up by his own bootstraps and who had then set about pulling up the bootstraps of the nation – the more I worked for this infernal writing machine, this actual living and breathing – there is no other word for it – *genius*, the more I was reminded of my own lack of drive and determination and brilliance and the more I came to despair of the possibility of ever making a significant contribution to the world of letters myself. I had long harboured dreams of becoming a writer, yet the only writing I did for myself now was the occasional postcard, my betting slips and IOUs. Writing for Morley, a master of the English language, I had become thoroughly disgusted with words. His facility both fascinated and appalled me. His achievements seemed incredible – and worthless. The last poem I had written consisted of exactly four words: 'Vexed ears/ Wasted years.' *The County Guides* were crushing me. I was beginning to feel no better than a broken, beaten dog.

My only consolation was that between books I was able to return to London, where I would enjoy all the things that city has to offer and would attempt to iron out the various knots and kinks that had formed in my mind and my body by consorting with the kind of people who had knots and kinks of their own to deal with – my kind of people.

Which is how I had ended up, on a Saturday night at the very end of October 1937, at the all-night vapour bath on Brick Lane in the East End.

CHAPTER 3

IT WAS EXACTLY WHAT I NEEDED. Frankly, if you can't get exactly what you need in the East End on a Saturday night, there must be something wrong with you – something *seriously* wrong with you.

After the relaxation and rigours of the vapour bath, I had adjourned to a pub nearby for light refreshments and to enjoy the company of people who certainly looked like, but who may or may not have been, thieves, prostitutes and ponces. One should never judge by appearances, of course, according to Morley. One should be open-minded. One should take people as you find them. The only problem is, when you take people as you find them, you'll often find that they'll already have taken you – in every sense – for everything. After a couple of hours of drinking and singing around the piano, I somehow found myself taking up the generous offer of hospitality and a bed for the night by a sharp-suited Limehouse chap I'd never met before and a couple of his lovely female companions. I did not judge them by appearances, being entirely incapable of doing so – and it turned out, alas, contra-Morley, that this sharp-suited individual with his female companions was indeed a ponce with his prostitutes, but I was determined I was not going to allow them to prove themselves also as thieves.

I awoke early after our long and largely sleepless night, having eventually fallen into an unsettling dream in which I was sitting with a man at a large glass table, drinking champagne, him wearing a silk suit and brightly polished shoes, and with a set of scales before him and saying he had a special present for me. At least, I think it was a dream. What woke me was the sound of birds.

At St George's, in the cottage that Morley had provided for me in the grounds of the estate, I would often wake to the sound of birdsong. All else there was silence, though if you listened carefully you could hear not only the sound of water bubbling and swirling in the faraway streams and in the cottage well, you could actually hear your blood coursing through your veins. It was unsettling, the country.

But in London: birdsong?

I remember being momentarily confused. I lay gazing at a crack in the ceiling above me, through which it would have been possible to insert my fist.

Was that the sound of birds?

Was I in Norfolk?

Or was I back in Spain?

Was I dreaming?

It was definitely the sound of birds. Lots of birds.

Out of the corner of my eye I could see empty beer bottles and cigarette butts piled in a saucer. The place, wherever it was, seemed dirty and unloved. I raised myself up on my elbow. There was a woman lying asleep beside me.

And then I remembered.

It had been a *very* long night.

I turned my head. My clothes lay discarded on the floor. The Limehouse chap and another woman lay sleeping in a bed opposite. There was a lighted cigarette smouldering in an ashtray on an upturned case by the bed, and what looked like a fresh glass of whisky perched precariously next to it.

I took some deep breaths and then coughed quietly in order to gauge any response.

Nothing.

Having thus determined to my satisfaction that my new friends were either fast asleep or at least innocently dozing, I rose quickly and quietly, intent on hanging on to whatever remained of my dignity and in my wallet, gathered up my clothes and fled from the room, down a dark stairway and along a corridor towards a door.

It was precisely at that moment, cold and ashamed, and the previous evening's activities returning clearly to my mind, that I determined that I should no longer live my life as a slave to my whims and desires, or indeed as a slave to the whims and desires of others, but that I should once again attempt to master myself and my destiny. It was then that I determined that I had had enough of being used by life, by London, and by everyone. Morley believed that on our grand tour we were surveying one of the great wonders of the world – *Great* Britain – and London of course, as it always has, believed it was *the* great city in this Great Britain, but at that time, in those years, it felt nothing like great and I felt nothing but forever lost and losing, a man condemned to life on a slowly sinking ship.

Stumbling as I reached the door, I thought I heard movement from my companions up above, and so fled from this latest prison of my temporary lodgings with new resolve – and into a scene of utter chaos.

CHAPTER 4

IT *WAS* THE SOUND OF BIRDS, and it was the sound as much as the sight that struck me, a cacophony of whistles and trills, accompanied by the bass-soprano of the voices of men and women, and the deeply disturbing sound of whimpering animals.

'Pretty foreign birds! Pretty foreign birds!'

Out on the street, as far as the eye could see, piled one upon the other, there were cages full of birds: larks, thrushes, canaries, pigeons and parrots. There were also dogs and cats in boxes, and chickens and snakes and gerbils and guinea pigs and weasels and tortoises, and goodness knows what else, animals of every kind everywhere. Here, a newborn litter of puppies tumbling over each other in a child's cot being used as a makeshift pen. There, a raggedy black rooster peering out of an old laundry basket. And endlessly, everywhere you looked, there were bulldogs and boxers and pit bulls straining at their leashes, restrained by men who looked like bulldogs, boxers and pit bulls straining at their leashes. It was a Noah's Ark, with flat caps and cobbles.

I'd forgotten about the market.

On Sundays, in those days, the centre of London shifted;

it went east to Bethnal Green and its environs, from the junction with Bethnal Green Road and Shoreditch High Street, onto Sclater Street and Chance Street and Cheshire Street: here, on Sundays, you could buy and sell just about anything. Petticoat Lane, down by Aldgate, became the people's Piccadilly, the mecca for cheap, cheerful and 'unofficial' goods: on Sundays, the East End became the dirty, cracked dark mirror of the West.

And here I was, in the midst of it, Club Row Market – the place where the working men and women of London came for their animals. A nightmare of containment and enclosure.

As I shut the door behind me and entered the chaos, I remember looking up and noting that opposite, across the road, there was a wet fish shop with the traditional, unnecessary sign outside, 'Fresh Fish Sold Here'. (This sort of signage was one of Morley's many bugbears, addressed in one of his popular, hectoring *Some Dos and Don'ts* pamphlets, *Shop Signage: Some Dos and Don'ts*. 'We know it's "Here", because it's here, we know it is being "Sold" because it is a shop, and if not "Fresh", then, frankly, what? So "Fish", in short, for a fish shop, will suffice.') A man in a white apron stood outside the 'Fish' shop, scooping jet-black, chopped, gelatinous jellied eels into white enamel bowls: the mere sight of it made me want to retch; I had to struggle to contain myself. Pausing mid-scoop, as if having sensed my dis-ease, the man in the apron looked across at me and scowled in disapproval. Gagging rather, I glanced away to see standing directly in front of me an elderly gentleman in a fez selling hot roasted nuts from a pan heated over a metal drum of embers set upon a simple wooden trolley. I could feel the heat on my skin. This man too looked directly at me and shook his head, acknowledging and also somehow regretting my very presence.

Which was when I realised I was naked.

Fortunately there were so many people jamming the street – it could have been a medieval fair, or a football crowd – that no one paid much attention as I huddled in the doorway and frantically pulled on my trousers, shirt, jacket and shoes. The problem was not that I was getting dressed, but that I was getting in people's way.

'Oi, oi,' came one cry.

'Oy, oy,' came another.

'Mind out the pave!'

'You on the bash, mate, or what?'

'Shove over!'

Hastily dressed, I looked back towards the hot-nut man, who nodded at my newly clothed state with calm approval. I put my shoulders back, took a deep breath, turned left and set off quickly down the street.

It was good to be back in the city.

People used to say that you could enter Club Row Market at one end leading a dog, lose it halfway down the street, and then buy it back at the other end. Certainly, it was a place where the usual rules of commerce did not necessarily apply: bruised and beaten dogs were covered in boot polish; cats were dyed; exotic singing birds turned out to be voiceless creatures, their song merrily whistled by their merry vendors as they merrily bagged them up and merrily took your money. Fortunately, it was a place where a man might easily get lost in a crowd.

It was a crisp, bright morning, though dark clouds on

the horizon suggested that some cold grey London rain was soon to arrive and turn crisp and bright into dull and damp. I barged my way along the street, continually checking over my shoulder for sight of the Limehouse chap and his ladies – sight of whom, thank goodness, there was none. I barged past men and women hawking animals, bicycles, knives, tea-sets, stockings, second-hand suits and the day's papers, all at half-price, fresh from outside newsagents in the West End. There were high-value goods at rock-bottom prices, 'genu-ine' articles almost as good as the real thing, and on every street corner urgent men and their accomplices were con-ducting Dutch auctions that left their customers with half of what they bid for, or nothing at all.

'Brand new, madam. Never seen daylight or moonlight, or Fanny by gaslight.'

'I'll tell you what, I'll even give you a bag to carry it away in.'

'Pretty foreign birds! Pretty foreign birds!'

It was as good as a trip to the circus, or a day at the sea-side. Traders were dressed to attract attention. There was a man singing 'Cohen the Crooner'; a tall black man with a walking stick yelling, 'I gotta horse! I gotta horse!'; and ye olde traditional English organ grinder with ye olde trad-itional English monkey. There was kosher restaurant after kosher restaurant: Felv's, Strongwaters, Barnett's. Enter-taining and enticing as it all was, my only aim was to get away and to clear my head. Buying a dog, bagels or placing a bet were most definitely not part of the plan. Other people had other plans.

'Hey! Hey! Hey, mate! Hey, hey! Buy a dog to keep you warm?' offered a man with a couple of shivering puppies nestling under his overcoat. He thrust the pups towards me. They were either extremely friendly or more than a little starved, licking frantically at my fingers in the hope of finding some trace of food there, their tails wagging.

'Look at that! They like you, mate. I could 'ave sold 'em ten times over this morning, but I want 'em to 'ave a good 'ome, see.'

'No, thank you,' I said, handing the puppies back and going to step round him.

'For you, because they like you, I'll do a special price.'

'No, thank you,' I said.

'What, what's the matter, mate? Not good enough for you?' he said, blocking my way.

'No, I just—'

'These are bloomin' good dogs, these. You sayin' there's somethin' wrong with 'em?'

'No, no.'

'Full pedigree, these.' Not only were they not full pedigree dogs, they were nowhere near half, a quarter, or one-eighth pedigree. 'I've got their pedigree right 'ere if you want to see it.' He patted his pockets.

Which made me think of my wallet. I checked in my jacket pocket – and was delighted to find it still safely there. Smiling with relief, I turned, triumphant, only to see the Limehouse chap approaching fast through the crowd.

A popular novelist might describe the Limehouse chap as swarthy and menacing, but this hardly did him justice. In the warmth and welcome of the East End pub the night before he had seemed the perfect drinking companion: garrulous, generous, good company. In the cold light of day I could see that he was in fact the sort of chap who looked as though

Petticoat Lane: The People's Piccadilly

he'd recently done some serious damage to good company and was intent upon doing exactly the same again, except worse, the sort of chap whose middle name would have been trouble, if he'd been the sort of chap who had a middle name, which I rather doubted. Even among the rather shady figures of Club Row, he stood out in the crowd like a dark silhouette.

Pushing past the puppy-seller – 'You fuckin' nark,' he called after me as I went, a traditional East End greeting – I ducked down, squeezed between some cages and slipped into a shop.

CHAPTER 5

THIS, I remember thinking, *this* sort of indignity, is *exactly* what I could do without. This was what I was trying to avoid. Running around London, running around the country, always running, always hiding, always skulking. It was not the life I wanted to live.

As luck would or wouldn't have it, this particular skulk-hole was a tailor's – a tiny tailor's shop, not much bigger than someone's front room, which I guessed was exactly what it was.

'Can I help you, sir?' asked a jolly round-faced man behind the counter, glasses perched on his rather sweaty forehead, waistcoat tightly buttoned over his belly, tape measure loose round his neck, tailor's chalk in one hand, cigarette in the other. Behind him two young Mediterranean-looking men were at enormous sewing machines, hammering away, hard at work, surrounded by swatches of fabric and vast lengths of cloth, piles of brown paper and, hanging everywhere, what appeared to be half-made garments. The place was like a fabric abattoir.

I glanced out of the window behind me. The Limehouse chap might still appear at any moment, in which case I'd be trapped in this tiny place, unable to escape. I looked at the tailor, with an expression that if not entirely pleading was certainly seeking understanding, and the tailor looked at me, and at my suit, with an expression that switched from curious to concerned to calculating.

It had been a relatively mild autumn and the moths from Morley's cottage had recently been making significant inroads into all my clothes, including this – once fine, now faded and moth-scarred – blue serge suit. Morley, of course, was something of an expert on the clothes moth, *Tineola bisselliella*, and on the many and various methods of deterrent: mothballs, camphor wood, bay leaves, cloves, lavender, conkers and all the other standard home remedies. But whatever the deterrent, the little larvae always seem to find a way through. You can wash and you can scrub, you can scatter mothballs far and wide, but again and again the moths will come, they will mate, the females will look for a nice warm place to lay their eggs, the eggs will hatch into larvae, and destruction will ensue. There was and there is, it seems, no solution to moths. Morley's article on the clothes moth, published in the now long-since defunct *Home Notes* in August 1939, is titled 'Eternal Vigilance: The War Against Moths', and makes for depressing reading. 'Eternal vigilance is required,' Morley would often say: it was one of his favourite phrases. 'Eternal vigilance. Or all is lost.'

Glancing at my suit for a moment, the tailor said nothing.

Then, 'Sugar lump, my friend?' he asked.

He indicated a bowl of sugar lumps on the counter top.

'No, thank you,' I said, again looking nervously behind me, and again he followed my gaze, then slowly took a sugar lump from the bowl, popped it in his mouth and crunched down on it with surprising force – *chromsht, chromsht, chromsht* – finishing it off with relish.

'Sir is desperate; for a new suit, perhaps?'

I couldn't possibly afford a new suit, even here. My suit was the suit I had bought when I inherited some money from my parents.

'Yes, that's right,' I said. 'I am desperate for a new suit.'

'Then sir has come to the right place.'

I glanced again quickly outside.

'Perhaps I can just use your changing room for a moment?' I said, and gestured towards a tiny cubicle on the left, hung with a heavy, faded moss-green curtain.

The tailor shook his head. 'No, no, no, sir. In order to fit the suit I would need to measure you up properly, in private. Total privacy. *If* you need a new suit.'

'I really need a new suit,' I said.

'Good. Then come. Come. Quick.'

He lifted a part of the counter top, kicked open a hinged door in the counter and let me through, past the men at the sewing machines, who paid us no attention whatsoever, and through a door into a windowless kitchen-cum-fitting room, piled high with yet more fabric and pattern paper, which almost obscured the two vast, ancient, weirdly ornate full-length mirrors set on either side of the space, which gave the room the appearance of decayed imperial chaos.

'Thank you,' I said.

'No need to thank me, sir,' said the tailor, who proceeded to measure me up for a suit I did not want and could not afford while discussing cut, buttons and what he referred to as 'suitage'.

Measurements completed, 'And when would sir like to collect his suit?' he asked.

I rather suspected that he knew I had no intention of coming to collect my suit. I also rather suspected that he had no intention of making me a suit.

'I can come—'

'We can have it ready in a week, sir.'

'Well. A week, then,' I said.

'By which time the coast should be clear,' he said.

'The coast?'

He nodded out towards the front of the shop.

'Ah,' I said.

'We do require a small deposit, of course, sir, for this special sort of service.'

'Of course.'

I turned away and checked my wallet. Farthings, ha'pennies, thrupenny bits – and two ten bob notes. It was everything I had.

'I'm afraid I don't have—'

I turned back to find the tailor, plus the two Mediterranean lads, grinning, blocking the door.

'We'll take whatever you do have,' said the tailor, leaning over and plucking the ten bob notes from my wallet.

I had entered the shop in order to avoid losing money to a merciless-looking thug: I'd ended up losing money to some harmless-looking hustlers.

I had enough money left to buy a cup of tea – and perhaps make a couple of phone calls, which I duly resolved to do. I was getting out.

The tailor and the two men turned and left, and I duly followed them, making my way back to the front of the shop, ready to leave.

'Your receipt, sir,' said the tailor, as I was opening the door onto the street. He was writing something on a pad.

I made no reply.

He then proffered the receipt towards me. 'And we'll see you next week, then.'

'Yes,' I said, turning back and taking the receipt, and turning towards the door again. 'Next week, absolutely.'

The coast appeared to be clear.

'Actually,' I said, as I reached the door, 'I wonder if I could just borrow your pad for a moment?'

The tailor swivelled the pad towards me.

'And a pencil or pen?' I asked.

He took his pencil from behind his ear, licked it ostentatiously and ceremoniously handed it to me.

'With pleasure, sir.'

And so I scrawled my resignation letter to Morley – courtesy of M. Skulnik, Sclater Street, E1, estd. 1928 – pocketed it and, checking in every direction to make sure the coast was clear, ventured outside.

I'd had enough.

CHAPTER 6

WITH MY FINAL FEW COINS I made my phone calls and adjourned to a pie and mash shop off Sclater Street, whose sole recommendation was that it claimed to offer the cheapest cup of tea on the market. Under other less trying circumstances, I might well have adjourned to one of my favourite East End eating establishments, Bloom's on Aldgate, or Ostwind's, with its bakery in the basement, or Strongwaters, or Silberstein's: a man could eat like a king in the restaurants around the Lane, while snacking on latkes and herring in between.

But I had rather lost my appetite.

The first call I made was to Willy Mann, a restaurateur and an associate of the infamous Mr Klein, an East End businessman in the loosest and broadest sense – which is to say, a crook – who had offered me work on a number of occasions since my return from Spain, work I had so far declined, on the basis it was beneath my dignity and against all my principles.

Mr Klein had wide-ranging business interests – in property, retail, wholesale, in precious metals and pharma-ceuticals, the import and export thereof – none of which enterprises particularly appealed, and several of which were both highly illegal and extremely dangerous, but which, crucially, did not involve endlessly sharpening the pencils of the country's leading autodidact, and which would, significantly, mean that I didn't need to travel the length and breadth of the country in order to make a meagre living, and could safely remain in London without fear of threat or retribution from people like the Limehouse chap and the many and various others whom I had foolishly offended. Out of the frying pan and into the fire – a desperate bid for freedom.

The second call was to Miriam.

I'd intended simply to let Miriam know that I wouldn't be joining her for our planned trip to Sussex, but she had somehow commandeered and then entirely redirected the conversation, letting me know that she needed to talk to me urgently, immediately and face to face. Which is how I had ended up, with Willy Mann, discussing the possible terms and conditions of working for Mr Klein, when Miriam arrived.

As always, one was instantly struck by her sheer raving beauty, her languorousness, her confidence and her charm. She had, as always, the appearance of someone who had recently raised herself to commanding heights from a position of reclining elegance – possibly reading Proust, or the *Picture Post*, with liquid refreshments, a handsome chauffeur and a strokable Pekinese all conveniently at hand. She certainly did not look like she belonged in an East End pie and mash shop, and she made no attempt to look like she belonged. She looked entirely – I think the phrase is – *à la mode*, in the most extraordinary red and white checked wool coat with fur shoulder detailing and a thick rolled red and white belt, over a creamy white crepe dress, and what appeared to me to be a hunting cap set with a monkey paw brooch. To say that she stood out against the white-tiled walls of the pie and mash shop and its many mirrors reflecting the dark, huddled masses inside and out, would be an understatement. She looked like a visiting dignitary, or indeed an ambassador not merely from another country but from an entirely other world.

'Miriam,' I said, getting up from the table. 'You're looking—'

'Sensational, Sefton?' she said.

'That's exactly what I was going to say.'

'Good.' She flashed me a smile.

'Miss Morley,' said Willy Mann, getting up and extending his hand.

'Have we met?' asked Miriam.

'In Essex, miss.'

'Ah, yes,' said Miriam. 'Never mind.' She settled herself at our table. 'One of your regular haunts, Sefton?'

'Not exactly,' I said. 'Would you like . . . some pie and mash?' Even the question seemed absurd.

'It's a little early in the day for me for pie and mash, thank you, Sefton.' She stared at our mugs of stewed tea, and at Willy Mann's plate of half-eaten burned brown pastry, grey minced mutton, creamy mashed potato and pool of thin green parsley sauce – and shuddered. 'Though thinking about it, *any time* is a little early in the day for pie and mash.'

'Can I get you anything, miss?' asked the café owner, who'd appeared at our table on Miriam's arrival, rightly anticipating that this was a customer who might expect a rather more attentive than average standard of service.

Before saying anything, Miriam looked up at the man, slowly and appraisingly. For a moment I thought she might actually finger his rather stained apron. He was a dark-skinned gentleman, extraordinarily handsome – perhaps from Ceylon – who spoke the most perfectly accented East End English. I was reminded of the old Jewish joke about the Chinese waiter in one of the East End's many kosher restaurants who spoke perfect Yiddish. 'Don't tell him,' the restaurant's owner begged his customers, 'he thinks he's learning English!'

'A cup of coffee would be wonderful,' she said, after another moment's pause. 'If you can manage it.' She had him, as they say, in the palm of her hand. The café owner flushed and became flustered.

'I could do you tea, miss,' he said apologetically.

'Do you know, tea would be *almost* as *equally* wonderful, thank you,' she said.

'Are you sure we can't tempt you, Miriam?' I said, gesturing towards Willy's pie and mash.

'Quite sure, thank you.'

The café owner departed, doubtless to brew some fresh tea for Miriam, rather than serving the swill that he was happy to dish out to the rest of us.

'So,' said Miriam. 'Here we are.'

'Indeed,' said Willy Mann, pushing around some mashed potato on his plate. 'Here we are.'

I'd told Miriam that I'd be free to meet her at one o'clock. It was now midday: for the first and last time during our long relationship, she was early. This was awkward. I'd hoped to have concluded my business with Willy before having to deal with Miriam. As it was, we were all now going to have to deal with each other.

While I stared out the window, still scanning the street for the Limehouse chap, Willy and Miriam eyed each other up. Or at least, Willy eyed Miriam up, and Miriam allowed herself to be eyed: this was one of her techniques. So many men found her alluring, she seemed to have found the best way to deal with them was to allow them their admiration – and then, like a praying mantis, she would crush them mercilessly. Her ruthless impassivity was a technique I had observed in practice many times and it was, invariably, devastatingly, outrageously successful. To see Miriam at work among men was to witness something like a Miss Havisham, who just happened to look like Hedy Lamarr.

'So what brings you to Club Row? Have you come for a dog, Miss Morley?' asked Willy, rather teasingly, I thought.

'Not exactly,' said Miriam, 'no.' She looked at me. 'Though I do love dogs. On more than one occasion a stray dog on the street has followed me home. Isn't that right, Sefton?' I had no recall of any stray dog ever having followed her home and wasn't quite sure what she was referring to. 'Dogs just seem to come to me,' continued Miriam. 'But they must be trained properly, don't you think?'

'Indeed,' said Willy, who had lost all interest in his pie and mash and who was now staring at Miriam, fascinated. It was always the way. I wasn't quite sure how she did it.

'I like dogs who are – what's the word, Sefton?'

'I'm not sure, Miriam,' I said. 'Docile?'

'No,' said Miriam.

'Ferocious?' offered Willy.

'No, no,' said Miriam.

'Loyal?'

'No.'

'Obedient,' said Willy.

'Yes. That's it. That's the word.'

'Obedience is important,' agreed Willy.

'Isn't it,' said Miriam. And she laughed, throwing back her head in studied abandon.

I was beginning to see that this was not really a conversation about dogs at all, except perhaps that like a dog spying an open gate, Miriam was taking off in whatever direction her whim took her.

'And, remind me, what is it you do, Mr . . . ?' she asked.

'Mann,' said Willy.

'Mr Mann. Curious name.'

'It's German,' said Willy.

'Ah. *Sprechen Sie Deutsch?*'

'I'm afraid not,' said Willy. 'My parents came here many years ago. Their first language was Yiddish.'

'Ah. The *Mame Loshn. Das schadet nichts,*' said Miriam. 'I do like to practise my German whenever I get the chance.'

Miriam's tea arrived, in an actual cup, in an actual saucer, with an actual jug of milk, the café owner also seemingly having donned a fresh apron for the sole purpose of visiting our table.

'Can I get you anything else, miss?'

'No, thank you,' said Miriam dismissively, returning to her captivation of Willy Mann. 'So what brings you here this morning, Mr Mann?' The freshly aproned café owner shuffled away. 'You have business in these parts?'

[31]

'I have business in many parts of London,' said Willy.

'Well, lucky you,' said Miriam. 'But here in particular?'

'Willy and his business partners help protect the local community from the Black Shirts,' I said.

'Is that right?' said Miriam.

'That's certainly a part of what we do here, yes,' said Willy.

'Well, that's very good of you,' said Miriam. 'And you do that entirely out of the goodness of your heart, do you?'

'We do, miss. Absolutely we do.'

'Gratis, for nothing and entirely for free?'

'Well, of course a business like ours—'

'A protection racket,' said Miriam.

'We wouldn't call it that, miss.'

'I'm sure you wouldn't,' said Miriam, taking a sip of her tea and wincing slightly. 'But I would. Go on.'

'A . . . service such as ours costs money, miss, as you can imagine.'

'I can imagine, yes,' said Miriam, who was looking around the café. 'How much, exactly?'

'Well, it depends, but let's say as little as a shilling a week for your safety.'

'A shilling.'

'Very reasonable, don't you think, miss?'

'I certainly do not think,' said Miriam. 'There are by my count almost forty people currently in this establishment. If each of them paid you just a shilling each you'd have two pounds; is that correct?'

'Your maths is impeccable,' said Willy.

'So that's two pounds per week, making eight pounds per month from the patrons of this café alone.'

'But not everyone in this café would be paying us a shilling a week.'

'I'm sure they wouldn't. They'd be far too sensible. And if they don't?'

'If they don't what?' said Willy.

'If they don't pay you their shilling. I presume there's the implied threat of violence.'

'We offer protection,' said Willy.

'Which of course implies a threat,' said Miriam.

'Not from us,' said Willy.

'Really?'

'Absolutely.'

'So all your clients have willingly entered into a voluntary contract with you?'

'That's correct.'

'A contract that essentially consists of you granting them protection in return for the payment of a small cash sum.'

'That's right.'

'So in effect your clients stand in relation to you and your associates as, say, children, or women – or indeed property – who are in some way incapable of protecting themselves and who therefore need protecting?'

'You could put it like that,' agreed Willy.

'Which makes them effectively chattels or slaves,' said Miriam.

Willy was about to speak but Miriam held up her arm, commanding silence, and then turned to me. 'I had thought, Sefton, that you might have kept rather better company.'

Willy did not look amused. He looked – well, he looked – emasculated.

'Anyway,' said Miriam, ignoring Willy's obvious irritation.

'I really shouldn't be barging in on you boys. I'm sure you have lots to discuss. Racketeering. Extortion. Fraud. White slavery, also?'

Willy got up from the table.

'You'll excuse me, but I have other more *serious* business I need to attend to,' he said.

'Oh, really?' said Miriam. 'What a shame.'

'It's been a pleasure, Miss Morley.' He didn't offer his hand.

'Hasn't it just?' said Miriam.

'Sefton, you know where to find me,' he said.

'I do, thanks, Willy.'

'Byesie bye!' said Miriam. '*Mahlzeit!*'

And with that, he was gone.

I noticed then that the hubbub in the restaurant had died down. We were drawing attention to ourselves. Or, rather, Miriam was drawing attention to us.

'Miriam,' I said quietly, 'you were really terribly rude to the poor chap.'

'Oh, come on, Sefton. He's big enough and ugly enough to take it,' said Miriam, not at all quietly. 'Well, maybe not ugly enough. But you know, you really have the most appalling taste in friends and acquaintances.'

'I'll take that as a compliment,' I said.

'And so you should,' she said. 'It's a mark of your character. Anyway, enough about him. I'm so glad you called.'

'Really?'

'Yes.'

'Why? What is it you wanted, Miriam?'

'Father's in terrible danger.'

CHAPTER 7

I HAD HEARD THIS LINE BEFORE. Miriam's idea of her father being in terrible danger included his being over-worked, underworked, unduly praised, under-appreciated, slighted, patronised, put-upon or indeed treated in any way other than the way in which Miriam treated him, which is to say with absolute, unquestioning devotion and utter disdain.

'Aren't you going to ask me what sort of danger, Sefton?'

'What sort of danger, Miriam?'

'He is being hunted.'

'Hunted?'

'Precisely.'

'Hunted by?'

'An American, of course.'

'Oh dear.'

'An American adventuress.' If Miriam had had pearls to clutch, she'd have been clutching them.

'I see.'

'Americans being undoubtedly the most dangerous among all the world's adventuresses.'

'Undoubtedly,' I said.

Morley was, admittedly, rather susceptible to the attentions of women whose interest and affection he was, alas, entirely incapable of returning. This had caused problems in the past, would cause problems in the future, and had indeed sown considerable confusion among a large swathe of the forty-plus, middle, upper and aristocratic single, divorced and widowed female population of Britain, Europe and North America.

'Honestly, Sefton, this one has more hooks in her than the proverbial poacher's hatband,' continued Miriam, 'and she is tickling him like a trout.'

'Like a trout, Miriam?' I said, smiling.

'Precisely, Sefton. Like a trout.'

'Tickling him?' I said, smiling again, though to no answering smile from Miriam, who was most definitely not in a playful mood.

'Like a trout, yes, as I said, Sefton. She adopts this low husky voice whenever she's talking to him.' Miriam had a low husky voice of her own, I should say, which she used to good effect, and indeed now for the purposes of mimicry. *"Mr Morley, you must have the biggest brain I have ever encountered."'*

'Oh dear,' I said.

'It's quite, quite disgusting,' said Miriam, raising an eyebrow, the fashion back in those days having been for eyebrows to be plucked to a single line, a fashion that Miriam had mercifully resisted. 'And anyway, where is Maryland?'

'Maryland?' I said.

'Where she's from, apparently.'

I wasn't entirely sure I could have identified Maryland on a map of the United States.

'Is it a land of Marys?' I asked.

Miriam ignored this weak joke, a sure sign of her being both irritated and distracted; usually she'd have pounced without hesitation.

'She was once a keen horsewoman, so she says, though frankly it'd take a shire horse now.'

'I'm getting the impression you're not over keen—'

'And she claims to be an expert on posture, of all things – she's the Lady President of the American Posture League. She's written a book, God help us. *Slouching Towards Gomorrah. And* she's a divorcee,' she said. 'Her first husband was called Fruity.'

'Was he?'

'I simply cannot take seriously a woman whose ex-husband is called Fruity, can you?'

'No.'

'And her second husband was called Minty.'

'Minty? Are you sure, Miriam? You're not making this up?'

'Of course I'm not making it up, Sefton.'

I only asked because Miriam herself spent much of her time during those years with various unsuitable Fruitys and Mintys, while I spent much of my time when I wasn't with Miriam in the company of Sluggers and Rotters and other ridiculously named low-life Soho characters. I rather miss the nicknames and sobriquets of the dog-end days of the thirties: they were, I see now, for all their squalor, the last days of innocence.

'The woman is mounting a campaign, Sefton,' Miriam continued, and she was certainly someone who knew a campaign being mounted when she saw one, so I suppose it must have been true.

[37]

'What sort of a campaign?'

'A campaign to marry Father, Sefton!'

'Really?'

'Yes! She might as well be wearing a veil and carrying a bouquet, for goodness sake. It's quite ridiculous.'

'Would you like another cup of tea, Miriam?' I thought this might calm her down.

'No, I don't want another cup of tea. I want you to take this threat seriously.'

'Of course I take it seriously, Miriam.'

'Do you, though?'

'Yes. Entirely.'

'She is bogus, Sefton, that's the problem.'

'Bogus?'

'Yes. She's a singer.'

'What sort of a singer?'

'Opera. Allegedly.'

'Allegedly?'

'Well, I've never heard her sing. She may be terrible. Father seems to think she's marvellous. *And* she's American – did I say?'

'Yes, you—'

'American *par excellence*. She's like . . . Uncle Sam—'

'Uncle Samantha, perhaps?'

'But I can tell you, I think her excellence is rather far from par.'

'Far from par,' I repeated.

'Correct. She is flirtatious and gay.'

'You're gay and flirtatious, Miriam.'

'Yes, but I'm twenty-one years old, Sefton, I'm supposed

to be gay and flirtatious. This woman must be – I don't know – fifty if she's a day.'

'Fifty?' I said.

'Fifty!' said Miriam. '*And* she's a terrible boozehound.' Like Morley, Miriam had a habit of adopting hardboiled slang more suited to the pages of *Black Mask* magazine. Her other favourite tough-guy Americanisms included 'the bum's rush', referring to what or where I never quite understood, and the term 'spondulix' for money. In later years she also adopted the habit of saying 'OK' in response to everything. I was surprised, though, I must admit, that this threatening American was a drinker. Morley strongly disapproved of what he called spiritous drink. She clearly had him under her spell, a spell that Miriam seemed determined to break.

'She is cloying and giddy,' she continued. 'She is dramatic and frowsy. She has this dreadful false laugh, and these ridiculous eyebrows, and eyes that just . . . winkle you out.'

'I'm getting the sense—'

'She is a mean, snobbish, vile, raddled, primped, crisped and bleached sort of a beast, Sefton.'

'I—'

'With this ludicrous heaving embonpoint. Constantly projecting.'

'She—'

'She belongs in a straitjacket, frankly.'

'That's a bit strong, Miriam,' I said.

'A bit strong, Sefton? She is fake, man. Completely fake! She recently sang the virgin in Gounod's *Faust*, for goodness sake.'

'But—'

'She is oval and—'

'I get the impression that you're really not keen,' I said.

'Whether or not I am keen, Sefton, is entirely beside the point. Theirs is a friendship that is frivolous, fraudulent, purposeless and dangerous.' A more accurate description of Miriam's own relationships with men it would be difficult to imagine. 'She has a dangerous hold on him, Sefton. Like Wallis Simpson. And you know what they say about her and her Shanghai tricks.'

'Speaking of friendships,' I said, not wishing to encourage Miriam to speculate any further upon Mrs Simpson's much rumoured amatory skills and virtuosities out loud in an East End pie and mash shop.

'Yes?' said Miriam, leaning forward in her chair. 'Might I cadge a cigarette, Sefton?' Cadge she did. 'Would you mind?' I dutifully lit her cigarette, she tossed back her head, took a deep gulp and relaxed. 'Go on,' she said, gesturing with her cigarette.

At this point, an almost total silence had descended upon the café, as more of the customers recognised Miriam's defining and indeed dominating presence among us.

'Miriam,' I said, lowering my voice, 'I'm afraid I'm going to have to resign.'

She did not respond.

'Did you hear me, Miriam?'

She blew smoke from her nostrils – a trick that she performed when alarmed, cornered, frustrated or otherwise excited. Out of the corner of my eye I could see a man making pies: chopping up eels, making mash, concocting parsley sauce.

'I'm leaving,' I said.

She laughed. It was not a pleasant laugh.

'Leave?' she said, fixing me with a stare. 'You can't *leave*, Sefton.'

Miriam couldn't leave: Morley was her father. But I could.

'I wonder if you might give this to your father,' I said quietly, handing her my resignation letter.

'This?' said Miriam with distaste, fingering my note written on the Skulnik receipt.

'It's my resignation,' I said.

'Hmm,' said Miriam. She held the letter in her hand, regarded it from a distance, without reading it, and then, with clear regard for the audience in the café that was now watching her every move, took her cigarette and used it to set fire to the little piece of paper, which flared, blackened, and which she placed carefully in the ashtray on the table. 'Oh dear,' she said. 'Sorry.' She fixed her gaze upon me.

The café owner at that moment approached our table.

'Everything all right here?' he asked.

'Everything's fine, thank you,' said Miriam, flashing him a smile. 'That will be all, thank you.'

The owner walked away, but looked back at me over his shoulder as he went, raising his eyebrows and widening his eyes, as if to say, 'I thought you were onto a winner there, but good luck with that, mate.' It was not an uncommon response to Miriam's provoking and unpredictable presence.

'You know I can just write another resignation letter, Miriam?' I said.

'You could, Sefton. But you won't.'

'Why not?'

'Because whatever reason you may have had for offering

your resignation, having now heard that Father is in danger, you won't even consider resigning.'

'Will I not? Why not?'

'Because,' she said, pausing for effect, 'you are a good man, Sefton.'

'I am far from that, Miriam,' I said.

'Well . . . If you say so. But if not because you're good, then because we need you, Sefton.' She placed her hand over mine, bit her lip, and looked away, as though overcoming silent tears. 'I need you.' This was another of her techniques: the pause, the hand, the lip, the look. I'd seen it all before. 'To be honest, I had rather hoped to be spending the autumn in Florence – there's no crush on the Cascine at this time of year and the faded light is quite magical.'

'I'm sure it is,' I said.

'I promise you, Sefton,' she continued, 'that this will be your final outing. If you could just help me prevent this dreadful woman from getting her claws into Father, we'll do Sussex, and then you can pop off and do whatever it is you want to do with Mr Mann and his dreadful schemes or whatever. And I can go off to Florence or somewhere. There we are. How's that?' She put out her hand for me to shake and seal the deal.

'I'll think about it, Miriam,' I said.

'Well, don't think about it for too long, darling.' With which she left, though not before I had to call her back in order to pay the bill, since I had no money.

'You can pay me back when we go to Sussex together,' she said, as she left the café.

'Rock and a hard place, mate,' said the café owner, as the door banged behind Miriam.

'Indeed,' I said.

I walked outside.

It was almost one o'clock. At precisely one o'clock the East End Sunday markets are supposed to close. At one o'clock, the market inspectors arrive and the traders and stallholders must pack up and leave; there is no more buying and selling to be done. And so at around ten to one there is a frenzy of final deals. This is the moment when 'pedigree' dogs change hands for pennies, when kittens are bagged up in job lots and when birds are offered, three for a tanner. Amid this chaos of buying, selling and bartering, on the other side of the road, I spotted a figure hurrying towards me.

It was the Limehouse chap.

Already exhausted from the conversation with Willy and Miriam, for a moment I almost thought it might be easier just to give up and abandon myself to my fate.

Then I decided to run.

And it was at that very moment that a large dog – a slavering boxer – a truly formidable-looking creature, quite enormous in size, broke free from its owner and came bounding towards me. Instinctively I stepped back, up against the window of the pie and mash shop. Without making a sound the dog reared up on its hind legs and placed its front paws squarely on my shoulders. Standing erect, the beast was as tall as me: we were face to muzzle.

I was trapped.

Which was when the Limehouse chap made his fatal mistake. Pushing through the crowd, he reached me just as the dog had settled its paws on my shoulders – and proceeded to grab the creature by its collar so that he could get at me.

The dog, believing that he was about to lose his new plaything, turned towards the Limehouse chap, gave a savage bark and butted him under the chin with his head. As I turned and began to slip away, the dog turned back towards me and the Limehouse chap found himself being pulled forward as he held on to the dog's collar, putting his other hand out in an attempt to steady himself. His fist went straight through the plate-glass window of the café. There was a crash, the man gave a blood-curdling cry, the like of which I had never heard before, and the dog, startled and disturbed, reared up under him, propelling him through the broken window.

My last look, glancing behind me, dodging among the crowds and animals of the market, was the sight of the marble floor of the shop turning a bright crimson.

Someone was screaming 'He's dead!' Whether it was the dog or the Limehouse chap I did not wait to find out.

CHAPTER 8

'SEFTON! What took you so long?' asked Miriam. 'Come on. Come on in.'

As Miriam ushered me into her apartment, an elderly, most striking-looking dark-haired woman, wearing an array of brightly coloured beads that may have been Mexican, and carrying a stout wicker shopping basket that was most definitely English, hurried past in the corridor.

'Well,' she said, in what sounded to me like a French accent but may indeed have been Mexican, but which certainly was not English, 'you kept this one quiet, Miriam.'

'Finders, keepers, Ines,' said Miriam. 'Finders, keepers. Far too young for you anyway.'

'They're never too young, my dear. It's just me that gets too old.'

'Hello?' I said.

Both the women ignored me.

'Can I get you anything?' asked Ines.

'No thank you,' said Miriam. 'We're going away for a few days.'

'Lucky you, my dear.'

'Work rather than pleasure,' said Miriam.

'The two are often the same, in my experience,' said Ines, waving a hand as she disappeared down the corridor. 'One of life's paradoxes.'

'Well, you've met the neighbours,' said Miriam. 'Come on then. Come in. Chop chop.'

The first thing that struck me about Miriam's new apartment was a slight smell. I couldn't quite put my finger on it, though it was a smell so strong that one might almost have put a finger on it. Miriam seemed oblivious.

'You found it then?' she asked.

'Evidently,' I said.

'Oh no, no,' she said, 'you're beginning to sound like Father, Sefton. Please, don't.' The last thing I ever wanted to do was to sound like Swanton Morley – his manner, alas, was contagious – so I shut up. 'Anyway, so we're all set,' she continued. 'What do you think: do I look OK?'

She looked extraordinary. Whatever it was she was wearing – Schiaparelli, probably – it was banana yellow.

'You look . . . all-encompassing,' I said, which was all I could think of.

'All-encompassing?' she said. 'Really? That'll do.'

'Do I look OK?' I asked, attempting irony. I was still in my blue serge suit.

She put a finger to her lips and studied me carefully.

'You look rather like you've spent the night sleeping rough, Sefton, actually,' which was a fair description, since I had in fact spent a few nights sleeping rough – mostly on friends' floors, but one night on Hampstead Heath, not to be recommended – having decided that it was probably best to try to keep a low profile, after the events at Club Row, and given my increasingly complicated relationship with a number of would-be employers, debt-collectors, former friends and newly acquired enemies. I loved London, but clearly the feeling was not mutual: every time I tried to make peace with the place, I seemed to become embroiled in some imbroglio.

Hence my decision to go back on the road with Miriam and Morley. At least then I'd be on the move and out of trouble. Miriam always told people that I had been saved by her ministrations and my work for her father. This was not in fact true. Basically, between 1937 and 1939 – like Britain and most of Europe – I was perpetually in crisis and continually on the run.

'Well, what do you think?' asked Miriam, referring not to her outfit, but to her apartment.

The new place was on Lawn Road, in Hampstead, in a most peculiar building called the Isokon, which, according to Miriam, was a triumph of modern design. 'Don't you think, Sefton? Isn't it a triumph!'

I wasn't sure it was a triumph, actually, though it certainly crushed and vanquished all the usual expectations of everyday human habitation, so maybe it was.

'It's the future, Sefton, isn't it? Isn't this what you were dreaming of when you were fighting in Spain? The International? The Modern? The New?'

It was pointless trying to explain to Miriam that in Spain, for whatever high-minded reason we'd gone, we all ended up fighting not for the International, the Modern and the New, but rather for own dear lives and for the poor bastards living and dying alongside us, and that whatever we were dreaming of, it was certainly not clean angles and white empty spaces, but loose women, strong drink and fresh food.

'Father's not a fan,' continued Miriam. 'He says it looks like the Penguin Pool at London Zoo.'

The Isokon did look like the Penguin Pool at London Zoo. It also rather resembled a cruise ship, and Miriam's apartment a cabin. Indeed, the whole place made you feel slightly queasy, as if setting sail on a stormy sea. The apartment was so small and so unaccommodating in every way that Miriam had dispensed with most of her furniture. 'I felt the furniture was disapproving, Sefton,' she explained, though I had no idea how or what disapproving furniture might be. Every surface in the apartment was flat, white and forbidding. The place looked like a . . . It's difficult to describe exactly what it looked like. Years later, with the benefit of hindsight, I suppose one would say that it looked like an art gallery, but at the time it was quite revolutionary even for an art gallery. Art galleries back then were still all oak-panelled and dimly lit. Even now a house that looks like an all-white ocean-going gallery would be unusual. And the Isokon was most unusual: above all, it was a building that took itself extremely seriously. It was a building that was clearly striving towards something, towards purity, presumably – which is always easier said than done. There was a bar somewhere in the place, apparently, and Miriam raved about the tremendous 'community spirit' among her fellow tenants, a spirit that found its expression in naked sunbathing, impromptu get-togethers, political discussions and all-night parties. Miriam loved it.

'You would *love* it, Sefton!' she insisted. 'We all get together and talk about art and literature.'

It sounded absolutely horrendous. Miriam often misjudged me: I had neither the money nor the inclination to become a part of the Isokon set. During those years I may have been debauched, but I have never, ever been a bohemian.

The place was quite bare and undecorated. Not only was there little furniture, there were no shelves, cupboards or mantelpieces for the many flowers, bibelots and thick embossed invitations that seemed to follow Miriam wherever she went. (It was often the case during our time together that we would fetch up in some out-of-the-way village or town, only for gifts and letters bearing invitations miraculously to appear within hours of our arrival.) In the Isokon, this temple to simplicity and stylishness, in which there was no place for anything, everything had been piled on a small round inlaid table in the hallway, which accommodated newly published books, manuscripts, gloves, scarves, jewellery and stacks of the aforementioned invitations. Above the table there was a sort of mobile hanging from the ceiling, which looked to me like a few large black metal fish bones stuck onto a piece of wire.

'That's . . . interesting, Miriam,' I said.

'Do you think? I'm trying to write a piece about it for the magazine,' she said.

'*Woman*?' I asked.

'Oh no,' she said. 'I don't write for them any more.'

'But I thought you'd just got a job as columnist?'

'No, no, Sefton. That was ages ago.'

'That was about two weeks ago.'

'Anyway. It was dreadfully dreary. They expected me to write about such terrible frivolities.'

'Really?'

'Yes, really.'

'Such as?'

'Accordion pleats or bishop's sleeves or whatever other silly thing is in fashion.'

'But I thought you were interested in fashion.'

'Of course I am, Sefton, but I'm not interested in writing about it. People who write about fashion seem to me about as dull as people who write about medieval patristics.' Thus spoke her father's daughter. 'People could go around in bustles and jodhpurs for all I care, Sefton – and I really don't care.'

For someone who really didn't care we seemed to spend much of our time packing and unpacking her clothes trunks.

'Anyway, you know me, Sefton.'

'I do?'

'I have a taste for much stronger stuff, Sefton.' Which was certainly true. 'No. I'm now a contributing editor for *Axis*.'

'*Axis*?' I said. 'Something to do with mechanics? Geometry?'

'It's an art magazine, silly. You must have heard of it.'

'I can't say I have, Miriam, no.'

'*Axis*? Really?'

'No.'

'*A Quarterly Review of Contemporary "Abstract" Painting and Sculpture*?'

'Oh,' I said, 'that *Axis*.'

From the teetering pile on the table she plucked the

latest issue of the magazine, which I flicked through while she went to finish her packing.

'That'll be an education for you,' she said, as she disappeared into her bedroom.

It certainly was. Most of the articles were entirely – one might almost say immaculately – unreadable, as if written from a strange place where the English language had been entirely reinvented solely to bamboozle and confuse. One contributor, for example, described some blobby sort of a painting as 'rampageous and eczematous'; another described an artist whose work consisted entirely of everyday household objects hung on washing lines as having 'traversed the farthest realms of the aesthetic to reinvent the very idea of objecthood'; Miriam's article was perhaps marginally less preposterous than the rest, though equally vexatious. She described some artist's series of abstract sketches as a work of 'profound autofiction': to me the work looked like a series of a child's drawings of black and white squares and triangles balancing on colourful balls.

Miriam's restless pursuit of knowledge of all kinds was of course quite admirable, her hunger for new experiences rivalling only her father's great lust for learning. Having endured a privileged, if rather peculiar upbringing and education at some of the country's best schools, and courtesy of one of the country's best minds, Miriam often expressed to me her wish that she had gone to Cambridge or to Oxford to study PPE (which, to my shame, I usually referred to as GGG, or 'Ghastly Girls' Greats', an easy alternative to Classics). 'All these women who go to Lady Margaret Hall do make one feel terribly inadequate, Sefton.' During our work together on *The County Guides*, Miriam slowly but surely reinvented herself, becoming more and more an autodidact in the manner of her father: she went to fewer tennis parties with girls called Diana and Camilla, took up the saxophone and the uilleann pipes, added Arabic and Mandarin Chinese to her many languages, and ranged widely in her reading, from Freud in German to Céline in French. She was naturally formidable: over time she became utterly extraordinary. It was sometimes difficult to see how anyone could possibly keep up with her.

When I occasionally asked why she had taken up with this unsuitable man or other, she would simply say, 'Because everyone else is so boring, Sefton.' Boredom was her *bête noire*. It could get her into terrible trouble. Her most recent boyfriend was a man so daring and adventurous that he had joined Britannia Youth, the neo-fascist group that specialised in sending impressionable young British schoolboys to Nazi rallies in Germany.

'Roderick was just such fun!' she said.

Roderick had lasted about two weeks.

'Right,' she said, barrelling out of her bedroom carrying a large handbag.

'Crocodile?' I nodded towards the bag.

'Alligator, actually, Sefton. Can't you tell? Are you ready?'

'I am. Is that all you're taking?' I was confused. Miriam did not travel light. Part of the challenge of travelling with

Miriam and Morley was travelling with Miriam's clothes: for even the shortest journey she would pack Chinese robes, leopard-skin hats and kid leather gloves.

'Yes.'

'That's it?'

'The rest is already in the Lagonda, Sefton. László gave me a hand last night. Do you know László?'

'I don't think I do, no.'

'You *must* know László.'

Miriam was always amazed when it turned out that I didn't know anyone she knew – because of course she knew everyone who counted. I did not, however, to my knowledge, know anyone named László.

'Bruno?'

'No.' As far as I was aware my life was both László- and Bruno-free.

'Serge?'

Ditto.

'Anyway, lovely chaps. They got the Lagonda all packed up for me. Now, what do you think?' She gestured towards a brooch she was wearing.

'It's very pretty.'

'Pretty, Sefton?'

'Very pretty.'

'Very pretty? For goodness sake, man, it's a nineteenth-century Tiffany orchid brooch with diamond-edged petals.'

'Yes, I thought so. And very pretty.'

'It was a gift from a friend, actually.'

'Very good.' Miriam was forever receiving gifts from friends, always men – and always jewellery, though once there was the gift of a De Dion Bouton car, which for a moment rivalled the Lagonda in her affections. The men came and went but the gifts remained.

'Do you know, Sefton,' she told me on more than one occasion, 'the perfect condition for a woman is either to be engaged, or to be widowed.'

We were about to leave the apartment, Miriam equipped with bag and key in hand.

'Oh, I almost forgot.' She dashed back into her bedroom and reappeared moments later carrying what looked like a small furry blanket clutched to her chest.

'What is that?'

'It's a Bedlington, Sefton.'

'A Whatlington?'

'A Bedlington. A Bedlington Terrier.'

'A dog?'

'Yes, of course a dog.'

'Oh, Miriam.'

'What do you mean, "Oh, Miriam"?'

'A *dog*, Miriam.'

'I like dogs, Sefton.'

'You didn't get it at Club Row?'

'I certainly did,' said Miriam, offended. 'There was a chap as I was leaving the market who was packing up for home and he had this little thing all on his own and—'

'From Club Row? You'll be lucky if he lasts a week,' I said.

'Sefton!' She covered the dog's ears. 'Don't talk like that around Pablo.'

'Pablo?'

'Picasso, yes.'

'You've named your dog after the artist.'

'Yes. Why shouldn't I?'

A dog that looked less like Picasso it would be hard to imagine: he was a dog that looked like *a* Picasso. Everything about him was wonky, or wrong: rather than a dog, he resembled a lamb, except he was a lamb with a bluish, velvety sort of coat, a high arched back, a narrow but bulbous head, a tail that tapered to a point, and ears that hung down to what looked like two little white pom-poms. He had a mild, bewildered expression on his face and was without a doubt one of the most peculiar-looking creatures I'd ever seen. Miriam obviously adored him.

'Take these,' she said, thrusting a brown paper bag into my hands. 'The chap threw in a bag of arrowroot biscuits.'

'Marvellous,' I said.

'Now. Pablo has left a *little* present in the bedroom.'

'Oh no.' So this was the source of the smell.

'And I just wondered if you'd be a darling and tidy it up, while I run down to the car? There're some old newspapers in there that should do the job.'

'Miriam!'

'Thank you, darling! See you in a min!'

Pablo's gift duly disposed of, I made my way down to the Lagonda, which was parked at the back of the building.

Miriam had donned her leather driving gloves.

'Are we not waiting for your father?' I asked.

'Oh no, no, no,' said Miriam. 'Sorry, I should have said. We're meeting him down in Brighton.'

'Right.'

'Come on, Sefton. In you pop. No time to lose!'

With Miriam driving, I was left in the passenger seat with the Bedlington, who instantly – quite understandably – became unsettled as Miriam started up the engine and gunned down towards Camden Town. I held on tight to the poor pooch and did my best to calm him: in return, he relieved himself over my trousers.

Damp and headachy, heading out of London, I listened as Miriam recapped for me some of the things her father wanted us to see in Sussex, including Arundel Castle – 'The archetypal English castle, Sefton, according to Father. Norman and Early English, Gothic and Gothic Revival, Victorian and Modern, absolutely unmatched' – and many other high points, including Beddingham, Seaford, Alfriston and Litlington, all places I'd never heard of and had absolutely no desire to visit.

'Do you know Elgar?' asked Miriam, somewhere around Crawley.

I admitted that I did know Elgar, forgetting, as so often, that for Miriam knowing someone of renown meant actually knowing them, rather than knowing *of* them.

'Marvellous, isn't he? Father and I have spent many happy hours with Elgar at Brinkwells in Fittleworth. He has marvellous views to Chanctonbury Ring. When did you visit?'

I had not visited. I had no desire to visit.

It had been a long day.

And I had no idea when we eventually reached Brighton that it was going to be an even longer night.

The Bedlington

A Late Night Sort of Town

CHAPTER 9

DUE TO CIRCUMSTANCES partly within my control (poor
map-reading) and partly without (slow-moving vehicles;
cattle being driven along the road on the way to an abattoir;
a family apparently moving house using a large cart, upon
which they had balanced a dog in a kennel, some rabbits in a
hutch, a canary in a cage, a goldfish in a bowl, some hens in a
chicken house, a garden shed, bags of logs and several sacks
of coal), we arrived rather late in Brighton. Fortunately for
us, Brighton was and is, and with any luck will always be,
the kind of town that stays up to welcome late-arriving visitors. Cruising into town on a chilly autumn evening around
10 p.m. – by which time most, if not all English towns and
villages have long since shut up shop, pulled the curtains
tight and retired safely to bed till morning – on the streets
of Brighton there were still dog-walkers, cyclists, courting
couples and children out playing. According to Morley in
The County Guides: Sussex, 'Eastbourne stands aloof, Hastings is of the people, but Brighton alone has a continental
character.' The place certainly had a character continental
that evening, as if it were an English town holidaying late
in the season somewhere in the south of France. And as it

turned out, the evening became more and more continental as it wore on.

Molly Harper, Morley's American adventuress, was giving a recital at the Theatre Royal, or, rather, had been giving a recital at the Theatre Royal. The performance was almost over by the time we arrived, which was a cause for great celebration on Miriam's part.

'Thank goodness for that, Sefton,' she said. 'I have absolutely no desire to hear the American Oval sing. It's bad enough having to hear her talk. Come on, let's find a quick drink, and then we shall go and rescue Father from her carmine clutches.'

We parked conveniently outside the theatre and persuaded – or, rather, Miriam persuaded – an usher to serve us in the bar, where we happily sat alone drinking gin cocktails until the audience departed, whereupon we made our way backstage and soon found Molly's dressing room by following the tinkling sound of laughter.

'Enter!' came the cry, as Miriam knocked briskly on the door.

The first thing I noticed on entering was the large presentation basket of fruit – Fortnum's, naturally – and numerous exquisite bouquets of flowers, which were most certainly not in season and therefore most certainly wildly expensive. Set among this extraordinary colourful display, like a life-size mascot Pierrot, was Molly Harper herself.

It has to be said that Miriam's description of Molly was not entirely inaccurate: she did indeed have eyes that looked like they might winkle you out; she did indeed have rather ludicrous eyebrows, suggesting a look of constant surprise verging on astonishment; and she did, in that American fashion, appear in every way to be a slightly inflated version of herself. She had a ready laugh, for example, that to English ears rang rather hollow, and she was seemingly equipped with endlessly bubbling reserves of the kind of enthusiasm that is entirely alien to the slow and long-cooled Brit. Her entire manner and appearance – her eyebrows, her hair, her enthusiasm, her vivid painted nails – struck one as being rather more suitable for the stage than for any average everyday activities. Larger than life, she was also rather larger than her tight, billowing black and white evening gown naturally allowed. With her white arm-length buttoned gloves, her perpetual look of astonishment, and her raven-black soignée hair, she had all the appearance of a rather sinister, pampered silken panda.

What Miriam had not mentioned in her description, however, was that Molly looked very much like an older, fuller version of . . . Miriam.

Swanton Morley of course looked precisely as he always did: he was someone whose success had been achieved entirely by dint of his own efforts and by unchanging daily habits and rituals, which meant that there was little about him that ever seemed to alter. Photographs of him aged thirty resembled exactly photographs of him aged forty and fifty – not so much Dorian Gray as an immovable and immutable Easter Island statue. He always wore exactly the same clothes, or at least exactly the same sort of clothes, a uniform that he had chosen as a young man and which he had stuck with ever since, the Morley Style: the sober-coloured suits in finest tweed or worsted, the tightly buttoned waistcoat with its additional notebook and pencil pockets, the sharply cuffed trousers, the tailoring always stiff, conservative and redolent of an earlier age. His tailor was a man in Norwich, a Mr Barton Bendish, who kept premises in an arcade near the city's market and whom Morley had known since childhood. Mr Bendish was, according to Morley, the equal of any tailor on Savile Row and a man capable of transforming even the stoutest and dowdiest John Bull into a super-sleek Sydney Greenstreet. He often suggested to me that he could provide me with an introduction to Mr Bendish, who would happily provide me with outfits similar to Morley's own, an offer I always refused since at the time I cultivated a studiedly care-free appearance that was quite in contrast to Morley's rather more sober-suited image. Though how I wish now that I had a Barton Bendish of my own. The only sartorial eccentricity Morley ever allowed himself were his brown brogue boots, always highly polished, and his bow ties, many of them pat-terned to resemble fine Scottish knitwear. This evening, at the Theatre Royal, he looked as well-tended as ever, in a three-piece light grey suit, with a red and white polka-dot bow tie – not merely smart, I thought, but actually elegant, as if the mere presence of a woman like Molly were slowly turning his tweed to silk.

Unchanging in appearance he may have been, but Morley was of course entirely unpredictable in conversation – and this evening was no exception.

'Billy Button buttoned his bright brown boots,' he was saying as we entered. 'Good evening, Miriam. Good evening, Sefton.'

Molly beckoned us into the dressing room.

'Billy Button buttoned his bright brown boots,' she repeated, after Morley. 'Your father is teaching me some English tongue-twisters, Miriam.'

'Is he now?' said Miriam.

'Betty Blue was beating butter,' said Morley.

'Betty Blue was beating butter,' repeated Molly.

'Miriam?' said Morley, nodding towards her. 'Betty . . .'

'I am not practising tongue-twisters, thank you, Father. It's far too late in the evening.'

'Never too late for tongue-twisting,' said Morley.

'Gig-whip, gig-whip, gig-whip, gig-whip,' said Molly.

'Oh yes, that's one of our favourites,' said Morley. 'Gig-whip, gig-whip, gig-whip, gig-whip. Sefton?'

'Gig-whip, gig-whip, whip-wig, wig-gip . . .' I gave up.

'Not as easy as it sounds, is it?' said Morley.

'Indeed,' I agreed.

'We've not met, have we?' asked Molly, breaking off from her tongue-twisting but remaining seated among the flowers and fruit and extending her hand.

'No. I'm Stephen Sefton,' I said, leaning forward, not entirely sure whether to kiss her hand, shake it, or kneel before her and receive a blessing.

'Ah, yes, Swanton has told me so much about you,' said Molly. No one called Morley Swanton.

We shook hands.

'All of it good, I hope,' I said.

'Hardly any of it good,' Molly said with a laugh. 'And all the better for that. Can I offer you a drink?' She indicated some unopened bottles – champagne, wine, lemonade – on the dressing room table.

I looked at Miriam out of the corner of my eye. She gave a sharp, vigorous shake of her head.

'I won't, thank you,' I said. 'It's been a long day. Miriam

and I have just motored down from London. We should probably retire.'

'You are clearly as self-disciplined as your famously abstemious employer,' said Molly.

'Perhaps not quite,' I said.

'You must have something,' she said. 'Here.' She got up, took two bottles of what looked like American lemonade, pushed down the marbles in the two bottle tops simultaneously, one in each hand, and thrust them towards us. 'A little trick I learned back home.'

'Flexibility of the lips is very important, you see,' said Morley, who was still on the subject of tongue-twisters.

'Oh yes, flexibility of the lips is very important, isn't it, Miriam?' said Molly.

'I have no idea,' said Miriam, rather huffily.

'Vowels as well as consonants suffer terribly from a lack of good lip movement,' said Morley. 'The lips are part of the resonating system, you see, which is what makes each human voice unique.' His own voice was as rapid as ever and as strange, rattling like a kettle on the range. 'The lungs and the diaphragm are the bellows, the larynx the vibrator, and this' – he tapped a finger to his head – 'the resonator. Molly has a magnificent resonator, Miriam.'

'I'm sure she has, Father,' said Miriam, as Morley and Molly started to make a humming sound together.

Miriam huffed.

Even by the high standards of embarrassment I had become accustomed to while working with Morley and Miriam, it was all rather embarrassing. Morley was clearly as fascinated with Molly as she was intent on fascinating him. They had first met, I later discovered, at a meeting of Morley's so-called Bonhomie Club, a group of friends whom he brought together once a month in London, for the purposes of discussion, playing chess, and listening to music. Molly had been invited by Morley to give a recital, and the two of them had quickly become inseparable.

'Your father, Miriam!' said Molly, breaking her gaze and her hum with Morley. 'He's incredible. I mean, his life, his experiences. His capacity for hard work! I'm surprised it doesn't simply sap all the energy out of him!'

'Oh, I'm sure you'll find other ways of sapping the energy out of him.'

'His knowledge!'

'A little knowledge is a dangerous thing,' said Miriam.

'"A little *learning* is a dangerous thing,"' corrected Morley.

'"Drink deep, or taste not the Pierian spring: There shallow draughts intoxicate the brain,"' said Miriam.

'"And drinking largely sobers us again,"' said Morley, completing the quotation. 'Sefton?' he asked.

'Dryden?' I suggested.

'Pope!' said Morley. '*Essay on Criticism.*'

'Marvellous!' said Molly, clapping her gloved hands together. 'You know, you're all just so . . . curious.'

'That's one word for it,' said Miriam.

'I'm terribly curious myself,' said Molly.

'Really?'

'Oh yes. I married my first husband entirely out of curiosity.'

'Isn't one supposed to marry for love?' said Miriam.

'One is supposed to do a lot of things, my dear,' said Molly. 'Do you know the final trio from *Der Rosenkavalier*?'

'Not off the top of my head,' said Miriam. 'No.'

'"*Hab mir's gelobt*",' said Morley.

'Indeed,' said Molly. 'In which the Marschallin gives up her young lover, Octavian, when she realises that he is in love with Sophie.'

Molly closed her eyes for a moment and then quietly began to sketch out the melody with her – admittedly – extraordinary voice, a soft, clear, luminous soprano. Morley closed his eyes and hummed along.

I thought for a moment that Miriam might actually be physically sick, but fortunately we had the Bedlington with us, who made his presence known at this point by attempting to climb up onto Molly's lap, interrupting the impromptu recital.

'Well, well, who is this little fellow?' Molly said, scooping him up.

'This is Pablo,' I said.

'Pablito, surely,' said Molly, petting him like a baby.

Miriam snorted derisively.

'I met Picasso at a dance in Madrid some years ago. Did I ever tell you, Swanton?'

'I don't think so, my dear,' said Morley.

'Yes. I'd been performing – Teatro de la Zarzuela – and there had been a dinner in my honour and we all went dancing in this wonderful little taverna, and Picasso was there and he really was quite a . . . bull of a man.'

'The minotaur of modern art,' said Morley.

'Exactly!' said Molly. 'The minotaur of modern art! How clever!'

Miriam sighed so loudly it sounded like a rushing wind had entered the room: her exasperation, I could tell, was reaching the point of no return and great regret. Thank goodness, there came a knock at the door.

'Enter!' cried Molly, though almost before she had uttered the word the door had already opened and a rather ugly bald-headed man with bulgy eyes poked his head around.

'This is Giacomo,' said Molly. 'He's my manager.'

'Good evening.'

The Bedlington leapt down from Molly's lap and snarled at Giacomo.

'Is he yours, Sefton?' asked Morley.

'He's mine, actually, Father.'

'I see,' said Morley, not entirely approvingly.

'I might need to take him outside, actually,' I said, having become keenly attuned to the dog's toileting habits during our drive down from London.

'Will there be anything else, madam?' asked Giacomo, ignoring the dog, and indeed the rest of us.

'Not tonight, thank you, no,' said Molly, with which Giacomo disappeared as swiftly as he had appeared.

'We're staying at the Grand, Father, isn't that right?' said Miriam.

'Yes,' said Morley. 'Perhaps I should come with you. Lots to plan for the next couple of days. We can take the dog, Sefton, if you'd be so kind as to ensure Molly gets back to her digs?'

'Of course,' I said.

'We'll take the Lagonda,' said Miriam.

'Do you have a driver, my dear?' asked Morley.

'Oh, don't worry about me, I can fend for myself,' said Molly, rising. 'And I have Giacomo, of course.' She bestowed triple cheek kisses all round. 'Now, we all have a busy week ahead of us. I shall see you tomorrow, Swanton. And you too, Miriam.'

'Hmm,' said Miriam.

And so Morley and Miriam departed, and I was suddenly left alone with Molly in her dressing room.

CHAPTER 10

'Well,' said Molly, taking a deep breath and gazing at herself in the dressing room mirror.

'Well,' I said.

She unbuttoned and peeled off her gloves. 'Would you mind, Stephen?' she asked, keeping her back to me, rather coquettishly, I thought. I didn't quite understand for a moment what I was being asked to mind.

'I'm sorry, I—'

'One can't afford to bring one's dresser with one everywhere,' she said, holding up her hair. 'Just gently,' she said, 'if you would, from the top.'

'Ah,' I said. 'Of course.'

I gently unzipped the dress, then turned around and faced the wall.

'Oh, don't be so English,' Molly said, in a ruffling of disrobing. 'I'm sure you've seen it all before, young man like you.'

I had indeed seen women in states of undress before, but – as all of us can perhaps testify – each and every time is rather different. I turned around as Molly was bending over to remove her shoes, leaning for support against the dressing table. She was clearly a woman who was more than happy in a state of half-undress, which on this occasion consisted of a pale silk slip, a black brassière, black girdle and stockings.

'Would you mind hanging this for me?' She handed me the dress.

'Of course, miss,' I said, mustering all my theatrical nonchalance, and hanging the dress on her dressing rail.

'Oh, come on. Do call me Molly. And do be a dear and open the champagne, would you?'

'Erm . . .'

'I'm *dying* for a drink, Stephen.'

'Of course,' I said, opening the champagne and pouring her a glass, while Molly rearranged her hair before the mirror.

'Wonderful!' she said, taking a sip of her champagne and turning and fixing me with a stare. 'You *are* going to join me, Stephen, aren't you?'

'I don't think so, no,' I said.

'Oh, but I never drink alone,' she said, pouring me a glass and handing it to me.

'No, thank you,' I said.

'It's terribly bad luck, drinking alone.' She raised her glass to me. 'Cheers.'

Matters were rather running away with me, I felt.

'Cheers,' I said.

She turned around now in her seat to face me and crossed her legs slowly in front of her.

'Now, would you pass me my blouse and suit?' She nodded towards the clothes on the rail. There were several blouses and suits to choose from.

'Which one?' I asked.

She came over and stood close by me. I could feel the warmth of her body next to mine.

'Mmm,' she said, skimming her hand across the clothes. 'Which one? What do you think?'

'I'm not sure,' I said.

'I think,' she said, reaching forward, 'I'll have . . . this.'

I watched, a little later, as she slowly buttoned her blouse, put on a dark, sober suit, smoothed it down all around her, and picked out a pair of matching shoes from a large selection underneath the hanging rail.

'Well,' she said, finishing her glass of champagne and gesturing for me to fill it up again. 'What do you think?'

'Very . . . smart,' I said.

'Smart? Really?'

'Yes, very stylish,' I said.

'Good.' She poured me a second glass of champagne. 'Tell me, do you find me attractive, Stephen?'

'I've only just met you, miss,' I said.

'I feel we've got to know each other rather well though, don't you?'

In the years I worked with Morley, out of a sense of duty, I often found myself in rather difficult and compromising situations. Also, during those years I did other things, shall we say, of an even more difficult and compromising nature, which meant that I was often on the lookout for the elderly, the infirm and young mothers with children to help across the road, in order to assuage my guilty conscience.

'I like you,' said Molly. 'I like you very much.'

'Well, thank you,' I said.

'You have that beaten look that people so admire and that is so hard to achieve.'

'Again, I am quite flattered,' I said.

She laughed. 'I think we're very similar, Stephen Sefton.'

'I don't know about that.'

'Here's to us!' she said.

We sat in silence for a moment, then Molly turned to the mirror and began first to remove and then to reapply her make-up, using little brushes in tiny pots.

'You're clearly not used to being around theatre people,' she said.

'No,' I agreed.

'Actors, musicians. We tend to be very *uninhibited*, you see,' she said.

'Yes, of course,' I said. 'I see.'

'The opposite of the English, really.'

'Indeed,' I agreed.

'Do you smoke, Sefton?' She turned back towards me, her dark eyeshadow and mascaraed lashes giving her a sleepy, languorous look, as if she were a femme fatale now relaxing after a long day's work.

I lit us both cigarettes and Molly half closed her eyes, champagne flute in one hand, cigarette in the other. She breathed deeply.

'Audiences these days only listen with their eyes,' she said. 'Can you believe I once sang Norina in *Don Pasquale*?'

I knew nothing about Norina in *Don Pasquale* and was now myself growing rather tired, so wasn't quite sure if the correct answer was yes or no.

'And Adina in *L'Elisir d'Amore*. Nannetta in *Falstaff*.'

'I can believe it, madam,' I hazarded a guess.

'Thank you. You're very kind, Stephen.'

We spoke about her various roles for a while, or rather she spoke about her roles and I listened, and eventually, after another glass of champagne she asked, 'People often ask me the secret of how I maintain my figure, Stephen. For a woman of my age.'

'Do they?'

'Two words,' she said. 'Actually, three words. Four. Cigarettes. Champagne—'

'Very good,' I said.

'And Gayelord Hauser. Have you heard of him?'

'I don't think so,' I said. I was pretty sure I'd have remembered the name Gayelord Hauser.

'Wonderful diet. You should try it.'

There came another knock at the door. Giacomo again peered round the door.

'Are you finished?' asked Giacomo.

Molly looked at me and then looked at the champagne bottle, held it up, shook it. 'We seem to have finished it off. Unless you would like some more, Stephen?'

'I think—'

'Come on,' said Giacomo. 'That's enough.'

I left them together and made my way to the hotel.

CHAPTER 11

ARRIVING DOWN FOR BREAKFAST in the Grand Hotel, I became immediately aware of a small fuss occurring in the far right-hand corner of the dining room. A large Philips radiogram, housed in an ugly walnut-veneer cabinet and half shrouded in dark green velvet, rather obscured my view, but – ugly radiogram in green velvet or no ugly radiogram in green velvet – I knew instantly the source of the fuss. For a moment I considered turning on my heel, leaving and making my breakfast elsewhere, but too late. A waiter approached and there was no going back.

'I'm with them,' I said reluctantly, and we began to make our way over.

It was Morley, of course, tucked away behind and beyond the walnut veneer and velvet. He was set up as usual with his typewriter, pad, papers, pencils and pens, having doubtless been there for many hours, banging away to the great annoyance of his fellow diners, working on some article or other, something about saints, or knights, or the relationship between the decline in hedge-laying skills in Derbyshire and the strange death of liberalism, or something on newts, or Newton, or the future of the steam-powered bicycle: Morley, irrepressible, indefatigable, and at it as always. With Morley there was Miriam, and Pablo the Bedlington, who seemed to be the immediate cause of the morning's commotion.

Miriam was busy remonstrating with a waiter as I approached, while Morley was busy writing, oblivious, half buried by papers. Morley travelled everywhere with what he called his *tel* – 'Arabic for hill, Sefton' – a mound of clippings and cuttings, which he used to stimulate his already highly stimulated mind. Part of my job was to keep the tel stocked and stoked with stories and articles from newspapers and magazines, like a fireman on a steam engine. Paper was Morley's great motor, his compost – and also a kind of impenetrable fortress. The table resembled the ruins of a small circulating library, or the aftermath of an incident at a newsagent's. Teacups and teapots had been set on the floor, for Morley or for the dog I wasn't entirely sure.

'Ah, Sefton!' Miriam said. 'Thank goodness. I've been explaining to this gentleman that Pablo has only just come into our care and needs constant supervision. Isn't that right?'

'That is . . . correct,' I hesitantly agreed.

'Dogs are not allowed in the restaurant, sir,' said the waiter.

'In which case I'll take him for a walk while you finish your breakfast, Miriam,' I said.

'You'll do no such thing,' said Miriam. 'We'll speak to the manager, thank you.'

'The manager's not available, I'm afraid, miss.'

'The manager's not available?' said Miriam. 'What sort of a place is this?'

'It's the Grand Hotel, Brighton, miss,' said the waiter, rather wearily.

'The *Grand Hotel, Brighton*,' repeated Miriam scornfully. 'Indeed.'

'And what do you think His Majesty would make of the Grand Hotel, Brighton?'

'I have no idea, miss.'

'Well, I think he might expect to bring his dogs to breakfast, don't you?'

'I—'

'Of course he would. *And* he would expect a supply of constant hot water, would he not?' Miriam always insisted that wherever we stayed should have a supply of constant hot water. Indeed, the very idea of a supply of constant hot water was for her a defining sign and symbol of modernity: anywhere that failed to supply constant hot water was *de facto* a place unsuitable for paying guests, stuck in the past, and should really be ashamed of itself. By Miriam's calculation, therefore, the Grand Hotel, Brighton was seriously struggling on a number of counts, though I thought the place tremendous. It had clearly recently been modernised: wainscoted walls, Lincrusta friezes and lots of what Morley would have called 'Tottenham Court Road' leather, with shiny bronze ashtrays absolutely everywhere, fixed to walls and indeed to the arms of chairs and sofas in a fashion I thought eminently practical but which Miriam had already declared utterly vile. Other signs of modernity throughout the hotel included a lot of tiling in the bathrooms, and lashings of chrome and Vitrolite – but all this was not enough for Miriam.

'By which I mean *constant* hot water,' she continued.

[76]

'Constant hot water, miss?' asked the waiter.

'Yes, *constant* hot water. What do you think *constant* hot water means, in everyday parlance?'

'Does it mean constant hot water, miss?'

'It does indeed. With the emphasis being on the word *constant*. Which your hot water most definitely is not—'

'I—' began the waiter.

'Being indeed entirely inconstant, like Shakespeare's moon. So, the manager, please.'

'I'm afraid the manager is not available until nine, miss.'

'Nine? What sort of a time is nine?'

I glanced up at a large, bright green Ferranti clock, mounted on the wall opposite the walnut veneer radiogram under its dark green velvet cloth. The clock suggested that this was going to be a very long breakfast. The waiter wisely chose to remain silent.

'Very well, if those are the hours you see fit to keep in the Grand Hotel, Brighton, I suppose we shall have to see him at nine.'

'Very good, miss. But in the meantime I must ask you to remove the dog.'

'The "dog", as you refer to him – he has a name, sir, which you might care to use, Pablo – will most certainly not be "removed", as you put it, and will be dining with us, thank you.'

'It's our rules I'm afraid, miss.'

I had found a breakfast menu amid the pile of papers on the table and was sheepishly glancing through.

'Father,' said Miriam, tapping Morley on the shoulder. 'Father,' she repeated, Morley being quite engrossed in his work. 'Father!'

'Yes, my dear,' said Morley, looking up from his notebook. He had recently embarked upon a planned two-year project of copying out the entire works of Shakespeare in his own hand, inspired by the example of Edward Capel, the eighteenth-century Shakespeare editor, starting with *All's Well That Ends Well* and ending with *Winter's Tale*, an enterprise that often occupied him after he'd completed his first article of the day at breakfast. It looked like he was working on a dog-eared copy of *Coriolanus*.

'Is there to your knowledge any law that prevents dogs from entering restaurants in this green and pleasant land?'

'Dogs in Shakespeare?' said Morley.

'Dogs in restaurants, Father,' said Miriam.

'Dogs in Shakespeare,' repeated Morley. 'Not sure if he was much of a dog person,' said Morley.

'Dogs in restaurants, Father.'

'Erm . . .' He consulted his mental filing system. 'Dogs in restaurants, you say?' He paused. 'What about them?'

'Laws regarding,' said Miriam.

'Hmm. Good question. Laws, you say?'

'Yes, laws, Father. Is there a law that prevents dogs from entering restaurants?'

'Not as far as I'm aware,' said Morley. 'Custom and practice, I think, rather than law, though one might reasonably expect the owners of any establishment to ensure there is no risk of contamination in food preparation areas.'

'Precisely,' said the waiter.

'Exactly,' said Miriam.

'I wonder if I might have a cup of coffee?' I suggested to the waiter, attempting to move things along in a slightly different direction.

'Are we in a food preparation area?' asked Miriam, who was not one to be moved in any direction other than the direction she had already embarked upon.

The waiter was silent.

'I said, Are – We – In – A – Food – Preparation – Area?' repeated Miriam.

'No, miss, we are not.'

'There we are then. Some crisp white toast then please, and a cup of coffee.' The waiter was about to remonstrate but Miriam held up her hand. 'The matter is closed, thank you,' she said. The waiter looked at me, at Miriam, at Morley, and at the Bedlington, and admitted defeat.

'And for sir?' he asked.

'A cup of coffee, please,' I said.

'Honestly,' said Miriam, as the waiter retreated. 'What is this country coming to?'

I took a moment to take a breath. Mood elevated, heart and pulse rate increased, pupils dilated: it was pretty much a typical start to a day with Morley and Miriam. They were like a drug – and I was an addict.

CHAPTER 12

'ANYWAY,' said Morley, unperturbed, unfolding a large map of the county. 'Ah, Sefton.' He didn't seem to have registered my presence till now. 'Trouble sleeping – or should I say rising – again?'

I often had trouble sleeping during those years and Morley was always keen to offer advice on how best to obtain a peaceful night's sleep, and how to wake before the crack of dawn fresh as a daisy, just as he was keen to offer advice on just about anything to anyone.

'I adopted a method from Seneca some years ago,' he said.

'Seneca the philosopher?' I asked.

'Are there other Senecas of your acquaintance, Sefton?'

'No.'

'Well then. Seneca, as in Seneca the philosopher, yes. Tutor to?'

'Nero?' I hazarded a guess.

'That'll be the one. We are at least on the same page with the same Seneca then, yes.'

'Very good, Mr Morley.'

'Anyway, Seneca performed a nightly confessional—'

'Oh dear,' said Miriam. 'Sounds awful. Was he a Catholic?'

'You know full well that Seneca was not a Catholic, Miriam. During his nightly confessional—'

'Not a Catholic confessional, Sefton,' said Miriam.

'He pleaded his case before the tribunal of his soul, retracing his words and deeds and subjecting himself to rigorous cross-examination – bad habits, any particular faults he had succumbed to, any troubles or problems that he had overcome. And then he would fall into a deep, tranquil, untroubled sleep, satisfied that his soul had answered to itself.'

'Not all of us are Seneca, Father,' said Miriam.

'More's the pity,' said Morley. 'More's the pity, eh?'

'A good morning's work?' I asked, before Morley was able to offer any more advice from the lives of the Stoics.

He explained that he was halfway through writing an article about crown green bowls – W.G. Grace, apparently, was a very good bowler for the London County Bowling Club ('He knew how to play up to the knob,' said Morley) – and that he had completed an article on hazelnut preservation. (You shake them off the trees – in case you want to know – stack them in their shells in jars between layers of salt, and bury them in the ground till Christmas.)

'Anyway,' he continued, consulting both his wristwatches – luminous and non-luminous – and his pocket watch. 'We're not *too* far behind schedule. So, plans for the day.'

'Let's just get to Lewes, shall we, Father,' said Miriam.

'We shall, Miriam, we shall. But there are some things I would like us to see first in this fine county. I can't wait to see the dew pond at Chactonbury Ring, and—'

'Yes, we've read the itinerary, Father. Haven't we, Sefton?'

'Yes,' I agreed. I had glanced at the itinerary with Miriam.

'Good,' began Morley. 'We shall capture Sussex, I hope, in all its glory over the next few days. We need to get to its very heart. To the very essence, to the bones and marrow of the place. The liver, the guts, the— '

'Let's not have talk of bones and marrow at breakfast, Father.'

'What do you think of when you think of Sussex, Sefton?' asked Morley.

This was one of his favourite questions whenever we arrived in a new county: 'What do you think of when you think of Norfolk/Essex/Sussex/Rutland/Northumberland/Lincolnshire,' etcetera, etcetera, *ad libitum/nauseam/ infinitum*. The truth was, I mostly thought of nothing. If I thought of the counties of England at all, which I did not, I think mostly what I would have thought of would have been Harold Larwood playing for Nottinghamshire and T.P.B. Smith bowling googlies for Essex. When Morley thought of the counties of England, on the other hand, he thought of just about everything: places, personages, customs, practices, bus routes, tram routes, lore, legend and myth; it was as if he contained within himself the entire historical, political, geological and deep paradoxical strata of the whole nation.

'You think of the Long Man of Wilmington, of course,' he said.

'Yes, I suppose I do,' I agreed, since agreeing with Morley was always easiest. 'The Long Man of Wilmington, of course.'

'A Sussex landmark,' said Morley. 'Said by some to be a memorial to a giant who lived round about, or indeed an actual outline of the giant's body as he lay there dead.

Some say he tripped and broke his neck on the crest of the hill, others that he was killed by a shepherd, or by pilgrims, or—'

'By those wishing he would go away and be quiet,' said Miriam.

'Quite,' said Morley. 'Or you think of striding across the Downs,' he continued.

'Striding, yes,' I said. 'Of course. Across the Downs.'

'Or of William of Normandy, striding up the beach at Pevensey?'

'William striding in particular, yes, absolutely, Mr Morley.'

'Canute at Bosham, the site of his encounter with the encroaching tide.'

'The encroaching tide, yes.'

'The Prince Regent at Brighton.'

'Mmm.'

'Daniel Defoe.'

'Daniel Defoe?' said Miriam.

'Defoe? Yes, of course, Miriam! His tour through the counties of England?'

'Oh yes,' said Miriam, 'one's mind is hardly ever off Daniel Defoe and his tour through the counties of England.'

'Sir Philip Sidney,' continued Morley. 'His house is in Kingston.'

'Is it, Father, really? Fascinating.'

'Or one thinks of the bee orchid, perhaps?'

'No one thinks of the bee orchid when they think of Sussex, Father,' said Miriam.

'Really? The most extraordinary flower: it mimics the appearance of the female bee, in order to be pollinated. A lesson there for females everywhere.'

'Really, Father? Is it?'

'Yes, yes.'

'Well, I can't think what it is,' said Miriam.

'The county flower of Sussex, Sefton?'

'The county flower of Sussex?' I said.

'That's right.'

'Erm. The bee orchid?' I suggested.

'Wrong! The Pride of Sussex. Round-headed rampion, *Phyteuma orbiculare*. Marvellous.'

Morley had by now warmed to his theme.

'Principal rivers of Sussex, Sefton?' he asked.

'Really, Father?' said Miriam. 'Shall we just leave this?'

'Well, if you can't remember—'

'The Adur, the Arun, the Cuckmere, the Ouse and the Rother,' said Miriam.

'You do remember! All those years of training have not gone to waste, then.'

'I wouldn't go that far, Father. And that is the end of that.'

During this exchange Miriam had mostly been absent-mindedly petting the Bedlington, but she now gave the discussion the benefit of her full attention.

'I'll tell you what I think of when I think of Sussex, Father.'

'Go on, my dear.'

'Resorts,' said Miriam.

'Resorts?'

'Yes. Sybaritic Sussex, home to the English at play.'

'Sybaritic Sussex,' said Morley. 'That's not bad, Miriam.'

'Thank you, Father.'

'Yes. That might be a separate article. A portrait of the retired gentlefolk of Eastbourne, the hard-working at rest in Brighton. Worthing, St Leonards—'

'I have no desire to visit St Leonards,' said Miriam. 'Or Eastbourne.'

'St Leonards? The first purpose-built resort in the country? And Worthing? We used to take you there on holiday as a child.'

'I have no recollection of Worthing at all, Father, thank goodness.'

'There used to be a wonderful little man there with a goat carriage made up to look exactly like a ceremonial carriage, and you used to love being drawn up and down the beach in it.'

'No, no memory of the goat carriage at all,' said Miriam.

'The old bathing machines pulled in to the sea? The hotel with the old leather bath chairs?'

'No, no, nothing,' said Miriam. 'Nothing at all.'

'They have these marvellous assembly rooms in St Leonards. I think I gave a lecture there once.'

'Fascinating, Father.'

'"On Modern Architecture and the Lives of the Architects". Do you not remember, Miriam?'

'No memory, Father, *what-so-ever.*'

'Do you know the De La Warr Pavilion in Bexhill, Sefton?'

'I can't say I do, Mr Morley, no.'

'You know Herbrand?'

'Herbrand?' I said.

'Harebrained,' said Miriam.

'Herbrand Sackville? Buck De La Warr?'

'No,' I said.

'The Lord Privy Seal? Mayor of Bexhill. Extraordinary man. Last time I was in Sussex was for the opening of the pavilion. Marvellous day. Welded steel construction. Triumph of the Modernist style – if you like that sort of thing.'

'Which we do, of course, Father.'

'Which you do, of course, Miriam.'

At this point my coffee and Miriam's toast arrived, brought by a new waiter, who had either been briefed by his colleague to say absolutely nothing, or who was simply wise enough to know not to get into any discussion of any kind over breakfast with the likes of Miriam and Morley.

'Now, the itinerary,' said Miriam, crunching on a piece of toast.

'Yes,' said Morley, 'the itinerary.'

'We both agree we need to skip some of the places you've suggested we visit.'

'Skip?' said Morley.

'That's right, Father.'

'Skip? As in skip over? Pass over? Miss out? Forgo?'

'Correct, Father. That, I believe, is the traditional meaning of "skip", certainly in this usage.'

'Skip!?'

'Yes, that's right, Father. Skip. Skirt around. Circumnavigate. Forget about. Avoid entirely.'

'But where on earth can we skip?'

Miriam reached down for her crocodile/alligator handbag and produced from it Morley's typewritten list of places to visit in Sussex – holding it out before her rather as though it were a contaminant in a food preparation area – and began scrutinising it, as an unhappy executor reading an unsatisfactory will, or a hanging judge preparing to pass sentence.

'Abbotsford Gardens,' she said, after long consideration, and with considerable disdain, 'I think could safely be skipped.'

'Really? Abbotsford Gardens?'

'Yes. *Utterly* pointless.' She took another determined bite of her toast. 'And the Balcombe Viaduct.'

'The Balcombe Viaduct!' said Morley. 'But the Balcombe Viaduct—'

'And Bexhill,' continued Miriam, 'Climping and Chailey.'

'Miriam!' said Morley.

'Father!' said Miriam. 'Listen, please.'

'Miriam!'

'Father, listen, please.' She held up a finger. Morley was silent. 'We are going to have to be much more disciplined if we're going to stick to our production schedule.' Miriam and Morley were the only people I ever met who referred to writing as a form of production. Then again, they were the only people I ever met who made a decent living from writing. 'If you wish to complete *The County Guides* by the time you retire we need to rationalise and streamline our processes.'

'Retire?' said Morley. 'I have no intention of retiring, Miriam.'

'You may not, Father, but I certainly do,' said Miriam, 'and I feel I've already spent far too much time on these blasted books.'

'But, Miriam—'

'Please!' The finger was raised again. 'We need a better system, Father.' Miriam knew that Morley was a sucker for systems. If she could get him to see the wisdom of some new system, the argument would be won. 'I am simply suggesting that we reduce our time spent travelling and increase our time researching.'

'But travelling *is* researching,' said Morley.

'Travelling is *not* researching, Father.'

'It's what we do.'

'It's a *part* of what we do, Father. Just to remind you, we have encountered nothing but trouble and difficulty in *every* county we have visited, and I see no immediate prospect of our troubles ceasing here in Sussex, or indeed wherever else we may find ourselves. In my opinion, you'd be much better staying at home and spending more time in the library.'

'But England is my library,' said Morley.

'Father, England is *not* your library.'

'Not only is it my library,' said Morley, stiffening rather and warming to his theme, 'it is my atlas, my dictionary, my thesaurus, my ready reckoner. It is my container, my crucible, it is the rock on which I stand, the source of my inspiration, the object of my attention—'

'You can pick one place we should visit before we drive to Lewes,' said Miriam.

'One?' said Morley.

'One,' said Miriam. 'And then we're going to Lewes.'

'One?' repeated Morley.

'One,' insisted Miriam. 'And we can bone up on the rest of it at home.'

It was a stand-off.

'What'll it be then?' said Miriam, taking a final decisive bite from her toast.

'This is mutinous, Miriam,' said Morley.

'It is practical, Father.'

'You're worse than Fletcher Christian,' said Morley.

'And you're worse than Captain Bligh, Father.'

'And I—' I began.

'Think not just of *The County Guides*,' said Miriam. 'Think of all the other books you're writing and wish to write. The book on Ireland, for example.'

'Ah, yes, the book on Ireland,' said Morley. 'Beginning with the *Táin Bó Cúailnge*.'

'Indeed,' said Miriam. 'And the book on Scotland.'

'Yes. The book on Scotland,' said Morley fondly. He had Scottish ancestors, the mere thought of which, when it occurred to him occasionally, as now, prompted him to misty-eyed reverie. At such moments, the quoting of the poetry of Robbie Burns was never far behind.

'Wales,' added Miriam quickly, saving us from Robbie Burns. As far as I knew Morley was entirely without Welsh forebears, which at least delivered us from the prospect of lectures on the *Mabinogion*. 'A brief history of China.'

'A long history of Europe,' said Morley.

'Of the United States. The anthologies. The compendiums. The guidebooks. The books on agriculture.'

'Horticulture,' said Morley.

'Viticulture,' said Miriam, sipping her coffee. 'You see. It goes on and on, Father. If you're ever going to get to where you want to get with all these books, we need to help you find a quicker route through.'

As it was, Morley moved through subject matter quicker and more efficiently than anyone I'd ever known, but even he was always looking to go faster.

'Yes,' he said. 'A quicker route would be good. Like an autobahn.' He was a great fan of the German road network, having visited in 1936 and written one of his more misjudged pamphlets, *Reichsautobahn: What the British Can Learn from the Germans*, now thankfully long since out of print.

'Exactly like an autobahn, Father.'

For all her efforts and arguments, I couldn't honestly see any way that Morley was going to agree to alter his itinerary. He never had. He never would. But then again, as my time with Morley and Miriam so often proved, I am not a good judge of character.

'Ashdown Forest, then,' Morley suddenly said. 'That's the one place I would choose to visit in Sussex.'

'Right,' said Miriam.

'One of the great secrets of Sussex.'

'Jolly good,' said Miriam.

'An ancient royal hunting ground, where even now one can still imagine the horses and hounds streaming across the slopes, the silver notes of the horn making English music, the echo of centuries long ago. Can you imagine it, Sefton?'

I did my best to imagine it, but Morley's imagination was perhaps more agile and accomplished than mine.

'Indeed I can, Mr Morley,' I said. 'Indeed I can.'

'A vast territory of heather and gorse and fir. A place of immemorial tranquillity.'

'Mmm, quite, quite. Fascinating, Father,' said Miriam, who now, triumphant, had returned her attention to petting Pablo. 'That'll be the place, then.'

Morley was showing me Ashdown Forest on the map.

'If you look here, Sefton, you'll see that Nutley is the major village in the forest – susceptible to fires in the dry season, alas. And you'll see that the highest ridge here' – he indicated what looked indeed, cartographically, like a high ridge – 'of the High Weald can be reached by car, along the B2026.'

'Very good,' said Miriam.

'And that geographically the heart of Ashdown is Gills Lap, which we shall visit and then of course make pilgrimage to Cotchford Farm which is the home of?'

'The Queen of Sheba?' said Miriam.

'Wrong.'

'Albert Schweitzer?'

'Wrong again, Miriam. A.A. Milne,' said Morley.

'Oh, no,' said Miriam, stroking Pablo. 'Not mopey Milne.'

'Do you know Milne?' Morley asked me.

'I don't, no,' I said.

'Anyway, you know the story of how Milne liked to walk with his son Christopher up to Gills Lap with his teddy bear. Hence—'

'Pooh,' said Miriam. Pablo gave a little bark here, which attracted the attention of the other diners.

'Pooh indeed,' said Morley. 'It'll be nice to see Alan.'

'Will it, though?' said Miriam.

'Bit of a cold fish, admittedly,' said Morley.

'Bit?' said Miriam. 'All I'll say, Sefton, is that he's rather more Eeyore than Roo, if you know what I mean.'

'Anyway, you'll enjoy Ashdown Forest, Sefton,' said Morley. 'This time of year, it's like an Impressionist painting.'

'Dull and hazy,' said Miriam, who had by now both finished her toast and petting Pablo and was preparing to leave, having seemingly forgotten all about her summoning the manager of the hotel for an urgent nine o'clock meeting about dogs in restaurants and the supply of constant hot water. 'Well,' she said. 'I'm so glad that's all sorted. I'm going to pack and then we can set off in – what? – an hour?'

'We have to wait for Molly,' said Morley.

'What?' Miriam froze as she was about to walk away.

'For Molly,' said Morley. 'We have to wait for Molly. She's going to be joining us on the journey down.'

'Oh no, Father.'

'What?'

'Really?'

'Yes, really.'

'She's coming to Lewes?'

'That's right, she's singing at the Hudsons', as you know.'

'But can't she make her own way there?' said Miriam.

'She could, of course,' said Morley. 'But I've invited her to travel down with us.'

'You invited her, or she invited herself?'

'I invited her,' said Morley.

'But she's got her manager fellow, Giacomo or whatever he's called, hasn't she? Isn't she better off travelling down with him?'

'He's going to be driving her luggage and costumes down and is going to meet us there.'

'Oh, Father,' said Miriam.

'What?'

'Come on, Father.'

'Come on what?'

'Let's be honest. She is dreadful, Father.'

'She is not dreadful, Miriam. On the contrary, she is quite delightful. And I would hope that you would know better than speaking ill of persons who are not here to defend themselves.'

Miriam huffed.

'What would Mother think?'

It was at this point that I decided I would take Pablo for a walk.

'If you'll excuse me,' I said. 'I'll perhaps meet you with the Bedlington in—'

'In an hour, Sefton,' said Miriam. 'We are leaving in an hour.'

'We are waiting for Molly,' said Morley.

I smiled and did what I should have done an hour previously: I scooped up the dog and departed.

CHAPTER 13

MOLLY, it turned out, would not be ready for some time. The life of an opera singer, it seems, does not involve early mornings. Or indeed, in Molly's case, mornings. While Miriam fumed, Morley suggested that he and I take a tour of Brighton.

We did all the usual things: Brighton Pavilion, though Morley strongly disapproved of George, the Prince Regent, and his relationship with Maria Fitzherbert, so much so that it was almost as though he were a family member who had betrayed him; the Pier, which was a 'shot-in-the-arm', apparently, though quite unlike any shot in the arm I've ever experienced; and Volk's Electric Railway, which, inevitably, I had to drag him away from.

On the way back to the hotel, Morley spotted a brightly coloured sign pointing down a side street, inviting passers-by to 'Come And Have A Look At My Little Stick of Rock', which, I had to explain, probably referred to the song 'With My Little Stick of Blackpool Rock', by someone called George Formby, an enormously popular and enormously ugly Lancastrian singer-songwriter and comedian. Morley was somehow not familiar with the work of Mr Formby:

there were some gaps in his knowledge. 'With My Little Stick of Blackpool Rock' contained rather salacious lyrics, which some readers will doubtless remember, including, '*A fellow took my photograph, it cost one and three./ I said when it was done, Is that supposed to be me?/ You've properly mucked it up – the only thing I can see/ Is my little stick of Blackpool Rock.*' This didn't amuse Morley, but nor did it deter him from insisting that we take a look at this little stick of Brighton rock, whatever it might be.

Rather disappointingly, it was a rock shop.

For anyone who has never enjoyed the pleasure of a stick of seaside rock, it is essentially a foot-long cylinder of hard, boiled sugar, about an inch in diameter, wrapped in cellophane, usually pink on the outside, and with a ring of bright red letters on the inside that spell out the name of whichever godforsaken seaside resort you happen to be visiting, and which somehow miraculously runs throughout the length of this vile confection. France has its pâtisserie, America has its cherry pie: England has rock.

'Are you here for rock or the tour?' asked the stout, red-faced, white-coated man in the shop.

'We're here for both,' said Morley.

'I'm not sure, Mr Morley,' I said, 'if we have time for—'

'Yes, yes,' insisted Morley, 'most definitely, rock *and* the tour. It's a tour of . . . ?'

'The rock-making factory,' said the man.

'Oh, goodie!' said Morley.

'We'll just be able to squeeze you in.'

There was no one else in the shop.

'That'll be sixpence each, then. Or a shilling for both of you.'

'But that's the same,' I said.

'The sixpence includes a stick of rock,' said the man. 'And so does the shilling.'

We handed over the money.

'So where's the factory?' asked Morley.

'Follow me,' said the man. 'Mind the crowds.' And he led us out of the front of the shop back onto the side street, onto another side street, and in through the door of a building that was clearly connected to the shop.

'Long way round?' said Morley.

'Is the best way in,' said the man. 'Isn't that what they say?'

Not as far as I'm aware.

'Now, lads, just stand back there, if you would,' he said, as we entered. 'You are entering a hazardous area. Frank! Frank!'

A young man who clearly answered to the name of Frank appeared from somewhere at the back of the room, which had all the appearance of a mechanics' workshop, though perhaps marginally less grimy.

'So, "How does you make your Brighton rock, you ask?"' said the man.

We had not asked, and certainly not in that fashion, but . . .

'Basically, you boils your water, your sugar and your glucose syrup, you colours it red and pink and white, you makes your letters from the red, puts the white all around it, rolls it all up, adds the pink, pulls it out, and chops it up, and that, my dears, is that.'

'Can I just ask—' began Morley.

'This is Frank, our apprentice. Say hello, Frank.'

'Hello, Frank,' said Frank.

'Very good,' said the man. 'Now, make yourself useful, lad. This, ladies and gentlemen, is Where The Magic Happens!'

I was beginning to get the feeling that the rock shop man was something of a frustrated performer.

Frank unplugged a stopper in a big copper still and allowed some greyish mush to flow out into a big copper bowl set on a trolley. It was a revolting sight. The mushy contents of the copper bowl he then transported and poured out onto a metal bench that could have been as much as twenty or thirty yards long; it certainly ran the length of the workshop.

'First, ladies and gentlemen—'

'There are no ladies present,' said Morley, who tended to take things literally.

'But the question is, are there are any gentlemen here, sir? That is the question!'

This stumped Morley. The man continued.

'We take our mixture of water, sugar and glucose syrup, which my lovely assistant Frank has prepared for us, and which has been boiled until it reaches a certain temperature.'

'And what is that certain temperature?' asked Morley.

'That certain temperature, Frank, is?'

'Around 260°F, Stanley.'

'Correct,' said the man. He looked like a Stanley. 'Next we take our hot syrup—'

'Hot syrup,' repeated Morley. 'Interesting. Are you making notes, Sefton?'

I wasn't, but then I did, though I should explain that the

[98]

process of rock-making as explained by Stanley almost takes longer than the actual process of making rock. The whole enterprise, from the moment the syrup was poured to pulling the rock took less than an hour: the commentary on the making of the rock made it feel like we'd been there for a week. Morley, needless to say, absolutely loved it.

'Which we call the batch, and which is poured onto this special metal table to cool it down.'

'Special in what sense?' asked Morley.

Stanley shook his head and beckoned us closer.

'This table,' Stanley said, 'is special in every sense, boys and girls.'

It was, I have to say, a pretty special table: at least a couple of inches thick, enormously long, and with a steel bar running all around the edge.

'This' – Stanley tapped the steel bar – 'stops the syrup from spilling over. And this' – he tapped the top of the table – 'is hollow, and can be heated or cooled by opening a couple of valves through which we run either hot steam or cold water.'

'Gosh,' said Morley.

'Gosh indeed, little lad,' said Stanley. 'This is English engineering at its best! What is it, Frank?'

'It's English engineering at its best, Stanley,' said Frank.

'We now add some flavouring to the mix – traditionally peppermint, ladies and gentlemen, though I prefer aniseed. Or Anna Seed, as her friends call her. I thank you. We're here all week.' Frank poured something into the molten mush from a small tin bucket and stirred it with a stick.

'Now as you can see, the batch begins to thicken as it cools down, becoming less like a liquid and more like my mother-in-law's custard, which means it can be safely handled – though, like my mother-in-law's custard, not safely consumed. Frank?'

Frank divided the batch into three parts, adding a small amount of red colouring to one part, a larger amount of red colouring to another part, and none at all to the third part. Coloured and divided into parts in this fashion, the stuff on the metal table now resembled nothing so much as the aftermath of an act of violent butchery.

'Now, ladies and gentlemen, the sugar-boiler shuts off the cold water which has been cooling the slab' – Stanley went and turned off a tap – 'and he opens up the steam valve to keep the batch at a steady temperature.' He turned on a different tap. 'So that the sugar remains workable. Why do we do this, you ask?'

'Because once sugar has cooled and hardened,' said Morley, 'it can't be softened again by reheating, because of the properties of sugar crystals, which—'

'Thank you, sonny,' said Stanley, who was busy rolling out the batches into manageable, rolled-rug-size proportions. 'We now give the rock to our assistant to pull.'

Frank then took what was by now a sort of enormous translucent sausage, draped it over a large hook that was fixed to the wall and proceeded to pull on it, lengthening it and folding it over itself, for a good ten minutes.

'And what's the purpose of all this pulling?' asked Morley.

'It gets the air into the batch, sir, encouraging the formation of those lovely sugar crystals that you seem to know so much about.'

In the process of pulling, the grey, uncoloured sugar sausage turned a milky white.

Once pulled, the batch was returned to the metal slab.

'Now,' said Stanley. 'Drum roll, please, Frank.' Frank tapped out a drum roll on the metal table. 'Up until this moment, ladies and gentlemen, you have merely witnessed cookery. Now, you are about to witness sorcery! You are about to witness what few people in the Western world have ever seen—'

'He's very good, isn't he?' said Morley to me.

I remained silent.

'The formation of rock letters that run through a stick of rock. In China and Japan, young men train for many years in their secretive culinary and martial arts. Here in England, I trained for no fewer than six years to become a lettered rock-maker. It is a difficult path, ladies and gentlemen, many are called but few are chosen.'

Frank gave a little round of applause.

In a funny way, the tension really was mounting: the closest I've ever seen to an act quite like it was when Morley and I toured the variety halls around Leeds for *The County Guides: West Riding*; I remember there was a very good act that involved dogs jumping through burning hoops, and another in which a woman opened jars in a most unusual fashion. Stanley stood before the metal table, much like a magician or an illusionist, with one large, opaque white roll of sugar mush, one slightly smaller, translucent pink roll of sugar mush, and a much smaller roll of red sugar mush. He took a slight bow and then – well, there is no easy way to describe exactly what Stanley did next. The simplest way to understand it would be to imagine a letter of the alphabet being formed, six foot long, made of red sugar, with the space all around it filled in with white sugar. Thus, the 'I', for example – which was easy – was made of a six-foot-long piece of red sugar, with two pieces of white sugar laid either side, the pieces joined together by being wiped with a damp cloth. You can only begin to imagine the terrible fiddle involved in making the 'B' and the 'G': the procedure, which involved shaping strips into rhombus shapes and ovals, is too complicated even to begin to describe in words, and indeed could barely be depicted in a diagram. Rock-making is a strictly heritable trade.

Morley was rapt. Even I was grimly fascinated.

Eventually, Stanley fitted all the different letters together, separating them using thin strips of white sugar gloop, to form a kind of thick white plank of unsightly stuff, six foot long and at least three feet wide.

'Come, come!' he said. 'Roll up, roll up!' He beckoned us closer and showed us the end of this thing, where one could just about read the words, 'BRIGHTON ROCK'.

This unwieldy construction was then rolled over, moistened with the damp cloth and rolled around the thin pink batch, to produce what was now recognisably a giant stick of rock.

'Another drum roll please, Frank!' said Stanley. Frank obliged, while Stanley hoisted one end of this monster rock up on some chains on a pulley, stretching it out and then hacking it apart into workable lengths with enormous scissors. More rolling and pulling continued until the rock was thin enough to be chopped into foot lengths and wrapped in cellophane, the words 'BRIGHTON ROCK' somehow intact inside.

'That,' said Morley, 'is *amazing*.'

'Thank you, gentlemen, thank you. Thank you,' said Stanley. 'If you enjoyed it, tell your friends. And if you didn't, tell them you did.'

'Bravo!' said Morley. 'Encore! Encore!'

I took him quickly by the arm, pocketed my stick of rock, and exited.

CHAPTER 14

Many, many hours later, Morley, Miriam, Molly and I were climbing into the Lagonda: Molly, as befitted a diva, had greatly delayed our departure; she had, in other words, won. She greeted me warmly with a smile and a kiss on the cheek. Neither of us mentioned the previous evening in her dressing room.

Miriam, as usual, was in the driving seat. She was – I can confidently state, having seen and experienced just about her every mood, from pleasing and pliant, through determined to furious and beyond – completely and utterly incandescent with rage. I sat up front beside her, with Morley and Molly in the back, like two naughty schoolchildren. However short the distance, the drive to Lewes was going to be a very long journey.

'Alas, since we are now departing so much later than we had planned we are not going to be able to stick to our itinerary,' said Miriam.

'But Miriam—' began Morley.

'Father!' Miriam raised a leather-gloved hand. 'We did discuss this earlier, at breakfast, if you recall.'

'Very well,' said Morley. 'But we're still going to Ashdown Forest.'

'I can confirm that we are *not* now going to Ashdown Forest.'

'But Miriam!'

'If we wish to make it to Lewes by nightfall, we are *not* going to Ashdown Forest.'

'But couldn't we—'

'Can you drive, Father?'

'No, as you know—'

'Molly,' said Miriam, twisting round to face her, 'can you drive?'

'No,' said Molly.

'I thought not. Which means I'm in charge, and which means we are not going to Ashdown Forest.'

'But we—'

'*You*, Father and Molly, will have every opportunity to visit as much of Sussex as you like over the next few days, but I am going to get us to Lewes on time for our appointment, or as close to on time as we're now able to get. Is that understood?'

'Yes, yes,' said Morley, doing his best to make light of the matter. 'You are *so* much going to enjoy Sussex,' he said to Molly. '"Something passes me and cries as it passes,/ On the chalk downland bare." Miriam?'

Miriam ignored her father.

'Sefton?' said Morley.

'Thomas Hardy?' I guessed.

'Masefield,' said Morley. 'Come on, Sefton. John Masefield. "On the Downs".'

'Of course, "On the Downs".'

Miriam was determinedly undertaking some last-minute adjustments to her make-up in the Lagonda's mirrors.

'Sussex is quite extraordinary,' continued Morley to Molly.

'Isn't everywhere, Father?' said Miriam.

'Quite different to her eight and thirty sisters fair,' said Morley.

'He means there are thirty-nine English counties,' said Miriam.

'And quite different to the United States, of course.'

'Of course,' said Molly.

'Unlike your own home country,' said Morley, 'England has a gentle temperate climate, with no extremes of variety in conditions. Our rivers are easily fordable, there are few marshes or mountain ranges—'

'He means it's deadly dull,' said Miriam, finishing off her lipstick.

'It is a unique habitat sculpted over centuries by man,' said Morley. 'The fells, the fields, the moorland.'

Miriam and I checked the map.

'Sussex, you will find,' continued Morley, 'is basically composed of these geological strips, Molly.'

'Strips?' said Molly.

'Strips, yes—' said Morley.

'I love a strip.'

'That run parallel to one another, east to west. You have the alluvial land that goes down to the sea. Then there are the Downs, which are a sort of rampart, if you like.'

'Rampart,' said Molly, cosying up to Morley.

'And then the Weald behind that, with marsh at either end

and rivers that run north to south, obviously. The Arun, the Adur, the Ouse and the Cuckmere and—'

'Excuse me,' said Miriam. 'Father?'

'Yes, my dear.'

'Before we go any further,' said Miriam, 'for Molly's benefit, of course, but also for yours, Father, if you don't mind, I'd like to lay down a few rules.'

'Rules, Miriam?'

'That's correct,' said Miriam.

She turned round again in the driving seat.

'Rule number one. Not too much of this.'

'Of what?'

'*County Guides* type stuff.'

'But we're writing *The County Guides*, Miriam.'

'Not in the back of the car we're not,' said Miriam, 'nor within my hearing.'

'But—'

'No ifs, Father, no buts, no . . .' For a moment Miriam seemed to have run out of things to forbid. But she soon picked up again. 'No *Ye Compleat Anglophile*. OK?'

'*Ye Compleat Anglophile*?' said Morley.

'You know what I mean.'

'I'm not sure I—'

'And no endless quizzing and questions about the route.'

'Miriam!'

'Your father is my *Baedeker*, my dear,' said Molly.

'I don't care what he is,' said Miriam.

'He is my *Guide Michelin*,' continued Molly, 'my *Encyclopaedia Britannica*—'

'Well, you will just have to consult him privately later,' said Miriam. 'Which I'm sure will suit you both perfectly.'

'Miriam!' protested Morley. 'Molly has never been in Sussex before and—'

'I was here for Goodwood, actually.'

'Some very pleasant Canalettos in Goodwood House,' said Morley. 'Did you make it to Chichester Cathedral?'

'I did not, no, alas,' said Molly.

'The only cathedral visible from the sea,' said Morley.

'Which brings us to rule number two,' said Miriam. 'No church crawling.'

'Church crawling?' said Molly.

'It's like pub crawling,' said Miriam.

'What's pub crawling?' asked Molly.

'There's going to be no crawling of any kind, pub or church, so it doesn't matter,' said Miriam.

'But there are so many churches in Sussex!' said Morley.

'I think you'll find there are churches just about everywhere, Father.'

'But you know that the one Sussex legend known to everyone—'

'Everyone?' said Miriam.

'Everyone,' said Morley, 'is the story that the devil was so enraged by the number of churches in the county that he dug a dyke to let the sea flood them, hence the Devil's D—'

'No dykes, real or imaginary, Father.'

'No dykes,' said Molly.

'None,' said Miriam. 'And no churches, flooded by the devil or not.'

'But the Sussex milestones, Miriam!' said Morley.

'The Whatstones, Father?'

'The churches in the Downs are called the Sussex milestones, Miriam.'

'I don't care what they're called, Father. Let me be clear, there is to be no church crawling on this trip.'

'Miriam!'

'Father.'

'St Andrew's in Steyning?'

'St Whosoevers in Wheresoever, no.'

'St Cuthbert I think it was who was supposed to have cared for his mother, pushing her in a barrow—'

'I don't care which saint did what to whom or where, we are not wasting our time on this trip with churches, Father.'

'Wasting our time?'

'Is what I said, Father.'

'But St Anthony's at Cuckmere Haven?'

'No, Father.'

'Magnificent fourteenth-century building, Molly.'

'Magnificent or not, Father. It's a no.'

'Lullington? Tiny little church, Molly. You could pop it in your waistcoat pocket. I think it's only about sixteen feet square.'

'A rather large waistcoat then, Father. Let me repeat, for the last time: *no* churches, however big or small.'

'What about castles?'

'Castles? No!'

'Sussex is peculiarly well-endowed with castles, Molly. It has a history of coastal defence and feudal lords. Amberley, Arundel, Hastings, Herstmonceux.'

'This is *not* going to be an Ancient Monuments, Tudor Cottages, Pewter, Oak, Ye Olde Inne and Kynde Dragons kind of a thing, Father. We are driving directly to Lewes and that's it.'

Miriam had turned back to face the front.

'Gardens?' asked Morley rather sheepishly.

'Are also *verboten*, Father.'

'Gardens!? But there are extraordinary gardens in Sussex, Miriam!'

'I'm sure there are, Father. But that's no reason for us to visit them. There were lovely gardens in Babylon and we haven't made a trip there, have we?'

'I think strictly speaking, Miriam – I think I'm right in saying – all recent scholarship would suggest that the Hanging Gardens of Babylon were a poetic construct rather than an actual place. As well to say that we haven't visited the Garden of Live Flowers in *Through the Looking Glass*.'

'You know what I mean, Father.'

'A better example might be to say that we have not visited the gardens at the Villa d'Este or the Humble Administrator's Garden in Soochow.'

'Father! No gardens.'

'What about Bateman's at Burwash, Kipling's place?'

'No.'

'But it has a superb kitchen garden.'

'I don't care if Mr Kipling grows actual kitchens in his kitchen garden, Father. We are not wasting our time visiting gardens.'

Morley, ignoring her, started singing a tune. He liked to sing. His usual choice were hymns ancient and modern, but the tune he was now running through sounded distinctly operatic.

Miriam turned back again.

'And rule number three,' she said, grinding her teeth. 'This is really for you, Molly, but also for Father. No singing.'

'But Molly's a singer, my dear,' said Morley.

'Indeed,' said Miriam. 'Though I like to think most of us could knock out a "Casta diva" or a "Nessun dorma", if we needed to – but we refrain from doing so in public, while people are driving.'

'But Molly's a *professional* singer, Miriam.'

'Which is precisely why she should be saving her voice for her performances over the next few days. We wouldn't want the vast, expectant opera audiences of Sussex being deprived of her dulcet tones now, would we? And as for you, Father—'

'Me, Miriam?'

'Yes, you, Father. I don't want to hear any more of—'

Morley continued warbling away.

'The catalogue aria!' said Molly.

'From *Don Giovanni*,' said Morley.

'Yes, we all know our Mozart operas, thank you, Father.'

'Molly is Donna Anna,' said Morley. 'Do you know the catalogue aria, Sefton?'

'I can't remember the whole thing, Mr Morley, no.' Or indeed any of the thing.

'Sung by Leporello. A list of Don Giovanni's conquests.'

'*Madamina, il catalogo è questo/ Delle belle che amò il padron mio;/ un catalogo egli è che ho fatt'io;/ Osservate, leggete con me*,' sang Molly.

'Yes, very good,' I said.

'*In Italia seicento e quaranta;/ In Alemagna duecento e trentuna;/ Cento in Francia, in Turchia novantuna;/ Ma in Ispagna son già mille e tre*,' continued Molly. '*V'han fra queste contadine,/ Cameriere, cittadine,/ V'han con-*

tesse, baronesse,/ Marchesane, principesse./ E v'han donne d'ogni grado,/ D'ogni forma, d'ogni età.'

'*Brava!*' said Morley. '*Brava!*'

'Or bravo,' said Miriam.

'I *love* the catalogue aria,' said Molly. (The gist of it, as Morley then insisted on explaining, is that the Don is a man with considerable appetites and the song is a catalogue of more than a thousand women – peasants, countesses, baronesses, women of every rank, size, shape and age – with whom he had consorted.)

Miriam started up the car.

'Well,' said Morley, in his usual way attempting to smooth things over and gee things up. I turned and noted that he had been clutching in his hand a book, *Baxter's Select Sketches of Brighton, Lewes and their Environs*. It looked like the sort of book that would contain a lot of wood engravings: just his sort of thing. He silently tucked it away by his side, a sure sign of defeat. He straightened himself next to Molly.

'Let us once more abandon ourselves to that oblivion of care, that solitude and that fond companionship that calls to us from the open road. There is surely nothing that has yet been invented by which so much human happiness is produced by so little human effort and—'

Morley always delivered some version of this little speech when we set off on one of our tours.

'And rule number four,' shouted Miriam.

'What?' said Morley from the back.

'Rule number four,' said Miriam. 'None of that.'

'None of what?' said Morley.

'You know full well what, Father.'

And with that, Miriam stamped on the accelerator and we were away.

CHAPTER 15

'THE TOWN OF LEWES,' to quote Morley in *The County Guides: Sussex* – and remember I'm abridging here, picking and choosing for the purposes of illustration, for though the book is certainly not bad, if I say so myself, it is *long* – 'is perhaps better set than any town in England. A solid, neat, substantial diamond displayed against the dark majesty of the primeval Weald [. . .] in Lewes we find perhaps the essential Sussex, prehistoric Sussex, Roman, Norman, Tudor Sussex, the Sussex of yesterday, today and, one hopes, of tomorrow [. . .] Just fifty miles from London, and situated on the slope of a hill, surrounded by the magnificent amphitheatre of the English countryside, the ancient keep may dominate the town, but this brightest and most precious of towns is kept, as it should be, by the country.'

Lewes excited and encouraged what one might call Morley's 'enraptured' prose style. At its worst, his writing, and indeed his conversation, rather resembled the Jacobethan furniture at his home, St George's, back in Norfolk: rather garish, rather ornamental and entirely unnecessary. Critics of his work occasionally referred to the 'Oriental' flavour of his work, meaning its excessiveness, and implying in some way that it somehow was not English. Certainly at his best he wrote rather like Marco Polo – and at his worst like a second-rate Victorian narrative poet. For Morley, everything about Lewes was either a 'graceful Georgian' this or an 'ancient Tudor' that. 'Lewes,' he writes in *Sussex*, 'is truly picturesque in that Italian sense of *pittoresco* – in the manner of a painter. Magnificently disorderly, the Georgian, the Gothic, the Tudor and the Norman tumble together, as if in constant play.' (So *pittoresco* is Lewes, indeed, that it features largely in Morley's book on *Irregular Beauty*, published in 1939, a celebration of raggedy-edge borders, rough-mown paths and wildflowers at the very moment at which all such things were about to be destroyed.) Basically, it was guff: entirely true of course, insofar as it went, which was entirely too far towards fancy and folderol for my taste.

Like so many of the English towns and villages and cities we visited during our years together working on *The County Guides*, Lewes is indeed a fine place, one of the best, indeed, and more than capable of speaking for itself. Our guides, it seemed to me, were often vast amplifications of places and of persons that required neither boost nor boast, and yet we often remained entirely silent on the very matters, the very sites, the scenes, the episodes and the incidents that affected us all the most and whose implications and consequences are felt even today.

In *The County Guides: Sussex*, for example, there is no mention of what was happening at the time in the county of Sussex as a whole or indeed throughout the *country* as a whole – the abdication crisis, the challenges faced by the National Government, an abandoned baby found on a hillside outside Worthing, arguments over planning consents in

Chichester – let alone events in Ethiopia, Spain and in China, news of which filled both the local and national papers. *The County Guides: Sussex* might as well have been written in 1837 or 2037 as in 1937.

And this was the problem, in the end, this was the great flaw in *The County Guides*: like any archive or record, however vast and seemingly comprehensive, however ambitious and *grand* a *projet*, the books were in fact partial, distorting and deceiving, acts of erasure and elimination just as much as they attempted to be honest and inclusive, exercises in pure fantasy and imagination just as much as they purported to be collections of memories, observations and facts. As Mr Chamberlain was soon to discover, to his and our great loss, every word and every sentence hides as much as it reveals.

There is certainly no mention in *The County Guides: Sussex* of Lizzie Walter, twenty-one years old, a teacher, daughter, sister, whose story has long since been forgotten, and whose destiny was about to become tragically entwined with our own. Lizzie Walter who drowned, in Pells Pool, on the night of 5 November, Bonfire Night, 1937: the night we arrived in Lewes.

According to Morley in *Sussex*, entry into Lewes is recommended in summer, in the morning, from the west by way of the magnificent old road that winds along the foot of the Downs, above the water meadows of the Ouse and through an avenue of beeches: magical. We in fact came into town from the east, having taken a circuitous route, under clouds, in autumn, and in foul moods: dreadful.

Miriam had driven wildly and recklessly the whole way from Brighton, enraged by her father and furious with Molly. It was something of a relief, therefore, when we finally made it to Lewes in the late afternoon, by which time preparations were well under way for the evening's merrymaking and mayhem: shops had been boarded up, crowds were already gathering, and vendors were setting up their stalls, selling sticky black toffee and hot chestnuts. It wasn't just me who was glad to have arrived safe and sound in Lewes: I think we were all relieved. Morley and Molly had settled down to harmless nattering in the back, and Miriam was slowly calming in her rage, bringing the Lagonda purring rather than roaring into town, where everywhere there were posters on billboards and newspaper stands, promoting and advertising the evening's activities, in the unlikely event that there might have been anyone accidentally passing through the town that day who was not already aware that 5 November in Lewes is renowned, spectacular, special and altogether a grand occasion.

My own favourite advertisement, which appeared in several shop windows, showed a young man with dirty bandaged stumps for hands and the motto, 'Never Mind! The Fireworks Were Worth It!' It wasn't entirely clear whether this was intended as a warning or an encouragement, but it was certainly arresting. Small boys with guys were collecting for the Cripple Fund – all proceeds going to the town's many stump-handed young men, no doubt – and Morley was doing his level best to explain Guy Fawkes Night to Molly, who was perhaps the person at whom all the advertisements were directed and targeted, since she had no idea of what it was all about or what to expect.

'Every year,' said Morley, 'the town of Lewes gives itself over to revelry—'

'Bacchanalian revelry, Father,' said Miriam, who'd had me light her a cigarette on our entry into the town, a sure sign that her rage was subsiding. I tended to smoke when tense, alarmed or alert: Miriam tended to smoke when calm or in the act of calming.

'Indeed,' agreed Morley, 'bacchanalian is probably the right term—'

'It is definitely the right term,' said Miriam, exhaling smoke.

'Oh, good!' said Molly.

'Don't get too excited,' said Miriam.

'To commemorate the Gunpowder Plot—' continued Morley.

'The Gunpowder what?' asked Molly.

'Oh for goodness sake, woman, read a book,' said Miriam, under her breath.

'Which is marked throughout England on 5th November, in commemoration of the events of 5th November 1605, when someone called Guy Fawkes – Prince of Sinisters! – was arrested with his fellow plotters, who were attempting to blow up the House of Lords and assassinate the Protestant King James I.'

'I see,' said Molly, who clearly did not.

'Here in Lewes on 5th November they also commemorate the local Protestant martyrs,' continued Morley, 'who were burned at the stake in 1557 as part of the Marian persecutions.'

'The Whatian persecutions?' asked Molly.

'Under Mary I, Bloody Mary, Catholic queen of England, 1553 to 1558?'

'Oh yes,' said Molly. 'Mother of Elizabeth I.'

'Half-sister,' said Morley.

'God help us,' said Miriam.

'There was a man called Dirick Carver, I think it was,' said Morley, 'who held prayer meetings in his home in Lewes, and he had his Bible thrown into a barrel on a bonfire and then he was burned in the barrel himself.'

'Oh dear!' said Molly.

'He managed to throw the Bible out; it's still on display in the local museum, I think. I hope so. That's one for us, Sefton.'

'Jolly good, Mr Morley.'

'So basically they're commemorating lots of horrible things,' said Molly.

'Yes, that's right.'

'That happened a long time ago.'

'Yes, that's it.'

'All together and all at once?'

'Precisely!'

'Horribly efficient,' said Molly.

'Ha ha!' laughed Morley. He seemed to laugh at Molly's every attempt to amuse, whether it was actually amusing or not, and she vice versa.

'Unlike some races and nations, we are capable of holding two ideas in our heads at once,' said Miriam, again under her breath, but just within my hearing.

'It's far too cold in England in the autumn and winter to be outside commemorating one thing only,' said Morley.

'Ha ha!' laughed Molly.

'Can I ask, are you of the Catholic persuasion yourself, Molly?' enquired Miriam, in another billow of smoke.

'Well, my dear grandparents were from Ireland—' began Molly.

'Well done them,' said Miriam. 'But the question is, are you a practising Catholic yourself?'

'I would describe myself as distinctly lapsed, my dear,' said Molly.

'Indeed,' said Miriam.

'So, yes,' said Morley, rather anxiously, 'the great South Down Saturnalia. The Capital of Bonfiredom. Lewes Bonfire Night is I suppose the closest thing in England we have to something like your Mardi Gras.'

'As in New Orleans?'

'Indeed,' said Morley. 'And as in many other countries with their carnival traditions. Ours is just a little bit—'

'Darker,' said Miriam. 'And bleaker.'

At that moment a firework came whizzing past the car. 'And much more dangerous,' Miriam added. 'Come on,' she said, pulling up outside the White Hart Hotel and extinguishing her cigarette. 'We're here.'

Morley, Molly and Miriam made it into the hotel unscathed by fireworks, leaving me to haul in their luggage and to survey the High Street.

Lewes, like every other town in England in those days had a fully functioning High Street, with a coal merchant, a timber yard, an undertaker, builders and decorators, a fishmonger, greengrocers, bakeries, a barbershop: it had *everything*. I have to say, I liked the place instantly.

Morley, Miriam and Molly were scheduled to meet Morley's friends the Hudsons in our hotel for a quick meal – Miriam referred to it as a 'scratch supper', Morley described it as 'tea', Molly described it as 'a dinner' – before the evening's excitements and activities. I was not invited to whatever it was, which was not a disappointment: the prospect of the meal did not appeal. The Hudsons were old friends of Morley's who had decided to turn their magnificent home a few miles outside Lewes into a venue for grand opera. Molly was to be the star of their opening, a performance of *Don Giovanni*, which had originally been scheduled for Bonfire Night itself, but which had been postponed for a few days due to 'technical difficulties'. To understand exactly why on earth anyone would want to turn their magnificent home in the country into a venue for grand opera, with all its attendant difficulties, technical and otherwise, it would be necessary to know Mr and Mrs Hudson, or at least to be familiar with their type. For anyone not familiar with their type, allow me to explain.

There is a very particular class, or at least a small, self-selecting sub-group of a very particular class in England, and indeed elsewhere, that one might describe as aristocratic impresarios. This type tend to be found outside the major cities, having either acquired or inherited vast country estates and wealth, usually from the proceeds of some dark eighteenth- or nineteenth-century industry or endeavour –

such as plundering the natural resources of far-off lands, or exploiting the labour of the home-grown working poor – but who have turned away from their ancestor's diabolical business towards the arts, or who have set about turning the arts into yet one more diabolical business. The great American families – the Rockefellers, for instance – are perhaps better known for this than their English counterparts, but the Hudsons were very much of the same breed and type, if not quite possessed of the same astronomical wealth. They were merely very – rather than fabulously or absurdly – wealthy. In the eighteenth and nineteenth centuries such English/Scotch/Welsh/Irish/Anglo-anything types would have contented themselves with building fake Roman temples, ruined medieval castles, or pineapple-shaped follies in their gardens: in the twentieth century they liked to indulge themselves as patrons of the arts, constructing theatres and concert venues to entertain their friends and occasionally the hoi polloi. This peculiar breed were on the whole more Miriam's type than Morley's but we seemed to spend much of our time during our years together dining with, entertaining and being entertained by such individuals, who ranged, in my opinion, from the merely irritating to the utterly intolerable, and who all seemed to be weirdly obsessed with the arts and music, without actually being artists or musicians themselves, in a way that I found patronising in every sense. Thus, although I had never actually met the Hudsons before, I felt I knew them already. As it turned out, I was to be proved entirely wrong: I knew them and their type not at all. I had no idea what they were capable of.

We had arrived shortly before dinner was due to be served in a private dining room up on the first floor of the hotel. Having checked in for Morley, Miriam and Molly, and having organised the delivery of their luggage, I was preparing to absent myself to my room for a couple of hours' well-earned rest and relaxation while they joined the Hudsons, but as I was about to slip away there was a brief *sotto voce* discussion between Miriam and the hotel's ruddy-faced sergeant major-looking maître d', who then approached me to inform me that the Hudsons had requested that I join their party for supper. It was a request I considered declining, rather fearing that it might be the sort of meal that involved oyster forks and *entremets*. But then I recalled with a rather sharp pang that my last meal had been my long-ago Brighton breakfast, which had consisted entirely of coffee, cigarettes and a walk of the dog, who I had by now safely stowed round the back of the hotel, under the attentive care of the kitchen staff, who were feeding him the finest scraps.

When in London I tended rather to subsist on a liquid diet, while at St George's in Norfolk with Morley mealtimes could be rather monotonous. (Left to his own devices, Morley's daily diet would consist of a spoonful of cod liver oil, one or two of his bottled plums, for regularity, a slice of bread and butter for lunch, one with paste and one with jam, and then a series of evening meals that his cook would produce week in, week out, with a predictability bordering on the insane: on Monday there was cold meat and milk pudding, on Tuesday a shepherd's pie and pea soup, on Wednesday vegetables, on Thursday liver and bacon, on Friday fish and on Saturday roast beef.)

So I decided that a dinner, of any kind, and in any company, would be most welcome.

CHAPTER 16

UPON OUR ARRIVAL UPSTAIRS in the small wood-panelled dining room there was much excited kissing of cheeks on Molly's part: she was an extremely enthusiastic kisser and hugger, one of the many things that failed to endear her to Miriam.

"'A complicated gentleman allow me to present, / Of all the arts and faculties the terse embodiment,'" Molly trilled, in her best D'Oyly Carte style, introducing Morley to anyone he hadn't met, while Morley bored anyone who didn't already know, and indeed anyone who already did – which included Miriam and me, since he had already bored us with the information on the journey down – with the dull fact that the great Thomas Paine had been part of a debating society, the Headstrong Club, which had met regularly in this very wood-panelled dining room in this very hotel during the late eighteenth century, before setting off to the American colonies to pen his great revolutionary works, *Common Sense*, *The Rights of Man* and *The Age of Reason*. Molly managed to look on enraptured as Morley explained how and why Paine was such an important political thinker, while I gladly accepted a glass of hock from a waiter and Miriam introduced me to a tall, handsome man, possessed of what one might think of as classic continental features who had of course instantly and instinctively gravitated towards her. He looked like he had recently stepped offstage at La Scala, Milan – and indeed he turned out to be the celebrated conductor Fritz Bauer, celebrated certainly by Miriam in her introduction to me, which included a long list of his most notable recent engagements and accomplishments and which ended, I thought, with a distinct diminuendo, 'And this, Maestro, is my father's assistant.'

'Assistant?' said Mr Bauer, unsmiling. 'Really?' He had long hair swept back from his face, and wore a tight-fitting dark suit and a white shirt buttoned to the neck with no tie. From the end of a long chain attached to his waistcoat he produced some pince-nez with which and through which he proceeded to scrutinise me.

'And with what exactly do you assist?' he asked.

'Oh, Sefton's our factotum,' said Miriam. 'He does absolutely *everything*.'

'*Everything?*' said Herr Bauer, indicating that he rather doubted my ability to do *anything*, and that anyway he had nothing to say to someone else's assistant. With this charming welcome he then turned abruptly away from me and began to usher Miriam towards the table. 'He's dining with us?' he asked.

'Sefton's our fourteen,' said Miriam to Bauer, and then to me, 'There were thirteen of us to dinner, Sefton, so we thought you might be our Kaspar.'

'Your what?' I said.

'Kaspar the cat? The Savoy cat. You know the legend of the poor chap who hosted a dinner at the Savoy for thirteen and left the table and was promptly shot dead? If you have thirteen to dinner at the Savoy you have to dine with Kaspar the cat.'

'A cat?' asked Bauer.

'A wooden cat,' said Miriam. 'At home we usually use an old mannequin for the same purpose, just to make up the numbers.'

'Well, thank you, Miriam,' I said, taking my seat at the table, feeling about as much use and as welcome as a tailor's dummy, or a wooden cat.

The other guests were all friends of the Hudsons, plus the director of the opera, the singer who was playing the role of Don Giovanni, who sported a colourful scarf knotted at his throat and who one assumed was a homosexual, and the singer who was playing the Commendatore, who was both notably American and notably black, it being much less common in those days in England to meet anyone who was either, let alone both. I was seated next to a man on my left who told me within moments of our being acquainted that he'd been at Balliol, had been a teacher, and that he was now the director of the Lewes Museum, and one of the stalwarts of the local Grey Shirt cadets, the Blackshirt Pippins, and the local amateur operatic society. His name was Michael Anderson. When I told Mr Anderson that I had recently been in Spain fighting with the International Brigade, conversation quickly dried up. As are so many dining companions on these sorts of occasions – certainly in my experience – the chap was perfectly pleasant and yet also, simultaneously, utterly repulsive.

During my many years with Morley I spent more time than I care to remember swirling venerable – and often less than venerable – wines in crystal glasses warmed by candlelight and the murmuration of voices, listening to the English upper and middle classes espousing the most peculiar and outrageous political views and ideas: fascism, crypto-fascism, Austro-, British, German and Italian fascism, anarchism, communism, occultism, communalism. The rich always seem to have strange ideas about how to organise society and how to run things, how to distribute wealth and what have you – though funnily enough, in all those years the one and only thing none of them ever liked to talk about was money. Money talk was strictly forbidden at all gatherings of all kinds. To talk about politics was permitted, to talk about religion, and – in some company, particularly among Miriam's sort of company – even to talk about sex, but to talk about money among the upper echelons of English society was instantly to demean oneself. Morley – who was essentially a working-class autodidact with Joe Chamberlain-style socialist sympathies and Merrie Englande ideas about the organisation of the social order – had no such qualms about talking about money, and so in polite society was often regarded as an ill-mannered arriviste. It was therefore often rather painful to dine with the rich and the privileged, whose manners, tastes and opinions were often, frankly, appalling; but I have to say that our dinner in Lewes on that first night was, on the whole, rather jolly and civilised. And the food was superb.

Mr Hudson welcomed us all to Sussex, claiming that there were five great continents – Europe, Asia, Africa, America and Romney-marsh – and that Sussex was not only becoming a hotbed of cultural activity, it was just about the hottest of hotbeds in the country, with Bloomsbury having long since set up shop in Charleston, Picasso and Henry Moore and some other people I'd never heard of at some place called Farley Farm House, Paul Nash and Edward Burra at Rye, Eric Gill at Ditchling, someone called Eric Ravilious somewhere or other, and Edward – James? James Edward? – at West Dean. Acknowledging Morley's presence, he paid tribute to all the famous and esteemed writers associated with Sussex: Richard Jefferies, Kipling, Belloc, Galsworthy.

'Esther Meynell,' added Morley.

'Hear hear,' said Miriam.

'Quite so, quite so,' said Mr Hudson. 'The contribution of the ladies to the literary and artistic history of the county should not be underestimated.'

Miriam raised her eyes to the heavens.

The meal consisted of something called 'Huffed Chicken', which is a local Sussex delicacy, apparently, and which is essentially a chicken pie, rather like a pasty, filled with sage, walnut and apple, and which was served with bread sauce, green peas and potatoes. Good hearty local hotel fare, and all the more welcome for being so.

'Do you know Florence White's book *Good Things in England*?' asked my Balliol-educated friend, between bites of huff.

'I can't say I do, sir, no.'

'Compendium of recipes – awfully good. The daughter of a local Sussex innkeeper, you know.'

'Really?'

'Yes.'

'How extraordinary.'

'Robert of course is good friends with Marcel Boulestin,' continued my companion, which meant nothing to me but

Miriam, who was sitting opposite, instantly perked up at the mention of this Monsieur Boulestin.

'Marcel Boulestin of the Restaurant Boulestin?' she asked.

'Of course.'

'Oh, that's one of my favourite restaurants!' said Miriam.

'Naturally,' said my dining companion. 'For it is surely one of the prettiest and possibly finest restaurants in all of London. A very decent fellow, Boulestin. He came and cooked for Robert and Marie one weekend at a house party. The escalopes were divine. Did you know he's started broadcasting programmes on the BBC television?'

'Has he really?' said Miriam. 'Television cookery? What will they think of next?' (Morley's disastrous experiments in the then new medium of television – including his once famously awful talk for the English Folk Cookery Association – have been discussed in passing by others, but there is much more to tell, though perhaps not here: both the radiophonic and the televisual form a large part of the background to the sad story that lies behind the elaborate façade that is *The County Guides: London*. Another time.)

On my right was my old friend the ill-mannered conductor, Fritz Bauer, who clearly felt that being seated next to a mere assistant was entirely beneath his dignity and who successfully managed to ignore me for the duration of the meal, until pudding, which was a Sussex pond pudding, no less, oozing with a buttery sugary sauce and dotted with currants, and which was so utterly delicious that Bauer was moved to speak even to the likes of me, deigning to remark on the pudding's sheer delectableness. '*Das schmeckt mir sehr gut*,' was his considered comment, which thankfully requires little if any translation and to which I deigned to reply with my own murmured 'Mmm'.

There ensued around the table a debate about the origins and purity of the Sussex pond pudding recipe, Mrs Hudson – who could trace her family's roots in the county back to the thirteenth century – declaring the addition of a lemon to be a recent aberration. Her mother's cook, apparently, used to make it with a whole apple inside, while Morley pointed out that, strictly speaking, the addition of currants made it a Kentish, rather than truly a Sussex pond pudding. There was then a discussion of the various other puddings for which the county is renowned – though, I'll be honest, it was the first I'd heard of it – including Ashdown Partridge Pudding, Sussex Bacon Pudding, Sussex Hogs' Pudding, Sussex Blanket Pudding, Well Pudding, Chichester Pudding and goodness knows how many other super-local variations of churdles, plum heavies and lardy Johns. The list went on and on. Indeed, it turns out that Sussex is so well known for all things suety and crusty that it is often said – at least according to Morley in *The County Guides* – that to venture into the county is to risk being turned into an actual pudding yourself.

By the end of the meal I was certainly beginning to feel rather puddingy and I dozed a little through coffee, awakening only with the bonfire assembly almost upon us and the sound of Mr Hudson asking guests before they departed if they could name the proverbial seven good things of Sussex. Once again, as with the Sussex puddings, I had no idea there were such good Sussex things, but there are, apparently, and it seems there are seven of them.

'The Pulborough eel,' said Morley.

'Correct!' said Mr Hudson.

'The Selsey cockle,' said Morley.

'Correct!'

'The Chichester lobster.'

'Correct!'

'The Rye herring, the Arundel mullet, the Amberley trout and the . . .'

Morley got stuck on this last.

'The . . .'

It wasn't like him. The pudding had perhaps defeated him also, or Molly was dulling his edge.

'No?' said Hudson.

'No, I can't remember,' said Morley.

'The Bourne wheatear,' said Hudson.

'Of course!' said Morley. 'The Bourne wheatear.'

Unable and unwilling to devote my full attention to the ensuing, doubtless fascinating wheatear chat between Morley and Mr Hudson, I found myself attempting another conversation with Mr Bauer as we got up to leave.

'How did you meet Molly?' I asked.

'I do not remember,' said Mr Bauer.

'It was through Rotha Lintorn-Orman,' offered Miriam.

'Oh yes, of course, dear Rotha,' said Bauer.

'It was a party,' said Miriam.

'Of course it was,' said Bauer.

'Rotha's parties!' said Miriam.

'Indeed,' agreed Mr Bauer.

There was then some brief mingling before we all departed for the bonfire processions and it was at this point that I met Molly's son, Henry, her son from her first marriage – or possibly second, or third, annulled, divorced, it was difficult to keep up and, I'll be honest, I wasn't paying much attention, except to note that Henry was a young man with what one might describe as a mid-Atlantic accent and east coast confidence.

'And what exactly is it you do, young man?' asked Morley, who had made it over to introduce himself to Molly's son, about whom he'd heard so much from Molly herself.

'I'm helping out on set design here for the Hudsons at the moment, Mr Morley.'

'Set design,' said Morley. 'Really? Marvellous. You don't know Appia's book, *Die Musik und die Inszenierung*?'

'I can't say I do, sir,' said Henry.

'Best book I think I've ever read on the subject,' said Morley. He had read most books on most subjects, though it has to be said that in the rather more obscure areas and topics his knowledge was often rather outdated.

'When was that published?' asked Molly's son.

'Some time ago now, I think,' admitted Morley. 'I remember I visited the Moscow Art Theatre some years ago,' he continued. 'I think I was reading it then, so that would have been . . . certainly back in the twenties.'

'Well, things have probably moved on since then,' said Henry, gazing over the top of Morley's head, I couldn't help but notice, presumably in the hope of finding someone else more up-to-date to talk to.

'I'm sure they have,' said Morley. 'Do you know, I'm sure my daughter Miriam would love to talk to you about your work, Henry, she likes to keep up with theatre. Miriam!' He called her over.

I saw her turn from her conversation with Mrs Hudson, note the presence of the tall, athletic – I believe the American term is 'preppy' – Henry, and promptly excuse herself and make her way over. She and Henry hit it off instantly, Henry explaining that as well as his budding career as a set designer he was also enrolled for doctoral studies in psychology at King's College London and was working as a tutor to the sons of various well-to-dos who happened to be friends and acquaintances of Miriam's. Henry Harper was, Morley later concluded, a young man with a bright future. He was both right and wrong.

During the mingling, Molly made a beeline for me. I wasn't quite sure which way the conversation might go. It went unexpectedly.

'A little bird tells me, Stephen, that you were on the Republican side in Spain, is that right?'

'That's correct,' I said.

'Can I ask' – she lowered her voice and leaned in close – 'did you kill anyone?'

'I beg your pardon?'

'I just wondered, if you killed anyone while you were there?'

'No,' I said.

'I was just curious. Research, really, for the *Don*.' She patted my bottom. 'Thank you, darling. That's all.'

And that was that.

The conductor, Mr Bauer, meanwhile, was eyeing developments between Miriam and Henry rather unhappily, and had drifted over towards us, the better to be able to survey the proceedings.

'And what is your latest project, Mr Morley?' he asked.

'I continue to work on a project called *The County Guides*,' said Morley.

'*The County Guides*?'

'A complete series of guidebooks to the English counties.'

'I see,' said Bauer.

I had learned from working with Morley that most people, when faced with a writer, find it difficult to come up with anything to say except 'I see', or sometimes 'Jolly good', or 'How interesting', and I fully expected Bauer's incurious 'I see' to be his complete and final comment on the matter of *The County Guides*. It was not.

'You do know England is doomed?' said Mr Bauer.

'Doomed?' said Morley in disbelief, though I had heard him say much the same thing on many an occasion. It is of course quite a different matter for an Englishman to speak freely and ill of his country than for a foreigner to do likewise, but Bauer was clearly someone who believed he possessed a kind of all-knowing, all-encompassing pan-European perspective and he was keen to share his superior insight. 'Doomed?' repeated Morley.

'Doomed,' said Bauer.

'Hmm. Well. I think not, sir. Though I can understand why you might have come to such a conclusion. Frankly, it's difficult to think of a time since the Great Reform Act when Britain did not seem doomed. Yet somehow we struggle on.'

'You are a tiny, vulnerable, isolated island, off the coast of Europe, where great changes are occurring.'

'Indeed,' said Morley. 'And built of coal, and surrounded

by fish, so we shall neither freeze nor starve in the cold winter that is doubtless coming upon us.'

Mr Bauer smiled. 'You'll excuse me, I have rehearsals to prepare for. Enjoy your Bonfire Night. Such a *quaint* custom.'

CHAPTER 17

QUAINT IS NOT THE WORD I would use to describe Bonfire Night in Lewes. One thinks of ivy-clad country cottages as quaint. Toy museums, perhaps. Victoriana of all kinds. Love spoons. Staffordshire dogs. Pianolas. Morley's fondness for Latin and circumlocution. Even Pablo the Bedlington might be described as quaint.

Bonfire Night in Lewes is not quaint. Bacchanalian, certainly. Strange, yes. Creepy, perhaps. And, alas – as it turned out that year – brutal and tragic. But quaint, no. English and German standards of the quaint are clearly not at all the same.

'Goodness,' said Miriam, as we ventured out from the hotel onto the street. The chaos that had descended since we had gone in to dine is difficult to describe: it was as if we had emerged from a state of slumber and tranquillity into a state of full public emergency, from a fairy tale into a nightmare. People were everywhere on the pavements, crushed and crowded, the road only kept clear by the considerable efforts of policemen armed with batons and good humour. As in any good old-fashioned English crowd, there was much lively trading of insults, or what according to Morley in *Sussex* is referred to locally as 'chavish', a sort of low-level chattering and exchange of abuse, largely consisting of the batting back and forth of various dialect terms, such as 'heggling', 'grummut', 'dubersome' and 'fluttergrub', the meaning of which one could easily work out by a simple process of substitution, certainly in simple sentences such as 'What do you think you're looking at? You sowing gape seed, you heggling fool?', and 'You great grummut, I wouldn't fancy your nunty.' Suffice it to say, the grummuts and nunties of Lewes were in good voice and full flow. (In *Sussex*, Morley makes the claim, entirely unsubstantiated as far as I can tell, and, I suspect, almost certainly influenced by his relationship with Molly, that there is a great similarity between various Sussex provincialisms and many words that we think of as uniquely and peculiarly American. Personally, I rather doubt that 'boffle', 'brabagious', 'bumblesome', 'gifty','impersome', 'sprackish' and 'snuffy' are at all common American terms, though there is doubtless more than a little of a Yankee tang to the oft-used Sussex 'dang', as in 'That is dang nonsense, Mr Morley, nothing but dang nonsense.')

Despite these signs of wit and good humour, the atmosphere in town was now rather dark and there were heavy hints of serious trouble ahead. The windows of the hotel had been fitted with wire blinds, for example, and a sturdy wooden barrier had been erected at the front entrance, manned by an equally sturdy-looking member of the hotel staff, who sported traditional cauliflower ears, a wide flat nose and mangled features – all of which were presumably intended to deter revellers from storming the building and damaging the premises. Fortunately, this same sturdy fellow – an 'absolute darling' according to Miriam, despite all evidence to the contrary – had earlier advised me to move the Lagonda to a safe place round the back of the hotel, otherwise it might already have been commandeered, requisitioned and set alight. Quite a trophy. When I say that the fellow had 'advised me' to move the Lagonda, what I mean is that when I asked him if I should perhaps move it, he had replied, 'I wouldn't misagree with you there, sir.' And when I had further enquired if there was likely to be trouble, his memorably gnomic response had been 'I'd say generally always yes and no, sir', a phrase that I had repeated to Miriam, and which she subsequently and enthusiastically adopted as her own, 'I'd say generally always yes and no' becoming something of a Miriam motto.

'My, my,' said Molly, surveying the crowd.

'Have you ever had wheatear, Sefton?' Morley asked me, seemingly oblivious to the dark carnival atmosphere that had now engulfed us, and still dwelling on the discussion of the seven good things of Sussex back in the hotel dining room. For someone capable of the most extraordinary focus and insights, he was also a man capable of ignoring and overlooking both the most obvious and most peculiar circumstances all around him. This of course is what made him great – and absolutely insufferable.

'Wheatear? I can't say I have, Mr Morley, no.'

'Rather like the ortolan. Have you ever eaten ortolan?'

'Again, I'm afraid not.'

'You have led a rather sheltered life, culinarily speaking, if you don't mind my saying so, Sefton.'

'I have indeed, Mr Morley, sir.'

'I can remember setting traps for the wheatear, many years ago. The shepherds would make little coops from turf and then simply set a horse-hair spring inside to catch the poor creatures. The high Downs were thick with coops back in those days. One might easily catch several dozen wheatears a day—'

A firework went whistling past our ears.

That seemed to catch his attention.

'Hmm. English fireworks,' he said. 'Best in the world. Brock's, Paynes. In my opinion there are no rockets or Catherine wheels that can possibly hold a candle, as it were, to—'

'Father!' said Miriam, taking Morley's arm and leading him past the hotel's makeshift wooden gatepost and out into the crowds. 'Come on! It's about to start!'

'Is all this strictly necessary?' Molly asked, surveying the dense crowd anxiously, and grasping my arm.

'It does rather look like they're preparing for war,' said Henry, her dutiful son, whose arm she was grasping with her other – and who had clearly never been to war.

'Swanton!' Molly called ahead to Morley. 'Is this really OK?'

'English high jinks, that's all, my dear!' called Morley back to her, as we pushed our way towards the front of the crowd. 'High jinks and jolly japes! We must give the Lewesians their head.'

The way Morley said 'Lewesian' made the inhabitants of the town sound rather like H.G. Wells-type aliens, and like aliens they indeed appeared, for at that very moment half a dozen men came hurtling – or in the local dialect, 'spannelling' – down the middle of the road, done up in the most peculiar fashion. They looked, in my opinion, rather like jolly jack tars in an amateur production of *HMS*

[139]

Pinafore, staged on Mars, or the Moon: Miriam thought they looked rather handsome. They were dressed smuggler-style, in striped guernseys, with white trousers and caps, and they were all wearing metal spark goggles – described by the man standing next to me, rather wittily I thought, as 'sparktacles' – which gave them the appearance of huge, knavish insects.

'Wow,' said Miriam, who was leading us slowly but surely towards the front of the crowd, with a natural authority that seemed to be instinctively understood by the overcoated locals, who parted in silence as she made her way through: she was as sharp-elbowed as she was sharp-tongued. She was also, on this occasion, absolutely right: this really was a wow, and indeed a gosh and a golly, for the Lewesians were not only done up all strange in their smuggler style, they were also dragging behind them on iron chains vast flaming tar barrels. It was – well, the only word is wow.

'It's like—' said Miriam.

'Walpurgisnacht,' said Morley.

'I was thinking more like some of the masked balls I've attended over the past few years,' said Miriam.

'Indeed,' said Morley, who wasn't listening. 'Promethean rebelliousness! Pagan in its origins, no doubt, coming so soon after Samhain.'

'What on earth is this?' asked Molly, huddling close to Morley as the Lewesians thundered past, the stench of burning tar thickening the air.

'It is perhaps really a symbolic marking of the summer's end and the onset of winter,' said Morley. 'People coming together to gather round fires, similar to what one sees celebrated in Ireland and the Scottish Highlands, where—'

'I think she means what *actually* is this, Father, rather

than symbolically or metaphorically,' shouted Miriam over the noise of the crowd.

'Thank you, my dear,' said Molly.

'Oh, *this*. This? *This* is the famous barrel run,' said Morley. 'These lads are the Bonfire Boys. You have the camera, Sefton?'

I did indeed, having taken the precaution of bringing it with me to dinner, but I did not alas have the necessary flash equipment, which meant that all our photographs of Lewes Bonfire Night were rather dark. They do at least capture the mood.

As the barrel run raced off down the street, crowds of Bonfire Boys came following, men rather than boys, lustily bellowing and singing songs, making what Morley in *Sussex* describes as 'a joyful noise' but which might just as easily be described as a terrible racket. It can sometimes be difficult to distinguish between crowds singing with joy and crowds chanting in fervent hate, though the words of the song were innocent enough:

> *For we're the men of Sussex*
> *Sussex by the Sea,*
> *We plough and sow and reap and mow,*
> *And useful men are we:*
> *And when you come to Sussex,*
> *Whoever you may be,*
> *You can tell them all that we'll stand or fall*
> *For Sussex by the Sea.*

As they reached the last line of this song-cum-chant-cum-infernal-roar, several of the Bonfire Boys attempted to push

The Mood of the Procession

each other over, and several indeed succeeded, one of them falling directly at Miriam's feet, who had of course now made it to the very front row of the crowd, having parted all before her, a female Moses in Schiaparelli. Strong drink, I think it would be safe to say, had most definitely been consumed by this poor prone fellow, who lay for a few moments, goggle-eyed and insensible, staring up at Miriam, until one of his fellow smuggler-styled companions pulled him up from the floor.

'Come on, Jack,' said his hale and hearty companion, who was a giant of a man blessed with the rough, roguish and sea-spray-weathered look of an actual smuggler.

'Sussex women,' mumbled Jack appreciatively, 'Sussex women.'

'Come on, Jack, leave this good lady alone,' said the giant sea-spray-weathered smuggler.

'It's perfectly all right,' replied Miriam.

'You know what they say about Sussex women, miss?' asked the gallant fellow.

'I'm sure I have absolutely no idea, sir,' said Miriam.

'They have wonderful long legs,' he said.

'Gosh,' said Miriam, caught momentarily off-guard. If it hadn't been so dark, one might almost have suspected her of blushing. 'Well, I'm not actually—'

'For pulling out of the Sussex clay,' mumbled Jack. 'You'd burnish nicely, miss.'

'Come on then, mate,' said the Bonfire Boy. 'Sorry, miss,' he called back, as he led his friend away. 'He's a little beazled, that's all.'

'That's perfectly all right,' said Miriam, giving him a little wave.

'The useful men of Sussex, eh?' said Morley disapprovingly. 'Useful for what one wonders?'

'Oh, I can think of several things,' said Miriam, gazing after the smugglish-looking smuggler, clearly rather impressed by his— 'Courtesy,' she added. 'They were very courteous, weren't they?'

'Very,' I said.

'Oh yes, terribly courteous county, Sussex,' said Morley. 'They'll now be throwing the barrels into the River Ouse. We won't make it down there. Let's wait here for the crosses, shall we?'

Seventeen large burning crosses representing the seventeen Lewes martyrs soon duly appeared, carried by men dressed in what was presumably intended to be some approximation of sixteenth-century Puritan costume – tall hats, frock coats, ruffs and all, the local Lewes tailors and costumiers having clearly been working overtime in the weeks leading up to Bonfire Night. If the sight of the burning barrels was strange, the sight of the burning crosses was truly shocking, and not at all the sort of thing one expected to see on the streets of the south-east of England; on the streets of the southern states of America maybe, but this was Sussex, not Montgomery, Alabama. At the sight of the crosses the crowd at first grew silent but then became quite ecstatic, cheering and clapping, as though welcoming the devil himself into town. Morley later recalled that he'd heard nothing quite like it since Ted Drake had scored the winning goal at Wembley for Arsenal against Sheffield United in the closing minutes of the FA Cup Final in 1936.

'This has nothing to do with the Klan?' said Molly. 'It is rather reminiscent. Of those terrible—'

'Oh no, no, no,' said Morley. 'Absolutely not. I blame D.W. Griffith for all that nonsense. These are English martyrs' crosses. Entirely different. Perfectly harmless.'

'We'll take your word for that, Mr Morley,' said Henry, who seemed, I thought, rather distracted and bored by the evening's proceedings.

We then followed the crowds, who were following the crosses, up towards the town square, where yet more people had gathered. '"A fair field of folk,"' remarked Morley.

'A field?' said Molly.

'*Piers Plowman*?' said Morley.

'Very good, Father,' said Miriam, quietly enough to be just out of Morley's hearing, 'but an allusion rather lost on your small round American friend, I think.' There were few moments during our time together in Sussex when Miriam did not take the opportunity to dig, to poke and otherwise attempt to undermine Morley's relationship with Molly. It was an entertaining, if not an edifying sight: Miriam was often at her best when at her worst.

Huge banners being held aloft proclaimed 'Our Faith and Freedom We Will Maintain', 'May We Never Engage in a Bad Cause or Flinch in a Good One', and numerous other similar slogans, all of a vague, perplexing and yet rather threatening kind, profoundly odd and profoundly Protestant, and richly illustrated with crowns and Bibles. The crowd remained silent during the megaphone prayers and condemnations of Roman Catholicism and Guy Fawkes that followed, conducted by various men in various sorts of regalia who seemed to be at least nominally in charge of proceedings from up on a podium in the middle of the square, and then the Bonfire Boys and the crowd took up a tune whose refrain seemed to consist of the repeated phrase, 'Bonfire Boys Are Out Tonight'.

'They most certainly are,' said Miriam.

All this was only the beginning. What followed was as confusing and chaotic an event as I ever attended during my years with Morley, years that included, I should point out, trips to the Appleby Fair, the Colchester Oyster Feast, May Day in Oxford, the Durham Miners' Gala, the Bridgwater Carnival in Somerset and the infamous Tissington Well Dressing, and many others, at which various events there were deaths, murders, robberies, outbreaks of mass hysteria and goodness knows what other kinds of bizarreries, strangenesses and shenanigans. The Lewes Bonfire Night was, in Morley's words in *The County Guides: Sussex*, 'a riot of rowdiness', which was an understatement. If you've ever perused Gustave Doré's famous illustrations to Dante's *Inferno*, you'll perhaps have some idea of the scene – except of course Bonfire Night in Lewes takes place live, every year, and in full widescreen Technicolor.

In summary of the chaos, or at least as Morley explains it in *Sussex*, Bonfire Night in Lewes is organised, if that's the word, by the various bonfire societies from different areas of the town, the Borough, Commercial Square, the Southover, the South Street Juveniles, Cliffe, St Anne's, as well as a number of other societies from nearby Barcombe and Burwash, East Hoathly, Halland, Edenbridge, Firle and etcetera. After the initial gathering of the societies and the flaming barrel run, these groups then parade individually and collectively throughout Lewes in a series of processions. The societies spend months preparing for Bonfire Night, building their bonfires all across the town, using scrap wood, faggots and brushwood collected from local groves and copses, and stockpiling petrol, fireworks and every other imaginable kind of flammable, sparking and incendiary material. In *Sussex* Morley rather sweetly describes this sort of activity as 'community building'. (He also takes the opportunity to reprint his popular article – one of his true hardy perennials – on 'How to Create the Perfect Fire', which bears no relation whatsoever to the bonfires of Lewes, but which, in case you haven't read it, advises that for the perfect hearth fire you need exactly 20 split hardwood logs, 2 large oak logs, 16 hardwood sticks at 3 inches in length, 20 assorted kindling sticks at 7 inches in length, some orange peel, some pine cones and some copper nails.)

On Bonfire Night, this 'community building' reaches its natural conclusion with members of the societies soaking torches in petrol, donning their smuggler outfits, and heading out onto the streets to denounce Guy Fawkes and the Pope and generally to carry on like pagans. As for the smuggler costumes, each society has its own slight variation on the theme, as well as a range of other fancy dress options: I spotted phalanxes of Lewesian Zulus and Red Indians parading that night, but there were also, apparently, Beefeaters and Vikings roaming abroad, and Morley claimed to have seen packs of women dressed in traditional Valencian costume, though it's possible of course that they may simply have been actual women visiting from Valencia. Each society also builds its own enormous effigy that gets paraded through town and then on to each bonfire site, where there are firework displays, yet more speeches and condemnations of the Pope, politicians and all other enemies of the people, until finally the effigies are violently beaten with sticks, have their heads blown off with fireworks and their remains cast to the flames, while the revellers dance around the fire, whooping, hollering and carousing until the early hours.

Quaint.

Almost as soon as the processions began that evening, I became separated from Morley, Molly and Miriam: it was impossible to stick together in the crowd, which surged this way and that through the narrow streets of the town, following a giant papier-mâché Hitler head this way, a blimp-like Mussolini that. Processions passed by with Lady Lancers, brass bands and firework wheels flaming, everywhere underfoot there seemed to be small boys skimming fireworks along the ground, and the chanting of various bonfire songs echoed throughout the town – 'Burn him in a tub of tar/ burn him like a blazing star/ burn his body from his head/ then we'll the say old Pope is dead!' – as did the repeated call and response, 'What shall we do with the Pope?' 'Burn him! Burn him! Burn the Pope!' I have never been to Belfast but I assume that the famous Orange marches on 12 July echo to a similar sound. Purely for the purposes of avoiding such sinister jubilations I found myself in and out of various local hostelries: the Snowdrop, the Anchor, the Bargeman's Arms, the Schooner, excellent establishments some of them, though I cannot alas recall which, but which I do recall were more like old country pubs, where the beer was kept in barrels in the cellar, accessed by steps down from the pub kitchen and brought up a glass at the time. Bare floors, a few old tables and chairs: one might almost have been drinking in the sixteenth century. Entirely without aim or intention, I eventually found myself with a bunch of local lads at a bonfire site some time in the early hours in the suburb of Cliffe. The masquerades and fireworks having long since concluded, small groups of men and women were running and jumping through the glowing embers of the bonfire. I dimly recall our all extinguishing the flames by the traditional method, while singing the National Anthem, and my returning to the hotel to find the doors firmly locked and bolted.

Making my way round the back to the old stables, past the undamaged Lagonda, I found where the kitchen staff had kindly settled Pablo the Bedlington on some old flour bags, and settled myself down beside him for the night.

CHAPTER 18

I woke, stiff and freezing cold, around five thirty, to the thoroughly unpleasant sensation of my pocketed stick of Brighton rock poking me in the ribs and my face being buried in dog fur – a choking, sickening sensation that I cannot recommend, and which was almost as bad as my throbbing hangover.

As I opened my eyes I saw that the kitchen staff were making their way into the back of the White Hart. I was sorely tempted to follow them immediately into the warmth and comfort of the hotel but then I got up to stretch and my whole body felt like a damp firework exploding. I thought Pablo and I might take a quick walk around Lewes – just to loosen up and to clear my head.

I nudged the dog. The dog did not move in response. So I nudged him again. Once more, no response. I patted him gently. The body felt stiff.

We never quite established the cause of death of the poor creature: it could have been the cold, it could have been the shock of the fireworks, it could have been that he was a Club Row dog with a Club Row constitution. It could have been anything. All I knew at that moment, on the morning after the night of 5 November in Lewes, was that I had a dead dog on my hands and I had to do something about it.

I headed over to the hotel kitchen.

The brutal fact is that a body, any body, begins to decompose immediately after death. I'd seen it in Spain – and alas on my various outings with Morley. A dead body soon starts to give off a foul, sickening odour and to attract insects, and the hotter the temperature, the faster the rate of decomposition. In Spain, you were really only looking at a couple of hours before you were facing a serious problem. Admittedly, November in Sussex presents fewer problems, and of course a dog is just a dog while a human is a human, but a dead body is a dead body. I also knew from my previous experience with Morley that rigor mortis sets in pretty quickly, so ideally if you're going to have to handle the remains at all you really want to get going before the full onset of stiffness and leakage. These are of course unpleasant matters to talk of – but then much of what is true in life is unpleasant.

There were three of them in the hotel kitchen. Two of them small and wiry, one of them an entirely more substantial sort of a fellow, a man who looked like he was capable of doing all his own butchery: I guessed kitchen porters and the chef.

'Gents, good morning,' I said. 'I've got a bit of a problem out the back here.'

I had to repeat myself. They weren't expecting anyone walking in the back door of the kitchen at five thirty in the morning: they were barely awake themselves. They looked at me, dumbfounded.

[151]

'Gents,' I said again, 'I've got a bit of a problem here. And I wonder—'

The bigger of the men approached me, and despite the fact that he was now wearing chef's whites rather than his smuggler costume, I immediately recognised that he was none other than the gallant gent who yesterday had picked up his companion lying at Miriam's feet. I was relieved – or at least momentarily relieved. The man stared at me with ill-concealed disgust. Admittedly, I was not looking at my best. I hadn't shaved, I was wearing the same faded blue serge suit I'd had on since we left London, and I'd slept outside in the cold, in the cart shed, and on flour sacks.

'Get out,' he said.

'I've got a bit of a problem,' I said.

'You're going to have more than a bit of a problem if you don't get out of my kitchen,' he said.

'I'm a guest,' I said.

'And I'm the King of Siam,' he said. 'I said get out.'

'It's the dog,' I said.

'What's the dog?' he said.

'A dog, a dead dog.' And I tried to explain that I was a guest staying at the hotel and that one of the other chefs had kindly accommodated my dog on the flour sacks out the back yesterday and that he'd died. The story was so strange and unexpected, I could see that although he was struggling to understand, he was also inclined to believe me.

'Come, come and see,' I said.

And so the four of us trooped outside to the cart shed to see poor old Pablo.

He looked like a sleeping lamb, curled up, his ears flat

against his long sad face, his fur its distinctive tinge of blue. The big fellow immediately took charge. He instructed one of his companions to go and fetch a sheet, and the other to fetch a bucket with some warm water and some rags.

'Well, I'll tell you what, this is a sorry business,' he said.

'It certainly is,' I agreed.

'Unaccountable bad.'

'Indeed.'

'You shouldn't have left the dog out in the cold like that, and with the fireworks and all.'

'I know,' I said. 'That was a bit of a mistake.'

'Bloody stupid is what it was.'

He said nothing more to me.

When his companions returned he set to work in silence, with me assisting, lifting the dog as he cleaned all around. I then helped him lift the body while the others laid out the sheet and we arranged the animal on the sheet, as if it were sleeping, and wrapped it up tightly. We then slid the body in its winding sheet into a flour bag and knotted it securely at the top with some string.

'Thank you,' I said.

'We can't just leave him out here,' said the big man.

'Obviously,' I said.

'But we're not putting him in the kitchen.'

'No, no, of course not.'

'We need somewhere cool and secure,' he said, glancing around.

'I suppose I could put him in the back of the Lagonda,' I said, nodding towards the vehicle, which I had conveniently parked behind the hotel the night before.

'This is yours?'

'It's not mine exactly, but it's . . . Well, yes, basically it's mine,' I said.

'That'll do then, if you're sure. Lads.'

And so we laid Pablo to rest in the boot of the car.

'Well, there you are,' said the big man when we'd finished and we were all standing around, smoking. 'We need to go and get on with the breakfast, lads. We're behind.'

'Thank you very much, gents,' I said. 'I'm Stephen Sefton.' I shook their hands.

'Ben,' said the first.

'Jake,' said the second. 'What breed of dog was that?'

'It was a Bedlington,' I said. 'A Bedlington Terrier.'

'I ain't never seen a terrier like that,' said Jake.

'No,' I said. 'I suppose they're not that common.'

'I'm Bevis,' said the big man, shaking my hand with obvious distaste.

'Thank you, Bevis. I really appreciate you helping.'

'I hope someone would do it for my dog,' he said.

'It's not actually my dog,' I began. 'I'm just looking after it.'

'Not your dog?' said Bevis. 'I thought you said—'

'Well, it belongs . . . Actually, gentlemen, if you'd excuse me, I'm going to have to clear my head,' I said, suddenly realising that I was going to have to work out how to break the bad news to Miriam.

'Go down to the Ouse,' said Jake, 'that'll do the job.'

'Or the park,' said Ben. 'Or Pells Pool. It's not far. Five-minute walk. You just go along Market Street. Nice spot.'

'It's not open though,' said Jake. 'They've been doing some work on the place.'

'Aye, not for a swim, but. It's a nice spot. That'll clear your head all right.'

I had no idea exactly how quickly it would clear my head – and how quickly a bad morning was about to become considerably worse.

CHAPTER 19

PELLS POOL turned out to be one of those so-called 'lidos' that seemed to spring up everywhere during the 1930s. The lidos, many of them now fallen into disrepair, were intended by the noble and multitudinous Pleasure Grounds and Baths Committees of this country's great local and borough councils to be necessary improvements upon and replacements for the old public baths and public park swimming lakes, many of which were themselves so far beyond disrepair at that time as to be most definitely unhygienic, if not entirely unusable. The lido craze had caught on everywhere: I remember back in London reading about the opening of a Tottenham Lido and a West Ham Lido, and I had myself on a number of occasions visited the famous Tooting Bathing Lake, which had been converted into a lido and become an unlikely south London tourist attraction.

Morley, perhaps surprisingly, was not a great fan of the lidos, believing them to be an example of the government interfering with and trying to control every Briton's inalienable right to swim in unsafe, unfiltered and often stagnant water wheresoever, whensoever and howsoever they wished, entirely for free and at their own risk. In his essay

'On Liberty and the Public Good' (*Amateur Philosopher*, January 1936), which does not mention the lido, but which does worry about the public park, he argues that 'To free individuals to act in accordance with their own best interests is a sure sign of a civilised society, just as to instruct individuals on how to use their freedom is a sure sign of the barbarous.' His ideas on such matters were, admittedly, subject to change and often contradictory but fundamentally he believed that everyone should be left alone to take responsibility for their own lives, though he also believed that we should support and provide for those who were, for whatever reason, unable to take responsibility for themselves. Basically he believed in duty and in charity and in generosity and rather distrusted what he called 'Bolshevik' ideas about social justice and equality. Thus, he was generally anti things like the lidos – though at other times, he could be pro. He was the kind of liberal who no longer really exists in this country, or indeed in any other: he believed in the Enlightenment ideals of rationalism, yet he also believed that men were always unlikely to work in their own best interests, let alone the interests of others. His strongest and abiding belief was in the simple idea of Englishness. If only we could educate our fellow men in English habits of discipline, self-respect and good manners, then all would be well; and maybe, in his strange, complex, muddle-headed way, he was right.

Anyway, Pells Pool was a fine example of everything that Morley both hated and admired: a square-set, brick-built, municipal-type compound, provided for the public good, but which one had to pay for the privilege to enter.

A stone plaque on the wall outside stated that a fresh-water swimming pool had first been established here – by public subscription – in 1860, which surely must have made it one of the oldest pools in England. I was keen to see inside. The new place had been opened as recently as 1935, and was surprisingly easy to crack into. I pulled myself up and over the main entrance gate, swanned past the ticket office and into the lido.

It was much, much larger than I'd expected – the pool was at least 50 feet wide and perhaps 150 feet long. There was a grassy lawn off to the right, with changing rooms signposted down at the far end. There were signs of recent building work or maintenance: piles of bricks, scaffolding planks, debris. The place was pleasantly cool and damp. I wondered idly if I might find the source of the spring that fed the pool.

(At St George's, during the years we worked together, Morley undertook a number of ambitious aquatic land-scaping projects of his own. There was a stream, for example, that was fed from a series of ponds that were in turn fed by various springs, that flowed eastwards down a slope past the north side of the house, ending in a large pool that had silted up. He spent hours – weeks, months – dredging that pool and using the silt and sludge to construct an island, upon which he eventually built a grotto-cum-bathing house, designed by someone who he claimed was a 'trained Italian grottoist', whatever that was, and who had imported decayed lava stone from Italy, constructing walls that glis-tened with water from hidden pipes designed to drip and cascade, depending on the weather. It was pretty awful. In an alcove sat a little marble Venus, being constantly spurted at. The place was inspired by a Moorish palace in Seville, according to the grottoist, though it might just as well have been inspired by a visit to the Windmill Theatre in Soho. But the pond became a very pleasant natural swimming pool, and I spent many happy hours there with Miriam over the years, lounging away what little remained of my youth. Looking back, I was a lucky man.)

Though it was still dark I could clearly see there was water in the pool. Looking closer it seemed to be only half full – just a few feet, rainwater perhaps, and there were leaves and branches, algae and scum floating on the top. I thought of the hundreds of boys and girls who had doubtless learned to swim here over the years.

I noticed that a large area of algae had collected down by the far end of the pool – a dark mass, darker even than the rest. I wondered if this might be the source of the spring water.

It was not.

It was a young woman, floating face down. She seemed to have something caught around her neck.

I waded in, fully clothed, and pulled the body to the side of the pool.

Lizzie Walter.

The Hudsons'

CHAPTER 20

I WAS EVENTUALLY TRANSPORTED – in what might now be called an unmarked police car, but which was in fact, as far as I could tell, simply a car, a Morris 6, if memory serves me right – to the Hudsons', a grand country pile about three or four miles outside Lewes. Fortunately, on this occasion, I hadn't actually been arrested, but I had been helping police with their enquiries: this became something of a theme during my years working on *The County Guides* with Morley, and I was already familiar with the routine of interviews and investigations. The Lewes police were like most of the police we encountered during those years: decent and firm but fair, with perhaps a *slight* emphasis on the firm. The phrase 'a rap on the knuckles', I can testify, derives from the once common practice of the actual rapping of actual knuckles. Similar derivations apply for phrases such as 'a quick slap round the back of the head', 'he tripped and fell' and 'to teach someone a lesson they won't forget in a hurry'.

Lizzie Walter had been murdered, it seemed, some time during the night of 5 November, strangled with a shoelace. My account of my discovery of her body was to be the subject of further investigation. The police were following a number of lines of enquiry.

It was by now about two o'clock in the afternoon. My arrival caused something of a commotion among the staff at the Hudsons'. The plainclothes policemen – hats, over-coats, pipes, and far from actual knuckle-rappers or indeed knuckle-draggers themselves – were insisting on speaking with Mr Hudson, local dignitary, and with Morley, as my employer, who had arrived up at the house with Miriam to look in on Molly's rehearsals for *Don Giovanni*.

The policemen were invited to wait in the library by the staff, while I was shown into the drawing room by a butler with a pencil moustache that seemed to express not only his dissatisfaction with his lot in life in general but his very especial displeasure with me. The Hudson party were relax-ing after lunch in what was a very well-appointed room, with large French windows running along one side, an enormous faded Turkish – Morley always insisted upon calling such a 'Turkey' – carpet, polished wood just about everywhere, a grand piano, of course, and a big brass fender in the fire-place with vast logs a-burning. I remember a lot of crimson velvet and mulberry, rose du barry, opaline blue, caca du dauphin – Louis XV sort of colours – drypoint etchings on the walls, and lots of extremely fine and expensive-looking furniture: gesso cabinets, mirror tables and an extremely fine, expensive-looking mahogany occasional table which sported an extremely fine, expensive-looking diamond-cut decanter, which contained what little remained of what had undoubtedly been some extremely fine vintage port. Much of the furniture seemed designed solely to hold and display the kinds of *objets* and knick-knacks inexplicably favoured by the wealthy, including statuettes of the likes of Apollo, Pan and the Dying Gladiator. It was a scene of moneyed calm and tranquillity. Miriam was deep in conversation with the conductor Fritz; Morley and the Hudsons were hunkered down in armchairs by the fire. And Molly and her son Henry stood smoking by the French windows, rather as though – I thought – about to flee.

'Ah, Sefton,' said Morley. 'We missed you this morning.'

The butler approached Mr Hudson, spoke quietly to him, and Mr Hudson then came to speak quietly to Morley. The two men made to leave – to speak to the police.

'Carry on,' said Mr Hudson. 'We'll be back in a moment.'

'Now, can I get you a drink?' asked Mrs Hudson, getting up and leading me in the direction of the port. 'The decanter was a gift from Molly. Isn't it lovely?'

'It's absolutely lovely,' I said. 'I won't though, thank you.'

The contrast between the Hudsons' delightful post-prandials and my own rather unpleasant morning in the Lewes police station was making me feel rather out of sorts.

'Everything's all right, is it?' she asked, perhaps sensing something wrong in my demeanour. 'Is there some sort of . . . trouble?' She looked deeply troubled by the prospect of trouble.

'It's probably best you speak to your husband, Mrs Hudson,' I said.

She poured herself a generous measure of port.

'It's not these ghastly National Trust people, is it?'

'No,' I said, having no clear idea what she was talking about.

'It's just they are very insistent. Even though we're trying to make a go of things with the theatre now. Not the plumbing?'

'Plumbing?'

'We're having terrible problems with the plumbing at the moment. It's the problem with these old houses, you see. All sorts of trouble with the valves and pressure. We get this terrible knocking at night.' Somehow she'd already finished her port. 'Morley says he's going to have a look at it later.' Morley fancied himself as something of an expert when it came to country house plumbing, having designed and installed some state-of-the-art system in St George's that was always breaking down. (His book, *Country Plumbing*, first published in 1930, and in print ever since, eventually paid for the professional replumbing of St George's, after many years of problems arising from his various avant-garde solutions.)

'So that's good, isn't it?' said Mrs Hudson.

'Yes, Mrs Hudson,' I said. She seemed to be in need of reassurance. 'That's very good indeed.'

'Sefton!' said Miriam, acknowledging my presence. 'Do you have Pablo with you? I was just talking to Fritz about him.'

'Erm . . .'

Fortunately, at that moment, Molly and Henry, having finished their cigarettes, wandered over.

'You'll perhaps be able to help us, Miriam,' said Molly.

'I doubt that very much,' said Miriam, smiling.

'Would you agree with me, Miriam,' Molly continued, 'Henry disagrees, that Zerlina is in many ways the counterpart of the Don?'

'Zerlina?' said Miriam. 'I don't know. Sefton? What do you think?'

I did my best to think on my feet – and failed.

'Zerlina?' I asked.

'In the *Don*,' said Miriam.

'Ah, yes, of course, in the *Don*.'

(For anyone like me who has perhaps momentarily forgotten some of the names of some of the characters in *Don Giovanni*, or – and unlikely as it seems, there may be some – who have absolutely no idea what it's about, or why it matters, I refer you to Morley's *A Beginner's Guide to the Opera*, one of his many popular *A Beginner's Guide to* series. *A Beginner's Guide to the Opera* was first published back in 1929 and remains in print to this day, since everyone, it seems, is forever a beginner in opera, or at least forever starting again. Personally, I've sat through several *Magic Flutes* and can still make neither head nor tail of the damned thing and how anyone can sit through the whole of *The Marriage of Figaro* is beyond me. The main plot of *Don Giovanni*, just to remind us all, concerns the efforts of a woman named Donna Anna and her betrothed, Don Ottavio, to identify the man – Don Giovanni – who has attempted to rape and seduce her and who has murdered her father, the Commendatore. Zerlina is a peasant girl who is one of the many other women who has attracted the Don's dubious attentions.)

'She wraps poor Masetto around her little finger, doesn't she?' said Molly. (Masetto – I refer again to *A Beginner's Guide* – is Zerlina's betrothed.) 'And uses her charms—'

'Her *certo balsamo*,' added the conductor, Fritz.

'Precisely, her *certo balsamo*,' continued Molly, rolling

and extending every Italian vowel and consonant that could possibly be rolled and extended, 'to soothe him.' (There is no mention of *certo balsamo* in Morley's guide, whatever the pronunciation, so I leave it to the reader's imagination.)

'Making Zerlina the equivalent of the rapist and murderer, Don Giovanni, is that what you're suggesting?' asked Miriam.

'In a sense, I suppose,' said Molly.

'Which makes absolutely no sense, of course,' said Miriam. 'Except in the obvious sense that the opera is all about dreadful people attempting to seduce one another.'

'Which it most certainly is,' said Molly.

'Surprise, surprise,' said Miriam, 'since most operas are all about dreadful people attempting to seduce one another, aren't they, Sefton?'

'Yes,' I agreed.

'I very much like this idea of Zerlina as the counterpart to the Don,' said Fritz.

'Though Zerlina is a lowly peasant woman and the Don is an arrogant, vile nobleman who can do whatever he wants, without fear of retribution?'

'But he gets his final comeuppance,' said Fritz. 'Remember, *Il dissoluto punito, ossia il Don Giovanni*: the rake is punished.'

'Yes!' agreed Molly.

'What, punished, as in the ridiculous ending when the Commendatore's ghost drags him down to hell – a kind of divine intervention, which we are clearly encouraged to view as a ludicrous joke?'

'A joke?' said Fritz.

'The opera was first produced when?' asked Miriam.

[166]

'In 178 . . .' said Fritz.

'Seven, I think you will find,' said Miriam. 'Which surely makes it both a critique of the old feudal Europe and a prescient harbinger of the French Revolution, does it not? And not so much a portrait of the war of the sexes as a damning indictment of the relationship between the privileged and the rest of us?'

'Ah, come on,' said Molly, sounding very defensive and very American. 'I think *Don Giovanni* is a portrait of the game of love, darling. I think you're taking it far too seriously.'

'And I don't think you're taking it seriously enough,' said Miriam. 'I would have thought that if *Don Giovanni* teaches us anything, it's that the social order is rotten, that women are not allowed to be active participants in what you call "the game of love" and that indeed the whole system is explicitly designed to repress and silence us.'

'Well, in that case we shall have to agree to disagree,' said Molly.

'Alas,' said Miriam. 'We shall, since I take *Don Giovanni* entirely seriously as a work of great art – and you seem to see it as a bit of a joke.'

I had not spent long with Mrs Hudson but she struck me as the sort of perfectly content rich sort of person who – though clearly an ardent lover of art and of opera, might equally enjoy a rubber of bridge, a round of golf and other nice things and good works – was not perhaps entirely accustomed to Miriam's rather more passionate and robust approach to the arts. I rather fancied the poor woman was developing a twitch.

'Would anyone like another drink?' she asked, having

magically produced another bottle of port from somewhere, and having already refilled her own glass.

'Why not,' said Miriam. 'Anyway, Sefton, as you were saying: news of the dog?'

This was clearly not the moment to explain what had happened to Pablo, but – and here was a problem I often encountered during our years together – it was extremely difficult under any circumstances either to refuse or to lie to Miriam. She would have made an excellent police inspector, I always thought, a natural metaphorical knuckle-rapper, or an army interrogator, or a spy: she had this relentless way of looking at you that quickly weakened one's resolve. I therefore, against my better judgement, explained to Miriam what had happened to Pablo, leaving out most of the more unpleasant details, to the sound of silence, except for the burning of logs in the Hudsons' generous grate.

Mr Hudson and Morley re-entered the room towards the end of my telling of the tale, their solemn presence only adding to what had quickly become a rather mournful atmosphere.

'We had a dog that died in the lake some years ago,' said Mrs Hudson, once I had rounded out the story with my own fond tribute to poor Pablo and his winning doggy ways. 'It was terribly sad. Do you remember, darling?'

'Remember?' said Mr Hudson. 'It is seared upon my memory. One of the worst things that's ever happened.'

'Robert and the children were out rowing on the lake, the dog leapt out of the boat, swam towards the shore, but the children were calling him back, and of course he turned back towards the familiar voices and exhausted himself, the poor thing.'

'Ah, yes. It was a most melancholy affair.'

'And this is a dreadful business altogether,' said Morley, looking rather sharply at me and presumably referring to the death of Lizzie Walter as much as to the death of the dog.

'Shall we have a drink?' asked Mrs Hudson.

'Perhaps we all need some fresh air?' said Mr Hudson. 'Come on, I'll give you a tour,' said Mr Hudson. 'You've not been down to the theatre yet, have you, Morley?'

Morley had not yet been to the theatre. And so down to the theatre we went.

CHAPTER 21

UNDERSTANDABLY, Miriam avoided my presence during our walk to the theatre through the grounds of the Hudson estate, instead huddling close to Henry, who sought to offer what comfort he could to a woman whose dog has unexpectedly died: an arm around the shoulder, a few tender words, and threatening glances in the direction of the person thought to be responsible for the death of the poor creature, which is to say, me. He was an odd sort, Henry. To borrow a Morley tag, *altissima quaeque flumina minimo sono labi.*

Morley, Molly and the Hudsons, meanwhile, were doing their absolute best to keep the party's spirits up. Morley was entertaining everyone with tales of his adventures: I had no idea that he had explored King Frederik VIII Land as part of a meteorological survey back in the early 1930s, or indeed that he'd met and befriended the nationalist leader Habib Bourguiba during his travels in the Maghreb and that they shared a great love of Tunisian checkers.

Neither Morley nor Mr Hudson made any mention to me of the death of Lizzie Walter.

Our final approach to the theatre was made through an

area that looked as though it were a woodland that had recently been felled.

'Is this what I think it is?' asked Morley.

'It rather depends on what you think it is,' said Mr Hudson. 'But if you think it is what I think you think it is, it most certainly is!'

'Really?' said Morley. 'A stumpery?'

'Indeed!' said Mr Hudson.

'It's a stumpery, Sefton!'

'A stumpery?' I said.

'Yes, yes, take a note. A stumpery!' exclaimed Morley, as though he were Howard Carter at the tomb of Tutankhamun.

'A stumpery?' I repeated, producing from my pocket the small German-made notebook that I kept about myself at all times for the sole purpose of jotting down Morley's remarks, enthusiasms and observations.

'Like a rock garden, Sefton, except made from stumps.'

'Right-o.'

'Marvellous for ferns, as you can see.'

'And mushrooms,' said Mr Hudson. 'We've had the most incredible crop this year.'

'I was thinking of developing one at St George's,' said Morley, who during my years with him redesigned his gardens at least half a dozen times. A stumpery would certainly have been an innovation.

'It's all about the quality of the roots,' said Mr Hudson, 'and what can grow among them. Oak is best, obviously. But you can also achieve tremendous effects with sweet chestnut. Beech. And then the plants just sort of take over. Ferns. Winter aconites, snowdrops, scilla, epimediums, uvularia. Mahonias.'

[171]

'We love a good mahonia,' said Mrs Hudson.

'Oh, me too, quite so,' said Morley.

'But the mushrooms,' said Mr Hudson. 'Look: like you wouldn't believe.' He pointed in the growing dusk towards what were indeed some unbelievable – enormous, multitudinous – specimens clinging around the sad and ugly stumps and I suddenly recalled a dark afternoon in Spain, gathering wood, sodden leaves everywhere, and suddenly coming across just a few spindly-stalked mushrooms and our Spanish compatriots becoming highly excited. They dried them over the fire and made tea from them, which they swore had extraordinary mind-expanding properties, but which I recall tasted largely of soil and produced little but a slight feeling of sickness and sway. I suppose I have been spoiled over the years by strong drink and advances in modern pharmacology.

Eventually, we approached the famous Hudson theatre, which had been famously converted from a barn. Converting a barn into a theatre is, I suppose, a process that might take an afternoon, a week, a month, or years, depending on the state of the barn and your idea of what exactly constitutes a theatre. The Hudsons' idea of what exactly constitutes a theatre was not inconsiderable and their barn was by no means average – and I speak as someone who is more than familiar with the average barn.

Morley's *Guide to the Farm Buildings of the British Isles* (1938) was yet another of his books that I expected to sell approximately no copies whatsoever, and which in fact sold in its tens of thousands, enjoying reprint after reprint – popular, presumably, not only with farmers and landowners but with country-dwellers, would-be country-dwellers and anyone else with an interest in cowsheds, pig sheds and threshing barns. *Farm Buildings* was in fact almost as popular as Morley's book on the Settle–Carlisle railway line, *72 Miles, 1,728 Yards* (1935), a perennial bestseller that eventually allowed Morley to indulge his own passion for rail and steam and to build a small miniature railway in the grounds of St George's. In similar fashion, the proceeds from *Farm Buildings* allowed Morley to update and upgrade his own farm buildings, a process of reciprocity and reinvestment that Morley called – hilariously – a sty for a sty.

I lived through the entire process of the writing and production of *Farm Buildings* with Morley, taking most of the photographs, writing most of the captions, and indeed large parts of the text, and it was for me what one might these days call a 'learning experience'. In my early twenties I would have been unable to distinguish between a barn and any other kind of a farm building. By the time I was thirty years old I could tell a brew house from a bake house, a cart shed from a coach house and if pushed would probably also have been able to identify a hemmel, a bee bole, a cheese room and a root store. To this day, if you are having trouble distinguishing between, say, a typical Breckland granary building and a Cumbrian salving shed, I'm your man.

In *Farm Buildings* Morley – or, rather, I, at Morley's request – attempted to identify a standardised set of features among British farm buildings, dividing them roughly into three categories: those buildings used for the storage and processing of crops (barns, granaries, hop kilns, oasts, cider houses, fruit stores, etcetera); those used for transport and machinery (cart sheds, mostly); and those used for the housing and managing of farm animals (cattle yards, stables, pigsties). Often, I discovered, farmsteads relied on one building to perform all such functions, rendering our system of identification if not entirely worthless then perhaps of merely scholarly value. Nonetheless, my extensive studies of the possible functions of farm buildings meant that I knew exactly what to expect in the Hudsons' barn: a series of internal subdivisions, with the doors opening to a large threshing bay, where the harvested crop would be beaten and the grain separated from the chaff in the cross-draught, with perhaps a small adjoining chaff house. In a barn converted into a theatre I suppose what I expected was perhaps a small stage, some scattering of chairs, and the threshing bay thoroughly swept and cleared of grain.

'So it's a sixteenth-century barn,' began Mr Hudson as we arrived, 'typical of its age—'

'Fifteenth century,' said Mrs Hudson.

'Sixteenth century,' insisted Mr Hudson.

'Parts of it are fifteenth century,' said Mrs Hudson.

'But it's mostly sixteenth century,' continued Mr Hudson. 'No foundations, obviously, when we began, so we had to remove the stone walls and the plinth—'

'Blue Lias plinth,' said Mrs Hudson.

'The Blue Lias plinth,' agreed Mr Hudson, 'and restore the frame—'

'The oak frame,' said Mrs Hudson. 'And the east end constructed in Coldwaltham sandstone, with galleting.'

'Roof redone,' said Mr Hudson.

'Hand-made clay peg tiles,' said Mrs Hudson.

'You note the catslide roof,' said Mr Hudson.

'Excellent,' said Morley. 'Wonderful.' In *The County Guides*, he describes the Hudsons' barn as 'one of the finest surviving barns in Sussex'. It was doubtless one of the most expensive – not least because inside its fully reconstructed exterior, the barn was a fully functioning proscenium arch theatre.

'Goodness me,' said Morley, as we made our way through the big restored barn doors. 'This is quite extraordinary.'

'Well, it's not quite La Scala or the Estates Theatre in Prague,' said Mr Hudson.

'Look at this, though!' said Morley, throwing out his arms in a gesture of appreciation and wonder. 'In a barn!' He threw his arms even wider. 'In Sussex!' And wider still, as if he might scoop the whole place up and embrace it.

'Well, we've been very lucky,' said Mr Hudson. 'We've been able to achieve most of what we hoped.'

Most of what the Hudsons hoped looked to me exactly like a West End theatre: a large stage and raked seating in place of the threshing hall.

'I thought it might simply be benches,' said Morley.

'Ah yes, the seats, yes. We were tremendously lucky with the seating,' said Mr Hudson. 'They were refurbishing a music hall in Brighton and we managed to snap up a lot of the fixtures and fittings. The seating, some of the lighting. The curtains, of course.'

At the west end of the barn was the raised wooden stage, with billowing red curtains forming the wings. Beyond the wings, linked to the barn from the backstage area was a one-storey building that housed the dressing rooms and a green room, and which had been converted from an old ice-house and a slaughterhouse, completely disassembled and reassembled 'brick by brick', according to Mr Hudson.

'Stone by stone,' said Mrs Hudson.

It was an incredible achievement: built with money, obviously, but clearly imagined and created with love and imagination.

Back in the barn, the arrival of the Hudsons had excited sudden and frantic activity among the various stagehands, technical staff, singers, costumiers, musicians and others who had previously been lounging and lurking in the shadows. Scenery was being hauled on- and offstage. Costumes – ball gowns, mostly, and the inevitable operatic doublets and hose – were being flung around and fitted on performers' bodies. Lights were being hoisted on pulleys. Stage directions were being issued. Instruments were being tooted, plucked and honked upon. Basically, lots of operatic-type stuff was happening.

'You'll excuse me,' Henry announced to our assembled company. 'Time to clock on.'

'Of course,' said Mr Hudson. 'The work of a set designer is never done.'

Molly had already disappeared, in a puff of perfume and a billow of her cloak, in the direction of the dressing rooms.

'One forgets sometimes,' said Morley, 'that the opera is in fact an even more labour-intensive and demanding activity than the theatre.'

'Oh one does, Father, yes,' agreed Miriam, who was avoiding looking at me or indeed acknowledging my presence in any way. 'It's like working in a coal mine.'

In front of the stage there was a large trestle table set up, where Fritz had joined a group of others in intense discussion.

'We're lucky, we're just in time for the *probe*,' said Mr Hudson, lowering his voice.

'The probe?' I said quietly.

'*Ja*, a *probe*,' said Morley. 'It's what they call a rehearsal in German, Sefton.'

'Ah.'

'Or *prova*, in *Italiano*,' said Mrs Hudson.

'Of course,' I said.

'Both words, in both languages, suggesting "trying" or "testing", I think,' Morley clarified.

'Very good,' I said.

'I was lucky some years ago to sit through the entire process of the production of *The Marriage of Figaro*, in St Petersburg,' said Morley.

'At the Mikhailovsky?' said Mr Hudson.

'Yes, that's right,' said Morley.

'Oh, how wonderful,' said Mr Hudson.

'You might take a note actually, Sefton, for the book.'

I produced my trusty notebook.

'So,' he explained, 'in any production, there's the *lese-probe*.'

'It's all in German?'

'Many of the processes and procedures have been codified and described in German, Sefton, yes, of course. Rehearsals are an art in and of themselves.'

'Of course.' During my time at college I had dabbled in amateur theatricals – farce mostly. Our rehearsals had always had the air of a sort of jolly jape, the director working haphazardly through any problems over a few drinks. It was all rather clubbable. Here, it felt rather more like a circus or a factory, with people working alongside, around and almost on top of one another in order to get things done.

'*Leseprobe*, you've got that, Sefton?'

'Yes, Mr Morley.'

'The reading rehearsal, and then there's the *sitzprobe*, the sitting rehearsal and now, what we have here, is the FD.'

'FD?'

'Final dress.'

'That's in English?' I said.

'Correct,' said Mr Hudson.

'And after that the production is frozen,' said Mrs Hudson.

'Frozen?'

'Whatever you see at the FD,' said Mr Hudson, '*should* be what you see on opening night – though between ourselves I can recall a few cases in which problems at the FD meant that the show could not be performed in front of paying audiences.'

'Really?' said Morley.

'It's very rare, of course,' said Mr Hudson. 'One usually says that the singer is ill or something similar. You know, a kidney infection or some such.'

'Well,' said Morley. 'I never knew.'

'Ssshhhh,' said Fritz, in our direction.

'Molly's amazing,' said Mr Hudson. 'We're so lucky to have her.'

There was silence as everyone shifted into position. Mrs Hudson excused herself while Morley, Miriam and I settled down in the front row of the stalls with Mr Hudson, close to the orchestra, which I was surprised to discover consisted of no more than about a dozen or so musicians.

'We've had to go for reduced orchestration,' said Mr Hudson to Morley.

'Of course,' said Morley.

'We're not quite a full opera house yet.'

'No, no, quite understandable,' said Morley.

To a man – and men they all were – the musicians looked as though they hadn't slept for several weeks and they were wearing both the clothes and the expressions to suit. Typical musicians. The music began with a thundering chord, though – as it turned out – not nearly thundering enough. No sooner had the poor blighters' fingers and lips hit their instruments than Fritz leapt to his feet.

'Darker!' he cried. 'Darker! We have discussed this already, yes?' Molly had explained in the car on the way from Brighton that the company had already spent a week or two in London working together, talking through how the music might work in the context of the staging, and how everything was now set. 'We must begin in darkness, as we end in darkness.'

'He's quite right,' said Morley, leaning across to me and speaking quietly. 'It is a very dark ending. You know the opera, of course?'

'Not perhaps as well as I would like,' I said, havering.

'The first note needs to *come* to us, yes?' continued Fritz. 'It needs to *come* directly to us. It needs to *pierce* us, yes?' He indicated the nature of a note coming to us and piercing us by jabbing at his heart with his fingers. The musicians then duly produced the opening chord again, rather heavier and louder, which I suppose might be interpreted as being piercing, and then moved into a Mozarty misterioso sort of sequence.

'We are in the garden of the Commendatore,' whispered Morley to me.

'Right.'

A man appeared onstage, in the obligatory doublet and hose, looking rather shifty.

'This is Leporello,' said Morley, 'Don Giovanni's servant. He is complaining about his master and daydreaming about being free of him: *Notte e giorno faticar*. "Night and day I slave away." The complaint about the master of course being a tradition that stretches back to the *commedia dell'arte*.'

'And which persists to this day,' I said.

'Indeed,' said Morley. 'He is keeping watch while Don Giovanni is in the Commendatore's house attempting to seduce the Commendatore's daughter, Donna Anna. Now, Don Giovanni enters, pursued by Donna Anna.'

Don Giovanni did indeed enter, pursued by Molly in wig and gown as Donna Anna.

'Don Giovanni is masked here, you see,' said Morley. 'And Donna Anna tries to unmask him, shouting for help.'

'*Non sperar, se non m'uccidi, Ch'io ti lasci fuggir mai!*' sang Molly, or something similar.

'"Do not hope, unless you kill me, that I shall ever let you run away!"' Morley translated.

'Gosh,' I said.

Don Giovanni then broke free of Donna Anna's clutches, ran offstage, with her following, only to appear back onstage moments later, followed by—

'The Commendatore,' said Morley.

It was the black American from the Hudsons' dinner playing the Commendatore and I have to say that his stentorian denunciation of Don Giovanni was really rather magnificent. If I'd been reviewing the opera, I'd already have identified the star.

As far as I could tell – although I have to admit by now I was already becoming rather bored – what happened next was that Don Giovanni killed the Commendatore, escaped with Leporello, Donna Anna returned onstage with her fiancé, Don Ottavio, was horrified to see her father lying dead and made Don Ottavio swear vengeance against the masked murderer, Don Giovanni. And this was the end of the action-packed first scene.

'Well, what do you think?' said Morley.

'It is certainly rather dark,' I said.

But not dark enough for Fritz, who was once again up on his feet issuing instructions to the cast, who had gathered together onstage.

'Good, good, yes it is *good*, but it is too *tentative*, *too too tentative*, too *dry*, too *nice*, yes? You have the toe in the water, but the whole body must be in the water, yes?'

Don Giovanni and Donna Anna and the others all nodded yes, as if this body in the water reference made any actual sense. To me, it seemed like a horror. I saw Lizzie Walter's face, the thin shoelace around her neck, everything fragile about her destroyed.

'We need more tone, more fullness, more resonance, yes?'

Again, they all nodded.

'It needs to *come* to me. It needs to *pierce* me.'

At which piercing moment, Mrs Hudson came howling into the barn.

'Henry's been taken away!' she screamed.

'What on earth's happening?' said Mr Hudson, leaping up.

'Henry's been taken away!' repeated Mrs Hudson. 'For the murder of a young woman.'

'What?'

Up onstage, Molly fainted. Miriam ran outside. And I turned to Morley, who had already disappeared.

CHAPTER 22

AFTER THE HULLABALOO at the Hudsons', Morley, Miriam and I drove back to Lewes in the Lagonda in complete and deadly silence. It was dark and it was cold. It was definitely November. The Downs no longer seemed so warm and welcoming: they seemed instead like a bad omen altogether. On the way to Lewes only yesterday, Morley had gone into raptures over the Downs: 'The Downs in many ways *are* Sussex,' he had enthused to Molly and to Miriam and to me, and indeed in *The County Guides: Sussex* he writes, in characteristic ebullient fashion, that 'We might visit any of this country's great counties and there find mighty forests and great rivers – any county in this great nation is blessed with such. But the Downs, the Downs belong to Sussex and to Sussex alone. You might perhaps find a verdant turf-covered chalk hill elsewhere, but nowhere are they as smooth and as easy, as calm and as spacious, as warm and as welcoming as the Sussex Downs.' There is a particular prospect, he goes so far as to claim in the book, up around Plumpton Plain, 'which I think may be the finest view in the whole of Europe'. (He made similar claims, it should be said, in other books, about various prospects and vistas from Land's End to John O'Groats.) Only hours before he had been quizzing Miriam and me on the 'great hymned' Downs and the famous lines by Galsworthy: 'Oh! the Downs high to the cool sky;/ And the feel of the sun-warmed moss;/ And each cardoon, like a full moon,/ Fairy-spun of the thistle floss.'

There were no hymns to thistle floss this evening. That night, it seemed to me that Dr Johnson had the Downs about right, quoted in *Sussex* by Morley only for the purposes of refutation: 'a country so truly desolate that if one had a mind to hang oneself for desperation at being obliged to live there, it would be difficult to find a tree on which to fasten a rope.' That night, the great humps and mounds of Sussex seemed like morbid symptoms of some terrible underlying disease.

Morley said only two words on the whole of the journey back, to correct Miriam when she referred to the ancient pathways that criss-crossed the landscape.

'Cross-dykes,' he said.

Somehow the words seemed to match our mood.

Mrs Hudson's shock announcement in the theatre had been followed initially by hysteria, then by confusion, high emotions, some heated exchanges with the local constabulary, and then stunned silence and outrage, after which we all retreated – cast, musicians, stagehands and all – to the comparative safety of the Hudsons' drawing room, where Mr Hudson loudly demanded of no one in particular which of his staff had spoken to the police, Mrs Hudson kept herself busy directing the dispensing of port, brandy, whisky and hot tea with lemon for Morley, and Molly desperately, operatically begged all of us to assist her in freeing Henry and clearing his name.

Over the course of several hours of shared conversations, and some shooter's sandwiches, a couple of large raised pork pies, some little Sussex churdles ('Made with hot-water-crust pastry,' explained the mustachioed butler; 'The working man's pastry!' exclaimed Morley), a Ten-to-One Pie, and lashings of something called shackle, a vegetable soup – the Hudsons not being ones to under-cater, even during the most difficult circumstances – the exact nature of the relationship between Henry and Lizzie Walter slowly emerged. Lizzie had been one of the volunteers working with Henry on the set design, a close relationship had formed over the weeks of preparation, they had spent some time together the previous evening at the Bonfire Night, apparently, after which Lizzie had disappeared, only to turn up at Pells Pool earlier that morning. There seemed to be no doubting the basic facts. The problem was establishing exactly what had happened, if anything had happened, between the pair between the hours of about 10 p.m. and 6 a.m. I was questioned more thoroughly by the Hudsons, Molly, Morley, Miriam and everyone else involved in the opera than I had been by the Lewes police, frankly, and by about ten o'clock I was so exhausted that I suggested to Morley that we retire for the night.

It was almost eleven by the time we arrived back at the hotel. Morley went straight to bed: he said he had books to read and review. Even his usual good humour seemed to have been shaken by events.

'Goodnight, Mr Morley,' I said.

'Mmm,' he replied, which was perhaps the shortest sentence I ever heard him utter.

'Sefton, I want a word with you,' said Miriam, as I was about to go up to my room.

'A word, Miriam? Will it not wait till tomorrow? It has been rather a long day.'

'Now,' she said.

She guided me firmly by the elbow towards the hotel's residents' lounge, which was entirely deserted and in darkness, lit only by the dying embers of the fire.

'So?' I said. 'You really do want a word.'

'Yes. I do.'

'I hope it's important.'

She settled herself onto a chaise by the window, her face illuminated strangely, cinematically one might say, by the fire and the streetlights outside. She looked . . . my mind drifted, as so often, towards memories of Hedy Lamarr in a film I had seen in Soho some years previously.

'If it's about the dog—'

'It's not about the bloody dog, Sefton.' She produced from her purse her favourite – Cartier – cigarette case, another gift from an admirer. The Persian-looking geometric patterns – lapis lazuli, gold? – caught the light. She produced a cigarette, without offering me one. 'Of course it's not about the dog.' Lit the cigarette. 'A young woman's dead, for goodness sake.'

'I know, Miriam,' I said. My ire suddenly rose. The face of Lizzie Walter swam before me. 'I know because I found her.'

'Yes, sorry.' She shook out the match. 'Rather insensitive. It has been a long day. Look, sit down, man. You're making me nervous. Come on.'

I sat next to her.

Miriam paused, took a deep breath, turned, and fixed me with a stare.

'This is strictly between us, Sefton. Do you understand?'

'Of course.'

'Strictly.'

'Understood.'

She took a long drag on the cigarette.

'Henry couldn't have killed the poor girl.'

'Why not?'

'Because,' whispered Miriam.

'Because what?'

'Because he was with me,' said Miriam, waving smoke away.

'What do you mean, with you?'

'He was *with* me, Sefton.'

'Are you sure?'

'Of course I'm sure.' Her voice was rising.

'You mean you're his alibi?'

'Keep your voice down!' She glanced towards the door of the lounge, which led towards the hotel reception. 'No, I'm not his bloody alibi. I'm just—'

'He was with you where?'

'Where do you think?'

'I have no idea. I was sleeping outside in the cart shed, with Pablo, if you recall.'

'In my room, Sefton.'

'In your—'

'I was with him all night, Sefton, OK? Can I put it any clearer, man? So he couldn't have killed her.'

'All night?'

'Yes! All night.'

'You were asleep?'

'What do you think?'

'Were you sleeping at all?'

'No, we were not sleeping, no. We didn't get back till gone two or three.'

'You weren't sleeping at all?'

'Sefton! Come on. This is intolerable.'

'As you said, this is a young lady who's been murdered.'

'I bloody well know that. I just don't want to get caught up in a . . . thing.'

'We're caught up in a thing already, Miriam,' I said. 'In case you've forgotten, I was helping the police with their enquiries most of the day, I was interrogated all over again at the Hudsons', and now—'

'Now what?'

'Now, you and your' – I struggled to find the right word here – '*activities* seem to cast a new light on things.'

'I did not mention this' – Miriam also struggled to find the appropriate term – '*episode* in order for you to lecture me about my behaviour, Sefton.' She seemed genuinely uncomfortable talking about this 'episode', which was entirely unlike her.

'I'm not lecturing you, Miriam.'

'Well, that's what it sounds like. You sound like Father.'

'I'm not your father.'

'No, but he is.'

'He's not going to lecture you either.'

'Sefton, come on! He lectures me on everything!'

'Yes, but—'

'Can you imagine, Sefton? Lot and his daughters? King Solomon's concubines. Tamar? Ruth? Dinah? Temple prostitutes! I'd never hear the end of it.'

The cauliflower-eared doorman appeared at the door of the lounge, perhaps alerted by the word 'prostitute' echoing throughout the hotel late at night; it is a word, after all, that does tend to carry and which can attract a chap's attention, for all the obvious reasons.

'Just checking everything is in order in here, miss.'

'Yes, thank you.'

'You're sure? You're not looking for a nightcap, miss? Sir?'

'No, thank you, not tonight.'

'Would you like me to stoke the fire, miss?'

'Yes, perhaps that would be good, thank you.'

The gentleman stoked the fire to a blazing fury, Miriam dutifully made polite conversation, and then we were left alone again.

'Anyway, look, Sefton.' Miriam spoke quietly. 'You and I are going to have to work together on this.'

'On what?'

'On a plan that protects my modesty, that allows Henry to walk free—'

'And which finds the murderer of Lizzie Walter?' I said.

'Yes, of course, Sefton. Yes, that most importantly of all. And which also keeps you from suspicion.'

'I found her, Miriam. I didn't kill her.'

'I know that,' said Miriam. 'But what do you think the

police are going to think once they discover your reputation?'

'My reputation?'

'You're not exactly someone who's unknown to the police, Sefton.'

'Well, assuming it wasn't Henry—' I began.

'It wasn't Henry,' said Miriam.

'Then who was it?'

This of course was *the* question, and a question that detained us for some time, as we attempted to draw up a list of suspects and to formulate a plan. Some of the names on our list – an actual list, jotted down in my German pocket notebook – were rather more unlikely than others.

'Mrs Hudson was shifting it a bit last night, wasn't she?' said Miriam.

'You don't think?'

'She was completely stewed, Sefton, by the time we left the hotel. She'd been on large whiskies with small sodas, if you catch my meaning.'

'But why?' I said.

'Well, it might just be the stress of building an opera house in a barn in your back garden. Women drink for the same reason that—'

'No, I mean, why would she have killed Lizzie Walter?'

'Oh, I don't know, Sefton. She'd have been quite capable of anything.'

'Or incapable,' I said.

'Or capable of forgetting all about whatever she'd done.'

'Sounds unlikely.'

'But perhaps unlikely is what we're looking for?'

'Possibly.'

'Oh, fiddlesticks,' said Miriam, sighing. 'I don't know. I mean, let's be honest, we're getting no closer to the kernel of the nut here, are we?'

'Not really,' I agreed.

She let out a low groan. 'Do you know what? I give up,' she said. She stretched out on the chaise. For a moment I thought she was simply lost in thought – but within minutes she was fast asleep, warmed by the fire. It wasn't long before I joined her.

I awoke thirsty, hungry and with a desperate need to pee. It was 5.30 a.m., the same time I'd woken yesterday, the fateful dawn of my discovery of Lizzie's body. The front door of the hotel was locked and so I made my way out the back, past the kitchens. On my way back in I saw Bevis arriving, the big man who'd helped me with Pablo. He was wearing what could only be described as a poacher's coat, with large pockets that looked like they might easily contain a ferret or a dead rabbit.

I watched him from the back door of the kitchen. He was intent on some hurried task: he took a bucket of what looked like vegetable parings and slops and offcuts from under a counter and then poured them into a pan, which he began to boil up, mashing the foul-smelling concoction ferociously with a big wooden masher, and thickening it with some sort of meal.

I watched him for some time. He was so focused that he didn't seem to notice me, until eventually I felt I had to cough to make my presence known. Hearing the noise, he wheeled round, seizing a knife that lay on a flat sharpening stone by the stove.

'It's you again,' he said.

'Yes,' I said.

'You startled me.'

'Sorry.'

'What's the problem this morning? Killed another dog?'

'No,' I said. 'There's no problem this morning.'

'No time for problems. The police were here yesterday, asking about you.'

'I see.'

'I told them what had happened. The dog.'

'Good. Quite right. Breakfast?' I said, nodding towards his bubbling pan.

He looked around.

'It's mash, for the pigs at home. The manager doesn't know, so . . .'

'Don't worry. I won't be telling anyone.'

Bevis grunted in response.

'Though I wouldn't mind a cup of tea,' I said.

He looked at me as if he'd rather make a cup of tea for Dr Crippen.

'All right,' he said.

As I settled myself in the kitchen, Miriam appeared at the service door through to the dining room. While I looked as though I'd slept the sleep of the damned, she somehow managed to look as though she'd slept the sleep of the blessed.

'Ah, Sefton,' she said. 'I wondered what had become of you. And good morning to you, sir,' she said breezily to Bevis, who was now changing into his kitchen whites. Underneath his coat he was wearing his striped bonfire jersey.

'Good morning, miss,' he said, rather sheepishly.

'Bit of a pong,' said Miriam, 'isn't there?'

'Yes, I'm just finishing off some . . .' Bevis looked towards me for support.

'I don't think you've met,' I said. 'This is Miriam Morley. And this is—'

'Bevis, miss.'

'Bevis, as in the giant of legend?' said Miriam. 'The warder at Arundel? Who waded to the Isle of Wight? Who ate an ox a week and drank two hogsheads of beer? Whose sword Morglay is in the armoury at Arundel? And whose bones lie beneath the park?'

'I was named after my uncle, miss.'

'Of course. But you are certainly a big fellow, Bevis.'

'Six foot eight, miss.'

'My goodness,' said Miriam. 'A giant among men.'

'I don't know about that, miss.'

'But you're the man in the jersey, of course!' said Miriam.

'I am a Bonfire Boy, miss, yes.'

'A friend of yours fell at my feet and you kindly scooped him up.'

'Of course, yes, miss.'

'Bevis is just making some tea,' I said, 'if you'd care for some, Miriam?'

'Do you know, Bevis, I could *kill* a cup of tea.'

Tea served, Bevis finished work on his swill and got on with preparing breakfast for the hotel guests. The other two kitchen porters, Jake and Ben, had arrived and set about their tasks, and Miriam and I were perched with our teacups on a couple of old chairs in the corner.

'You don't know someone called Lizzie Walter, I suppose?' Miriam asked Bevis.

'Of course, miss,' said Bevis. 'Lewes is a small town, miss.'

'Everyone knows Lizzie,' said Jake. 'Terrible tragedy.'

'Dreadful unaccountable happenings,' said Ben. 'I hope they get the bastard who did it. Excuse my language.'

'That's perfectly all right,' said Miriam. 'Bastard is probably the only appropriate word in such circumstances.'

'I can think of some others,' said Bevis.

'Indeed. And how did you know her, Bevis?'

'Everyone knows her.'

'She's a teacher at the school,' said Jake.

'You never spent any time with her, or . . . ?'

'No,' said Bevis. 'I didn't.'

'I'd see her out some mornings,' said Ben, pausing in his hand-grinding of coffee beans, the aroma of which was gradually dispelling the stench of Bevis's pig feed. 'Exercising.'

'Exercising?' said Miriam.

'There're a few girls in town, miss, they've made themselves into some sort of a keep fit society. The Women's League of Health and something or other.'

'They all wear these white shirts and black satin shorts,' said Jake, who was busy slicing bread.

'That's quite a sight, first thing in the morning,' said Miriam.

'Certainly puts a bit of pep in your step, miss, that's for sure. If you don't mind my saying.'

'Not at all,' said Miriam. 'You chaps are out and about early every morning, I suppose?'

'That's right, miss.'

'And who else do you usually see up and about at this ungodly hour?'

'No one else really, miss,' said Jake.

'Well, there's always the milkman, of course,' said Ben.

'Yes, of course,' said Miriam.

'And the bakers, I suppose,' he added.

'The butchers,' said Jake.

'The greengrocers,' said Ben.

'The fishmongers,' said Jake.

'And we get deliveries of blocks of ice,' said Ben. 'From the iceman.' (The iceman. Like so many things that we took for granted, the icemen of England, dripping wet in leather and sackcloth, have long since disappeared, like the telegraph boys racing around on their bikes with the old orange-coloured envelopes in their hands, and the muffin men walking through town with their high-sided trays. It seems like yesterday, but this was all a long, long time ago.)

'It seems like Lewes is a veritable Piccadilly Circus first thing in the morning,' said Miriam.

'That's right,' said Bevis, who'd been carefully following the conversation while wiping down the kitchen surfaces with a cloth. 'A working town, for working people.' Not like the two of you, being the implication, sitting around in a hotel kitchen at all hours with nothing much to do, sipping tea.

Breakfast prepared, Miriam and I excused ourselves to go and prepare for breakfast.

'Well, it turns out there's rather a long list of potential suspects,' said Miriam, as we made our way up to our rooms.

'And witnesses,' I said.

'Good,' said Miriam. 'I always knew we'd come up with a plan, Sefton.'

CHAPTER 23

WE AGREED THAT while Miriam would set about charming the various butchers, bakers, fishmongers, greengrocers and the icemen of Lewes, in the hope of finding someone who might have seen something suspicious on the morning of 6 November, I would accompany Morley to Lizzie's school, where he had been scheduled to give a talk on the unprepossessing subject of 'Sussex: Then and Now'.

Wherever we went on our travels, Morley always insisted on visiting the local schools and colleges to deliver some such encomium or to award some prize: in many ways, schools and colleges were his natural territory. In the grand country houses and literary salons of England he was often treated as something of an adornment, or an amusement, the pet autodidact, the rare working-class specimen of the genus writer. Specialists and scholars had little time for him or his work, regarding what he produced as little more than cheap entertainment for the masses. They were not entirely wrong. R.G. Collingwood he was not, but then who now reads R.G. Collingwood? There were – I'll admit, as the author of more than one or two of them – some inaccuracies in the books. Quotations often came closer to paraphrase than they did to absolute accuracy. Broad generalisations often took the place of careful discussion. He was prepared to swoop low in his rhetoric, just as much as he was prepared to swing ludicrously high. Often humourless, and entirely lacking in satirical aim and intent, he could yet be enormously funny and piercingly keen in his insights and ideas. Children, obviously, loved him.

Mr Johnson, the headmaster of the school, was a man who rather strained towards a military bearing, I thought: ramrod, flinty, no-nonsense. Barrel-shaped, red-faced, he struck one as the sort of man who might have a full set of Blakey's in his shoes: heel plates, toe plates, dozens of treble hobs; a strider and a stamper; a strict disciplinarian; the sort of chap who prided himself on taking no nonsense, no prisoners, and little or no pleasure in anything, like so many teachers back then, sharp of tongue and dull of mind. He explained to us on our arrival, after a perfunctory handshake and welcome, that though many of the children were aware of the death of Lizzie Walter, he and his fellow teachers were not discussing the exact circumstances of her 'demise' – his word – since so many of the children had learned to swim in Pells Pool. He would be grateful, he said, if we made no mention of recent events.

'Of course,' said Morley, clearly offended that anyone would assume that he would make mention of such a terrible tragedy to young children. 'Under no circumstances, sir.'

'We don't want to put them off getting into their swimming togs.'

'Indeed we don't,' agreed Morley.

'Healthy and wholesome exercise,' said the headmaster,

jutting out his chin, puffing out his chest, and straightening his posture.

'And a sort of performance, of course,' said Morley, rather pointedly. 'Of the self, in public.' He knew a fellow spoofer when he saw one.

The talk took place in the school hall, with Morley encouraging the children to persevere, to study hard, to be good Christians and citizens: it was boilerplate stuff, yet in Morley's hands, and in front of this audience, it seemed to have an electrifying effect. There was barely a fidgeter in the hall, and no call upon the teachers to impose discipline or to remind anyone not to do this or that or the other. The children sat, cross-legged, arms folded, heads unscratched, pigtails unpulled and noses entirely untended, staring up at this man whose words they had only previously read, or heard read aloud from books and newspapers. It was as if the good Lord Himself had suddenly stepped forth from the pages of the *Children's Bible* – in tweeds, brogues and with a broad Empire moustache. Underneath it all, underneath the words and the outfit, the manner, in his speech, as in his prose, through its many varnished layers, you could still discern in Morley the figure of the child. Which of course is why children loved him: he was exactly like them.

During my many years with Morley, he spoke rarely of his own childhood and upbringing – only ever, in fact, when speaking to children. I suggested to him on a number of occasions that he should consider writing about his memories of childhood but he was always amazed at the suggestion. Surely every word he wrote stood as a testament to his childhood? There was no need for further elaboration. Like a child, he was curiously uninterested in his own past: he was somehow innocent of himself. The past made little or no claim upon him, though this morning he spoke movingly to the children of growing up in the sawmills and timber yards of Norfolk, full of energy and optimism, and how, without opportunity for education or advancement, the world had become his textbook and his teacher.

People often tried – adults, that is – to penetrate to the true meaning of Morley and his work, to try to work out what he was really all about. Because he appeared so self-contained and was not susceptible to self-revelation or to self-analysis, it meant that he could sometimes seem cool and aloof and uninterested in others. Yet the opposite was the case. He really was, very simply, like a child, a part of and yet entirely apart from the realm of adult thoughts and concerns. There was always more association than logic in his thinking, for example, his speech and his sentences that morning leaping from one to another, with the carefree joyousness of a small boy kicking a stone down the road. Capable of extraordinary absorption in a subject, he was also infinitely distractible. The children clearly recognised in him one of their own. They recognised that he was not using them for any purpose: he was simply enjoying their company.

The teachers were in fact the first to fidget. I noticed the early signs – some tell-tale eye rolling – when Morley embarked upon a story about a trip he had once made to Iceland, during which he claimed to have met the *huldufólk*, the hidden folk.

'Sussex is thick with little people like that, with fairies and stories of fairies, just like Iceland. The Pucks and the Pooks and the fairy rings on the Downs.'

The teachers began to exchange disapproving glances.

'The little people are written into the landscape in Sussex as perhaps nowhere else, children – Iceland excepted. You have Pookhill, Puxsty Wood, Puckscroft—'

A little chap put up his hand.

'Yes, young man?' said Morley.

'Pucksroad,' he said.

'Very good!' said Morley. 'What's your name?'

'Sidney, sir. Pucksroad,' he repeated.

'You live on Pucksroad?'

Sidney shook his head, suddenly aware of the sentinel stares of his teachers.

'No?' said Morley sympathetically. 'Near Pucksroad? By Pucksroad? You made it up?'

He nodded.

'Good. Good! Stand up!' said Morley.

Sidney stood, abashed.

'A plucky little chap from Pucksroad!' said Morley. 'Well done! Let's give him a round of applause.'

The children erupted into applause.

Sidney looked like the sort of little chap who was probably unaccustomed to the applause of his classmates: he looked indeed the sort of little chap who might more usually have spent much of his time being pummelled by his peers. He now beamed in the glow of their regard.

'Very good,' said Morley. 'Now, sit down, Sidney,' and Sidney sat down. 'In Iceland,' continued Morley, 'they're the *huldufólk*. In Ireland they're the leprechaun. What other names do you have for the fairies here? If you tell me, I shall write their names in a book.'

Lots of little hands shot up.

Morley picked out a young girl.

'Yes, my dear, what do you call the fairies?'

'Pharisees, sir.'

'Pharisees? As in the Pharisees?'

'Pharisees,' said the girl again.

'Wonderful.' More applause. 'Sefton,' he said to me. 'Make a note.' Which I duly did. More applause. More disapproving glances.

I noticed then that there was a sort of tapping that continued on beyond the applause. Sitting at the front of the hall with Morley, I could see what neither the children nor the teachers could, but which everyone could hear, which was the headmaster, in his gown, ramrod, flinty, no-nonsense, rocking backwards and forwards on the Blakey's on his shoes, and tapping at his watch, indicating that it was time for Morley to conclude. Morley glanced at his own watch. And then his other watch. And then his pocket watch. He had been asked to speak for half an hour. He had so far spoken for only twenty minutes. The headmaster had made a serious miscalculation: you didn't challenge Morley over time.

The next ten minutes – exactly – of Morley's talk were a bravura performance, packing in history, economics, natural history, art, science, music, agriculture, and encompassing encomiums to the Sussex lane (which are 'haunted by the ghostly swoop of the barn owl at night', apparently), the Sussex stook (a term which was entirely new to me, but which seems to have something to do with the harvesting of corn), tales of Sussex grey ladies and black dogs (which sounded similar to the tales of grey ladies and black dogs we encountered in every other county we visited, but anyway), and a tribute to the Greyhound Inn at Tinsley Green, which had hosted – who knew? – the World Marble Championship since 1932. Details about the marble championship went down particularly well with the children, all of whom solemnly vowed to practise their marble skills in time for the next championship, to bring glory to their home county, Morley leading them in a chant of 'Marbles! Mibsters! Ducks and Taws!', the headmaster's tapping effectively drowned out by the sound, which was presumably Morley's intention.

With just minutes of his allotted time to go, Morley concluded with what can only be described as an improvised prose poem on the wonders of the Sussex dew pond, which might easily have come from the lips of Edith Sitwell herself – if, that is, Dame Edith had had any knowledge of Sussex country crafts, country lore and primitive engineering. (Readers keen to experience this prose poem for themselves in all its glory, and indeed at much greater length, can do so by reading 'The Sussex Dew Pond: A Brief History' in the *Countryman*, January 1938.) Like most people, I suspect – and certainly like the children in the school hall, whose attention was, at this point, finally beginning to wander – I was unaware of the history of the construction of these very particular and peculiar Sussex structures, these 'mirrors of the Downs' as Morley described them, these 'wonders of nature and culture', these 'testaments to the skills and determination of the Sussex men and women of yore'. I had no idea, for example, that the holes, having been excavated long ago, had been laid with chalk, to be crushed by oxen and carts drawn around and around in circles, with water being continually doused upon the surface until the mush resembled a smooth thick cream and was left to harden like

A Dew Pond on the Downs

cement. Sensing that he had perhaps rather lost his audience with his story of the dew pond, Morley concluded with a final flourish, asking how many Cinque Ports there were. When came there no answer he turned to me.

'Sefton?'

'Five?' I hazarded a guess.

'Seven!' cried Morley, much to the children's uproarious hilarity, though none of us really knew why, except we were perhaps all relieved that it was over.

Very occasionally I heard Morley despair of his skills and capacities. He would sometimes repeat the criticism often made of him by others: that by lecturing and writing so much, and about so much, and so fast, with such enthusiasm and abandon, he somehow betrayed himself as essentially lacking in seriousness. His critics seemed to believe that education should be the product of pain and anguish, yet with him the work was always the product of joy. It also counted against him, even among those one might have expected to have approved – teachers, for example – that he sought only to educate the young, the poor and the undeserving. It was felt to be rather beneath the dignity of a serious writer to want to educate and encourage those who were without education and in want of encouragement. Even those who had benefited from his work in their own lives, as they continued on in their journey towards knowledge seemed to feel that he was merely a starting point or an early staging post along their journey's way. Morley and his work were therefore often abandoned and stranded in that very place that no serious middle- or upper-class writer ever wishes to inhabit: neither quite literature nor simply entertainment, destined to be merely a memory, as something one *used* to read. As he concluded his talk to the children that morning, I realised that as well as welcoming them into his world he was also simultaneously bidding them farewell.

After the talk, as the headmaster was briskly escorting us out of the school down one of those stinky, interminable and forbidding school corridors that seem to grow no less stinky, interminable and forbidding the older one gets, Morley asked if he might rest and recuperate for a few minutes before setting off again. He seemed suddenly and uncharacteristically tired.

'Yes, of course,' said the headmaster. 'You must come to my office.'

'No, no, we wouldn't want to disturb you,' said Morley. 'You are clearly a very busy man, Mr Johnson. Perhaps we might just rest in an empty classroom, if you have one,' said Morley. 'Just for a few moments.'

'Well,' said Mr Johnson. 'It would be no trouble to—'

'Ah, here we are,' said Morley, pushing open the door to what was indeed an empty classroom and stepping wearily inside, almost as though he were about to collapse. 'Perhaps I could ask your secretary to bring us some tea?'

'Yes, that's—'

'No milk or sugar for me, thank you,' said Morley. 'And my assistant will have—'

'I'm fine, thank you,' I said.

'Very good,' said Morley. 'Goodbye, Headmaster.' And he ushered him out the door and into the corridor.

As soon as the sound of Mr Johnson's footsteps had disappeared down the corridor, Morley – apparently miraculously restored to his former self – leapt up and dragged a desk across the door.

'What on earth are you—'

'No time for questions, Sefton, we've got about eight minutes, by my calculation.' He checked both his watches. 'Let's just hope the secretary knows how to make a proper pot of tea, eh? Come on, Sefton, kettle's on.'

As he explained to me later, Morley, on Molly's insistence, in an attempt to clear Henry's name, had embarked upon his own investigation into the death of Lizzie Walter, and had quickly decided that the best approach was not to seek evidence or clues of any unusual activities on the night of 5 November, but rather to study and try to understand Lizzie's habitual behaviour – thus, beginning in her workplace. There was likely to be only one empty classroom in the school we were visiting that morning, he reasoned, which would be the classroom that had been used by Lizzie. By creating a simple diversion we might have a few moments to see if there was anything interesting in her classroom. In fairness, as a plan, it made about as much sense as Miriam and I drawing up a long list of possible suspects and witnesses from among the early morning men and women of Lewes.

Our first challenge was to somehow crack into the locked stationery cupboard behind Molly's desk, a classic piece of school furniture, a big old beast of a thing, of the kind small boys have since time immemorial enjoyed locking each other inside.

'Now,' said Morley triumphantly, producing from an inside pocket a thin sliver of metal he kept concealed for just such purposes – though, alas, it turned out to be the wrong tool for this particular purpose.

'Wrong tool,' he said.

'A workman never blames his tools, Mr Morley,' I said.

'Pot's warming, Sefton,' he said, consulting his watches again. 'No time for levity. Chop chop. Where would you leave a key?'

'Under a plant pot?' I said.

'That's no good,' said Morley.

I pointed at the many plant pots lined up on the window-sill in the room.

'Aha!' said Morley.

There were no keys under the plant pots.

'So, if you had the keys and you didn't want the children to get hold of the keys,' said Morley, 'where would you . . . ?'

He reached up by the side of the blackboard and sure enough produced a keyring from a small hook, half concealed behind the frame of the board.

Within seconds, we had the stationery cupboard open, only to find that it was indeed a stationery cupboard full of stationery, rather than a clue to the inner workings of Lizzie Walter's mind. Morley became momentarily distracted by the stationery – he was an obsessive when it came to the paper and the pens and the inks and the nibs required for the smooth running of his writing business. Since I was responsible for the smooth running of the smooth running of his writing business, I too became something of an expert in such supplies: we had accounts and orders with the biggest stationers in London, Germany, Paris and Geneva. (It was also my job to update weekly Morley's endlessly updated Catalogue of Items Read, which required a very particular layout, with bibliographical references, quotations and questions, as well as the notes and a series of marginal keywords: the ledgers in which we recorded this information had to be specially imported, at great expense, from Milan.) The stationery cupboard at the King's Road School in Lewes was far from a treasure trove, but it was more than enough to fascinate Morley, and for me therefore to have to remind him of the urgency of our search.

'Mr Morley,' I said, looking at my own watch. 'I think the brew's on.'

'Ah! Yes!'

He turned towards Lizzie's desk: neat, tidy and paperless.

'Does that look like a schoolteacher's desk to you?' he asked.

Before I could answer he had jemmied open the locked desk drawers with his thin sliver of metal, which indeed was the right tool for this particular purpose. Inside, the drawers were crammed with pencils, pens and paper.

There is, alas, only one phrase to describe what we did next, though Morley would object to the cliché: we rifled through the contents of the drawers.

Mid-rifle, as the door of the classroom noisily banged into the desk that had been wedged against it, Morley lifted up the back vents of my jacket, thrust some papers into my trouser waistband, and rushed over to the door.

'Apologies!' he called. 'Apologies! Didn't want to be disturbed. Just taking a quick nap. I was quite overcome.'

The desk pulled away, Mr Johnson's secretary appeared at the open door, holding a tray with a cup of tea.

'Miss?'

'Hunter, sir.'

'Miss Hunter, thank you so much,' said Morley. 'That is so kind.'

'That's perfectly all right, sir.'

Miss Hunter gazed into the room, as if bewitched, but would not cross the threshold.

'I'll . . .' She was staring at the desk. Not at the drawers, which we had been rifling, but behind the desk, in the area in which a teacher might be seated, or standing at the blackboard.

'Ah, yes. It must be difficult, of course,' said Morley.

'This was her room,' she said.

'Yes,' said Morley. 'A terrible loss for you. For the whole school.'

'Yes.'

'Did you know her well, Lizzie? Miss Walter, I mean.'

'We used to go out together,' said Miss Hunter. 'Me and my fellow and her with hers.'

'Henry?' said Morley.

'Who?'

'Henry? The American. Son of Molly Harper, the singer?'

'No. Her boyfriend was Michael, up at the museum.'

'The man from the museum?' said Morley. 'Which museum?'

'The town museum. They'd been going out for a long time. I thought they were engaged, but you know how these things go.'

'Alas,' said Morley. 'I do. You have been most helpful. Thank you. Sefton?' He nodded to me that we should leave.

'What about your tea?' asked Miss Hunter.

'No time, I'm afraid, Miss Hunter. We have much to do in Lewes. Thank you again.'

Young scholars

CHAPTER 24

'WHEN THIS IS ALL OVER,' said Morley, spying a Welsh rare-bit being served with a cup of tea to an adjacent table, 'on our way home, we shall return to Brighton and I will treat you both to a Welsh rarebit at the King and Queen. The best Welsh rarebit in Britain, in my opinion.'

'That sounds lovely, Mr Morley,' I said.

'Brighton is boring, Father,' said Miriam.

'Brighton, boring? The Mecca of the excursionist? The rapid recuperator of the fatigued and the overworked? The lung of London?'

'It's boring, Father.'

'We almost sent you to Rottingdean, Miriam.'

'Almost,' said Miriam.

'But not quite,' said Morley.

'I rather liked Brighton,' I said. 'From what I saw of it.'

'You would,' said Miriam.

'Brighton, don't they say,' remarked Morley, 'has the look of a place that has won the jackpot and then squandered it.'

He leaned back in his chair.

'Precisely,' said Miriam. 'That's precisely why Sefton likes it.'

'While Lewes,' continued Morley wistfully, gazing around, 'wears the badge of lost innocence.'

We had reconvened in a tea shop on the High Street, where Miriam was recounting tales of her early morning rounds of the early morning tradesmen of Lewes. She had spoken to a milkman.

'Marvellous fellow!' she said.

'And did he hear or see anything—' I began.

'A terribly underrated sort of a job,' said Morley. 'Milkman.'

'Absolutely,' said Miriam. 'I was quite amazed. The chap deserves a medal, as far as I'm concerned. He fits people's false legs, first thing on his round,' said Miriam. 'Knocks them up. Gets them up.'

'Lights their fires?' asked Morley.

'And puts out fires!'

'There we are,' said Morley. 'Underrated.'

'And a terribly jolly chap. Three milk bottles in one hand, three in the other, cigarette clamped tight in his mouth' – Miriam imitated the milkman's stance and manner – 'and he was whistling, just like a milkman!'

'Whistling being traditionally associated with professions of the night, of course,' said Morley. 'Witches, prostitutes. Milkmen.'

Miriam proceeded to whistle a florid bit of Bach, and then Morley joined in. I looked around at the other customers in the tea shop, more than a little embarrassed, as Miriam took the top line and Morley experimented with some counterpoint. Thank goodness, the tune soon broke down.

'Harpo Marx is a tremendous whistler, you know,' said

Morley. 'Virtuoso really. He can hum at the same time. Lovely chap also. He was always my favourite.'

'You know the Marx Brothers?' I asked.

'Father's long corresponded with Groucho,' said Miriam.

'Eccentric, of course,' said Morley. 'But a wonderful correspondent.' There was no one, it seemed, that Morley hadn't met, or corresponded with, dined with, travelled with, or otherwise encountered on some enterprise or other. It gave him extraordinarily broad horizons – but also alas meant that he was an expert, for example, on the history and culture of whistling, much of which knowledge he had acquired from his old friend Harpo. 'I think it's in the Canaries, Miriam, isn't it, that there are communities who whistle to one another across the valleys? *Homo sibilans*, I suppose the term might be—'

I coughed loudly. I often had to try to interrupt and redirect their wandering conversations. It was an essential part of my job. The flow of words between them and around them was seemingly never-ending. Miriam of course was happy to debate with anyone anytime on anything, and Morley simply spoke incessantly, while working, while walking, standing, waiting, in transit by vehicle, on land and sea and, I rather suspected, in his sleep. On those exceedingly rare occasions when he was sick, he would continue to talk, on and on, from his bed, often to himself, and often while writing. Both Miriam and Morley also had freakish memories, seemingly accumulating everything and losing absolutely nothing, able to recall facts and quotations and remarks that people had made years before, and continually shaping and polishing every piece of information and every incident and episode into stories that could be reused for multiple purposes, in order to illustrate and illuminate some little nub. It made actually getting to the point of anything tremendously difficult.

'So, did the milkman hear or see anything unusual on the morning of the 6th?' I asked.

'Nothing, no,' said Miriam. 'But he did let me have one of these.' She produced a milk bottle from her handbag. 'Look at the legend, Father. I thought it would amuse you.' The milk bottle bore the legend, in black Gothic script, 'The Milk is Thine, the Bottle Mine'.

'Wonderful!' said Morley.

'Anyway,' I said.

Miriam had also spoken to three brothers, Bill, Bob and Bernard, one of them a blacksmith, one a saddler and one an ironmonger, again tremendous characters all of them, according to Miriam, and none of them having seen anything suspicious or unusual. *And* she'd been to a high-class green-grocer – *the* high-class greengrocer – in Lewes.

'Virginia goes there,' she said.

'Virginia?'

'Woolf,' she said. 'Sussex is absolutely stuffed full of Bloomsberries, Sefton: Leonard and Virginia are just up the road at Rodmell, there's Vanessa and her friends at Charleston.'

'We should really go and visit Leonard and Virginia,' said Morley.

'Well, they can be a bit . . . much, Father,' said Miriam, 'can't they.'

'They can,' agreed Morley. He rather disapproved of the Bloomsbury set, though he did admire the work of the

Hogarth Press and spoke very highly of Leonard Woolf's skills as a printer and publisher. 'Dear Leonard,' he said.

'Pozzo Keynes and his crazy Russian have got a place somewhere nearby,' said Miriam. 'They're great fun.'

'That's one way of describing them,' said Morley. If he rather disapproved of the Bloomsbury set, then it would be safe to say that Morley very much and very particularly disapproved of John Maynard Keynes, describing him to me on various occasions as a 'beast', a 'swine' and a 'blackguard', though in fairness many of Keynes's friends would probably also have described him as such. Keynes was a man, shall we say, in those years, with a certain reputation.

'Perhaps Virginia Woolf saw something suspicious at 5 a.m. on the morning of the 6th, when she was out shopping for her leeks and potatoes?' I asked.

'I don't think so,' said Miriam. 'She doesn't strike me as an early riser.'

Our own cups of tea arrived, *sans* rarebit.

'So,' said Miriam. 'How did you get on at the school, chaps? How was the headmaster?'

'I would describe the headmaster,' said Morley, 'as a man like Chaucer's Sergeant of the Law, who—'

'Seems busier than he is. I've heard you tell that one before, Father. Bit of a waste of time then?'

'Not at all,' said Morley. 'We know now that Lizzie had a boyfriend.'

'A boyfriend?' said Miriam. She dabbed at the corner of her red-lipsticked mouth with a napkin. 'Is that right?'

'Apparently so. Some chap at the museum. Michael. We're going to go and visit him, obviously. But first.' Morley checked around that no one could overhear us. 'Sefton?' He nodded at me.

'What?'

'Your trousers, man. Look at this, Miriam.'

'What?'

'Ah, yes,' I said, reaching round to produce the papers from my waistband.

'What on earth?' said Miriam. 'I thought you were going all Keynes on me for a moment there, Sefton. And what on earth's that in your pocket?'

'It's a stick of Brighton rock,' I said.

Miriam raised both her eyebrows.

The papers we had filched from Lizzie Walter's drawer included mostly blank sheets of paper, but also a few local newspaper cuttings, some sheet music ('Kitten on the Keys', 'Let Me Call You Sweetheart', 'O Lovely Night', and several other undistinguished tunes), and, most significantly, a copy of something called the *Blacklist*, which appeared to be a conspiratorial, right-wing sort of a journal and which contained an article by a certain 'LW' titled 'Knowledge For All'. We passed the article around. It was really rather good. 'Education should provide an equal opportunity for all to rise to the top,' wrote LW. 'I submit that knowledge should not be the monopoly of the well-to-do, but available to all our children, as part of their birthright as true-born Englishmen and women.'

'Perfectly reasonable,' said Miriam, which indeed it was, except perhaps for some references to 'foreign influences and ideas' diluting and spoiling the purity of the British educational system, and its – entirely contradictory – praise for the German model of education, with its emphasis on a sound body and a sound mind, which was claimed to be preventing national decline. I rather expected Morley to approve of the gist of the article. He most certainly did not.

During the late 1930s, Morley attracted all sorts of unsavoury characters, drawn to him by his various ideas about localism, his strong favouring of 'the common people', and his general distaste for big business and middlemen. These were the years when many good men and women – myself included – drifted inexorably towards the extremes politically, while Morley did his best to steer a steady middle course, which, as always in politics, as in life generally, cost him dearly. Throughout this time his work and his ideas were claimed by all sides and he was often accused of betraying some cause or other. His great friend Chesterton, for example, eventually disowned him, and by 1939 he was increasingly intellectually isolated and alone, particularly in his ideas about England and about Englishness. Perhaps Morley's clearest statement on the subject came in a book that he worked on continually during those years, returning to it again and again, like a dog to its vomit or a sow to its mire, but which was never published, alas, because he rather feared the effect it might have on British morale. These were the years of big books on big themes: John Strachey's *The Coming Struggle for Power*, George Dangerfield's *The Strange Death of Liberal England*, Walter Brierley's *The Means Test Man*, Gollancz's *Handbook of Marxism*.

Morley's big idea – the title of his great unpublished work was *The Invention of Britain* – was that Britain was invented, or 'confected' in his words, in order to give credibility to the Union and to sustain the Protestant religion, and that despite it all, however much we cooperated and coexisted, the Scots would always be Scots, the Irish Irish, and the Welsh forever Welsh. According to Morley, this idea – that Britain was an idea – did not invalidate the idea of a United Kingdom, but on the contrary recognised its great power as a story, rather than as a fact. Morley would often insist that the three of us debate this idea on our journeys together around the country in the Lagonda, in order for him to develop the finer points of his argument.

'I'm with Lord Acton,' he liked to say.

'We're all with Acton,' Miriam would retort.

'Sefton?'

'I'll abstain,' I usually said.

'I believe that our nation, like all other nations, is a kind of invention, a creation. No less magnificent for that, but an invention nonetheless. An act of the imagination. I like to think of Britain, indeed, as a kind of imagined community.'

'An imagined community, Father?'

'Yes, what do you think, Miriam?'

'As an idea? It'll never catch on.'

It never did catch on. His belief that Britain and the British are essentially the product of the stories we choose to tell about ourselves rather than some immutable national identity based on race, or religion or ideology, was unwelcome at the time and has remained so ever since. Morley basically believed that anyone could become an Englishman if they adopted certain habits of mind and behaviour, and if they understood certain aspects of the country's history and culture – hence *The County Guides*.

But back to Lizzie Walter's article in the *Blacklist*.

'Balderdash,' said Morley. 'If you combine a passion for education with an obsession with birthrights and an idea of national decline linked to the influence of foreigners and immigrants, I'm afraid you have a very dangerous mix indeed,' said Morley.

'Oh,' said Miriam, whose attention had shifted to the one remaining unexamined sheet of paper in our haul. 'Yes, I'm sure you're right, Father. What is *this*?'

She held up the sheet for us to examine. It was a sheet of notepaper. Quality notepaper. It appeared to be a list of women's names – about a dozen in total.

'Why on earth would she have written such a list?'

'*If* she wrote it,' said Morley. 'We don't know if this is Lizzie's handwriting.'

'But what *is* it?'

'Well, you know what it reminds me of?' said Morley, taking an innocent sip of tea.

And so Morley launched into what I now recognised as the catalogue aria from *Don Giovanni*:

> *Madamina, il catalogo è questo*
> *Delle belle che amò il padron mio;*
> *un catalogo egli è che ho fatt'io;*
> *Osservate, leggete con me–*

'Oh, that woman's dreadful influence, Father,' said Miriam.

Morley paused in his recitation, looked as though he were about to go on, but then lapsed into silence.

'What?' asked Miriam.

'Actually, I'm sure this is nothing, my dear,' said Morley, pocketing the piece of paper. 'Just some list she'd drawn up for some reason.'

'But what reason?'

'Who knows, Miriam? It's a . . . mystery. Anyway, why don't Sefton and I meet you back at the hotel in, say, an hour or so and we can wander up to the museum and talk to this boyfriend chap. In the meantime, I think Sefton and I are going to go shopping for a trug.'

'A trug?' said Miriam. 'This is no time to go shopping for a trug, Father.'

'I would have thought this exactly the time to go shopping for a trug, Miriam. The trug-makers of Sussex are renowned worldwide.'

'Are they really, Father?'

'Of course. The trug.' Morley savoured the word. 'Rectangular-shaped wooden basket, made from willow and chestnut, beloved of the lady gardener.'

'Right, yes, we all know what a—'

'Incredible craftsmanship involved.'

'In trug-making?'

'Absolutely. It would take years to become an expert.'

'Years?' said Miriam

'At least,' said Morley.

'Years, though?' said Miriam.

'Have you ever felled a tree, Sefton?'

'I can't say I have, Mr Morley, no.'

'Stacked and seasoned logs, Miriam? Split and sawn them into boards? Sefton?'

'Erm . . .'

'No, thought not. So it is probably safe to say that the pair of you have little or no idea about the manner and method of trug manufacture, would that be true?'

'No idea and care less,' said Miriam.

'Well.' Morley rose from the table. 'In an hour at the hotel, Miriam, and in the meantime Sefton and I are going to go and meet someone who does possess such knowledge and who does care.'

CHAPTER 25

'AND WHO, MOREOVER, might be able to tell us some-thing about his daughter's tragic death,' said Morley, out of Miriam's hearing, as we left the tea shop.

'Pardon, Mr Morley?' I said.

'We're going to go and talk to Lizzie's father,' said Morley.

'Right. Is that really a—'

'I have taken the precaution of making enquiries, Sefton, and it turns out that Lizzie's father is a trug-maker. Which is fortuitous, is it not, since we are simply tourists in Lewes out trug shopping?'

'Erm . . .' Sometimes I couldn't see exactly how his mind worked, though I could see that it was working. Sometimes it was better not to think about it too much.

'Not a word about Lizzie, understand? Trug shoppers, merely.'

'Very well, Mr Morley.'

Mr Walter's trug shop was a short walk from the White Hart, down a steep narrow street. The shop had clearly been a house at some time in the recent past, and in all probability was at least a semi-house still, having become an emporium of trugs with the simple addition outside of a sign and inside with an array of trugs. And arrayed they most certainly were: rectangular trugs, round trugs, square trugs, oval trugs, long shallow trugs, short fat trugs, stacked on the floor, piled on tables and chairs, and hanging from hooks in the ceiling. Morley and I manoeuvred ourselves inside with some difficulty. It was more like a trug cave than a trug shop, or a 'truggery', according to Morley, who was, obviously, completely and utterly thrilled by the place.

'Good day, sir!' he said, to a man sitting with his head low behind a table in the corner, by a fireplace lit with a poor fire. He was hunched, busy eating something, which he put aside when Morley spoke, looking up at us and slowly wiping his mouth on his sleeve.

'Is it?' he said.

'Is it what?' said Morley.

'A good day, you said.'

'Indeed,' said Morley.

The man looked out beyond us. 'A goin' to rain,' he said.

'Well, yes, perhaps, but . . .' said Morley. 'Anyway, don't let us interrupt you.'

'It's my elevener,' said the man.

'Would that be a Sussex churdle, might I ask?'

'Would be and is,' said the man.

'Liver and bacon?' asked Morley.

'And apple,' said the man.

'And do I detect sage?' Morley sniffed.

'Bit reeky?' said the man, sniffing at the churdle and then

producing a well-used handkerchief from his apron pocket and placing it carefully over the half-eaten pie.

'There. Now, can I help you?'

'Is it Mr Walter?' asked Morley.

'It is.'

(And I will tell you what I thought then, to my shame. I thought, this – a man eating a churdle – does not look like a man whose daughter has been murdered. I'm ashamed now even to admit it, years later, to admit that what I expected to find was a *grieving* man, whatever that might be, for a man or a woman who has suffered such a terrible loss, what are they supposed to look like? How are they supposed to behave? This is one of the great lies of literature, actually, one of its many illusory promises: that people can be read and understood, that they will appear as they truly are, or at least if interpreted rightly. If I learned one thing working with Morley for all those years, producing all those words together, all those millions of words of seeking and under-standing, it is this: that literature is a gigantic, terrible lie. No human can tell another human's story. No place, no person, no face ever fully reveals itself. And it is a disgust-ing assumption, actually, that they should, like assuming that a man whose daughter has been murdered will always and should always look like a man whose daughter has been murdered. Mr Walter that morning looked like nothing so much as a man hunched in the cold, in the corner of a shop, eating a Sussex churdle.)

'Excellent!' continued Morley, who always took people and places at face value. 'I am looking for a trug.'

Mr Walter simply raised an eyebrow and gestured towards

his amazing stock, as if to say, are you blind, or stupid, or both?

'Which size?' he asked.

'About . . .' Morley stretched out his arms.

'We've got everything from a pint up to a bushel, sir.'

'Something in between a pint and a bushel, I would have thought.'

'A number 6 or a number 7 then.'

He pointed up to a range of what were, apparently, number 6s and number 7s.

'And they're all willow and chestnut?' asked Morley.

'That's what a trug's made from, sir, yes.'

He got up slowly and brought down a couple of trugs from their hooks.

'And where do you get your willow, may I ask?' said Morley.

'From the marsh,' said Mr Walter.

'Of course,' said Morley. 'The marsh.'

'And the handle and the rim are sweet chestnut there. That's the traditional method. Willow strips, chestnut frame and trim.'

'Yes,' said Morley, holding the admittedly very fine trug that Mr Walter had handed him. 'Very fine, sir. Very fine indeed.'

'We do all different shapes, as you can see, as well as different sizes.'

'Well, I think this traditional shape is the one to go for, don't you, Sefton?'

'Yes,' I agreed.

'The word trug, after all, I believe, is derived from the Anglo-Saxon *trog*, meaning "boat-shaped vessel".'

'I wouldn't know about that, sir,' said Mr Walter.

'I think I'm right in saying that the trug derives from the practice in the late eighteenth century – early nineteenth century? – when people would hollow out pieces of timber to make boat shapes and fixed handles to them, for various purposes.'

'People use them to carry grain and measure out for planting mostly, sir,' said Mr Walter. 'But they did used to be made from a single piece of timber, sir, that's correct. So they could measure liquids as well.'

'Hence the pint-size trug?' said Morley.

'I suppose, sir.'

'I don't know if you're familiar with the history of the modern trug, Sefton?'

'I can't say I am, Mr Morley, no.'

'Well, I think they became popular – you'll correct me, Mr Walter, if I'm wrong – after a Mr Thomas Smith of Herstmonceux showed them at the Great Exhibition in 1851 and Queen Victoria was so taken with them she ordered several for members of the royal family.'

'I wouldn't know about that, sir,' said Mr Walter.

'Legend has it he made his delivery of trugs from Herstmonceux to Buckingham Palace in a wheelbarrow.'

'Dubersome folk, in Herstmonceux,' said Mr Walter. 'I should get back to work here, sir.'

'Yes, yes, we don't want to keep you, Mr Walter.' Morley produced his wallet. 'Yes, we're just shopping for trugs.'

'That's what brings you to Lewes?'

I saw Morley peering out the back of the shop – the front room – towards the kitchen and beyond.

'And we are writing a book about Sussex actually.'

'Are you, now? You'd make a fine oration of anything, I'd say.'

'I wonder if we might have a look at your workshop.'

'I wouldn't, sir,' said Mr Walter. 'It's a bit of a rattlebone place back there.'

'That's perfectly all right,' said Morley, who was already striding towards the kitchen and into the yard beyond. 'The more rattlebone the better.'

Out back, in a tiny yard that had been converted into a tiny workshop, a man sat shaving away at a thin board. He was knee deep in wood shavings, as though he were emerging from a sea of pink-white foam.

'Good morning!' said Morley.

The merman looked up, nodded, and went back to work.

'This is the heart of the operation, then,' said Morley to Mr Walter. We had followed him outside – what else could we do? 'The old HQ, eh? Just talk me through the process, would you?'

Mr Walter looked at me and looked as though he wasn't sure where to start, but then which of us could explain our jobs from start to finish?

'To start?' asked Morley.

'You take your sweet chestnut poles,' said Mr Walter. 'We call them batts.' He pointed towards a pile of long sticks.

'Very good,' said Morley.

'And we split them in two using a froe.'

'A froe?' said Morley.

'That's a froe,' said Mr Walter, pointing towards what looked like a long-bladed axe, leaning up by the chestnut poles. 'And a cleaving brake.'

'A cleaving brake?' asked Morley.

'Stops the poles splintering.'

'Actually, I'm going to ask my assistant to make some notes, if that's all right with you, sir?'

And this, *this* I realised was the reason for our visit, and for the whole trug-shopping expedition: before I could reach for my German pocket notebook, Morley thrust into my hands the piece of notepaper we had pulled from Lizzie's drawer, with her list of women's names upon it.

'You can use that, Sefton.'

'Are you sure, Mr Morley?'

'Absolutely sure. Waste not, want not. I think Mr Walter said a froe, Sefton. Isn't that right, Mr Walter?'

'That's right, sir.'

I wrote down the word froe, at the bottom of the page, underneath the list of names.

'Now let me have a look,' said Morley. 'I'm afraid my assistant's writing is sometimes difficult to read. Just check that spelling for me would you, Mr Walter?'

And he held the piece of notepaper before him.

Mr Walter looked at the piece of paper and happily nodded his head.

'That looks right,' he said, without hesitation.

'Just there,' said Morley, pointing to the word, 'below that list of names.'

'Yes, that's right,' said Mr Walter. 'Froe. I have my letters, sir.'

And so we had what we needed: proof that the list was not written by Lizzie, for what father seeing his recently deceased daughter's handwriting would not be shocked?

But we then had to persist for another twenty minutes in the charade of being interested in the making of a trug. Or, rather, *I* had to persist in the charade of being interested in the making of a trug: Morley really was interested, of course. I allowed my mind to drift while Mr Walter demonstrated the use of the wooden shaving horse, clamping the chestnut in and using a knife to trim the handles and the rims of chestnut to exactly the right width and thickness, and then the use of a steamer – a fire beneath an old iron drum – to bend and shape the wood for the frame, the willow boards cut and soaked and nailed into place . . . You certainly had to admire the craftsmanship.

'What's this book about Sussex then?' asked Mr Walter, as we were preparing to leave with both our trug and our newly acquired trug-making knowledge.

'It's a guide to Sussex,' said Morley.

'What sort of a guide?' asked Mr Walter.

'A guide for admirers of nature, for lovers of antiquity, and for friends of the arts,' said Morley.

'Not for the likes of me, then,' said Mr Walter.

'Well, I—'

'I'm not an educated man,' said Mr Walter.

'You must have been very proud of your daughter then,' I said, realising immediately that I shouldn't have said it.

'What?' said Mr Walter, his face suddenly contorting. 'My daughter?' He raised himself to his full height, his fists clenched. 'What about my daughter?'

'We – I – heard people saying something about . . . In the hotel.' All I wanted to do now was to get out of the place as quickly as possible, now that the man's pain was suddenly apparent.

'Get out, the pair of you,' he bellowed, 'before I throw you out!'

'I assure you,' said Morley, 'that we came here with good intentions, sir.'

'And I assure you, sir, that if I ever see you near here again I will beat the both of yous senseless. Get out!'

And so we exited, through the truggery, with our trug.

CHAPTER 26

'How was your shopping then, chaps?' asked Miriam, once we were back at the hotel.

'Excellent,' said Morley. 'Excellent. Look at this magnificent trug.'

'Hmm,' said Miriam. 'Yes. Quite magnificent, Father. Fabulous, in fact. Astonishing.'

'Now now,' said Morley.

'Was that really the best use of your time, though, Father? Trug shopping? Fiddling while Rome burns?'

'I think if you're referring to the proverbial, *apocryphal* story of Nero, Miriam, you'll find that Rome burned around AD 64, fiddles weren't invented for another millennium, and that anyway Nero wasn't anywhere near Rome when it was burning.'

'But my point still stands.'

'It would, my dear, except for the fact that we managed to make some considerable progress on important matters.'

'Which important matters?'

'I think we'll save that for the moment, Miriam. We need confirmation on a couple of things.'

'I think we might need confirmation on more than a couple of things, Mr Morley,' I said. I still had no idea in what direction Morley's investigation was headed.

'Well, let's get to the museum, shall we, have a quick word with this chap, Lizzie's boyfriend, and then we can regroup and see where we've got to?'

The museum in Lewes is by Lewes Castle, which is entered by and through a magnificent barbican which, according to Morley in *The County Guides: Sussex*, is highly sketchable. So highly sketchable, indeed, that before we entered the museum, Morley paused to sketch it.

'Look at that flint work, Sefton.'

'Indeed,' I said.

The flint work looked exactly like flint work.

One of Miriam's rules for dealing with her father, which she had explained to me when we first set out on our adventures together, was never to let him get on to flint work. There were a lot of other forbidden topics, it has to be said, ranging from anthropometrics to Ottoman history. (Notably, in the context of our trip to Sussex, we were supposed never to allow him to discuss Piltdown Man. Morley was with Ramström of Uppsala, in believing that though the skull may have belonged to prehistoric man, the jaw definitely belonged to an ape. Piltdown Man was an absolute no-no.) The trouble with Morley was that he was simply too curious about everything, which was an affliction rather than a skill or a gift, and which meant that, say, the study of flint work might easily occupy as much of his time and money as, say,

Some Highly Sketchable Flint Work

the study of world political and economic systems, or the future of farming in an age of scarcity.

'He is obsessed with blasted flint work, Sefton. Knapping, coursing, cobbling and goodness knows what else-rying.'

Back at Morley's home in Norfolk I had indeed already enjoyed many conversations with him on the subject of flint knapping, so I always did my best, wherever we were, to steer him away from flint work. On this occasion, however, Lewes Castle had caught me off-guard. From bitter experience, I knew that the only thing to do, once the subject of flint work was introduced, was to try to steer him immediately into a conversation about some other building material. Exactly which building material, and indeed what was the building, was irrelevant.

'Mmm,' I said, looking around. 'Look, Mr Morley—'

'Yes, black-glazed bricks,' said Morley, nodding towards a building, which I hadn't even noticed, to our left.

'Yes.'

'But the flint work, Sefton!'

'Yes,' I agreed. 'But what about the . . .' I pointed randomly towards the top of the barbican.

'Machicolation?' said Morley.

'Yes, exactly, the . . .'

'*Machicolation*,' repeated Morley. 'I am right in thinking that you did study history at school, Sefton?'

'I did, Mr Morley, indeed.'

'And French?'

'And French, sir, yes.'

'So, machicolation, from the French *mâchicoulis*, isn't it?'

'Yes, yes, I think so.'

'And it is therefore . . .'

'It is . . .'

'The opening between the supporting corbels of a battlement. There, see?'

I eventually saw what he was pointing to.

'Yes, yes,' I agreed.

'*Machicolation*. Through which rocks or boiling oil can be dropped on attackers at the base of the wall.'

'Lovely,' I said.

'Very common in France,' said Morley. 'Less so in England. Which is what makes it so remarkable.' He then went on to explain the differences between English and French fortifications and defensive tactics during the Middle Ages.

But at least we avoided the flint work.

Lewes Museum was housed in the Barbican House, a big red brick building, which according to the small brass plate outside was officially the home of the Sussex Archaeological Society. We entered the building through a magnificent stone-floored hallway, hung with paintings and with some rather half-hearted displays of pottery ware and old flint arrow heads in half-empty display cabinets: a typical English provincial museum. So typical, in fact, that, typically, there didn't seem to be anyone about.

'Hello?' called Miriam. 'Anyone there?' There came not a sound, not a peep, not a creak, not even the slightest museum echo. 'Hello? Anyone in? Shop?'

Morley was already venturing up the ancient staircase, taking the steps two at a time.

'This way!' he called.

'Father!' said Miriam.

'This'll be the way,' he said.

And he was, as so often – when he wasn't utterly incorrect – absolutely correct.

At the top of the house there was a vast room with great tie-beams. 'Look at the tie-beams, Sefton!' said Morley, and look indeed I did, and I can confirm that the tie-beams of the Barbican House in Lewes are truly great tie-beams. The room resembled a library, though with rather fewer books, and at the far end, working at a table with a heavy serge cloth upon it, haphazardly piled with books and papers, and looking for all the world like Dürer's *St Jerome in His Study*, though without the lion, and some years younger, and with a full head of hair, was Michael Anderson, Lizzie's boyfriend – the rather weak-featured fellow we'd already met at the dinner at the White Hart.

'I really don't see what she sees in the chap,' whispered Miriam to me.

Michael, for his part, was delighted to see us.

'Mr Morley!' he said, getting up from his chair. 'How delightful. And Miriam. And . . .'

'Stephen Sefton,' I said.

'Yes, of course, the assistant.'

'We couldn't leave Lewes without a look round the museum,' said Morley.

'Well, I am truly honoured,' said Michael.

'So you are the director? The curator of this . . . ?' asked Miriam.

'I am officially employed by the Sussex Archaeological Society, which is one of the nation's great ancient societies.'

'How old is the Sussex Archaeological Society, Mr Anderson?' I asked, reaching instinctively for my German notebook, in the full knowledge that if I didn't quickly start taking notes, Morley would soon be asking me to take a note, so I might as well start.

'We were founded in 1846.'

'Not that ancient, then,' said Miriam. 'Not that much older than Father.'

'Thank you, Miriam,' said Morley.

'We were founded after the discovery of the ruins of the Cluniac Priory of St Pancras at Southover, when the railway was being developed. You know the story of the priory of course?'

'Henry VIII decided he had the right to the priory's wealth, and Thomas Cromwell had it destroyed?' said Miriam off-handedly.

'Yes,' said Michael, with something of a snort. 'In a nut-shell I suppose that's it.'

'And how did you end up here, Mr Anderson, in this wonderful place?' asked Morley. 'You're not local? I'm not picking up the accent.'

'The house once belonged to my great-uncle, actually.'

'Ah,' said Miriam.

'But he – having no children – was succeeded by my father, who was the son of his brother, who was an 8th Hussar, reputed to be the bravest officer in the British Army.' He gave a bitter little laugh.

'Very good,' said Morley.

'And who as a young subaltern eloped with the colonel's wife. Hence me, and hence . . .'

'I see.'

'I was a teacher at the Berlitz School in Brussels for a while, and then I returned to London, where I was living in Chelsea.'

'Well done,' said Miriam.

'I then ended up in Crawley, whose only distinction is that it's halfway between London and Brighton, but it allowed me to pursue my studies.'

'Oh dear,' said Miriam. 'Bad luck. Crawley's awful.'

'I don't think Crawley's that bad, Miriam,' said Morley.

'No, no, you're quite right, Miss Morley,' said Michael. 'I'm afraid Crawley is rather Limbo-like. But, by various means, I ended up back here in Lewes. So it's a sort of homecoming, I suppose.'

'And what's your specialism, may I ask?' asked Morley.

'Actually,' said Michael, 'I'm not so much an archaeologist as a geologist. I'm a bit of an expert in flint.'

'Oh no,' groaned Miriam.

'Flint!' said Morley. 'Really? Marvellous!'

'A fellow enthusiast?'

'Absolutely!' said Morley. '*The* great sedimentary rock.'

'Lot of competition?' asked Miriam.

'A naturally occurring mineral that can be used as a weapon and as a tool?' said Morley. 'A grey shapeless shape that yet contains within it darkness and sharpness and edge? Can you name another such sedimentary rock?'

Miriam gave a loud groan.

'Do you have a cigarette, Sefton?' she asked.

'Well, you're certainly in the right county for flint, Mr Morley,' said Michael. 'The great hill called Cissbury Ring is of course one of the great repositories of flint in England.'

Miriam looked at me, appalled.

'Anyway, Mr Anderson, perhaps you'd give us a tour?' said Miriam, desperate to avoid any more flint talk.

So Michael began to show us around.

'Now, do you want to start with the shield bosses, or perhaps some brass rubbings? We have an extraordinary collection of old ankle fetters. Take your pick.'

'Be careful what you wish for,' I whispered to Miriam, who was now in full fug and furiously smoking.

'I noted your flint arrow heads downstairs,' said Morley.

'Oh yes,' said Michael. 'Plenty of flint arrow heads. But I suppose for the general public the most remarkable exhibit is probably the mummified hand of a murderess – everyone wants to have a look at that.'

'Oh, yes!' said Miriam. 'Let's have a look at the mummified hand of the murderess.'

'But if we perhaps come over here first, we have a little display – that I must say I'm rather proud of – about Togidubnus, who was a local chieftain who was friendly with the Romans . . .'

The display consisted of some handwritten documents and some black and white photographs laid out on a small green baize-topped table.

Miriam yawned.

'Downstairs, miss, there are lots of etchings and some very fine watercolours—'

'If you think because I'm a woman I'd be more interested in etchings and watercolours,' said Miriam, blowing smoke in his general direction.

'No, not at all,' said Michael. 'I just thought—'

'Apologies for my daughter,' said Morley. 'If she'd been born a few years earlier she'd doubtless have been a suffragette.'

'Ah, well, you might be interested in our little display on radical Lewes then,' said Michael, leading us towards another green baize-topped table, similarly set up with some typewritten documents and copies of engraved portraits.

'The author of *The Rights of Man*?' said Morley, indicating one of the engravings.

'Correct. Though perhaps more famous for our purposes here in Lewes as the winner of the Headstrong Book, which was an old Greek Homer awarded to the most obstinate haranguer at the White Hart evening club, where we were the other evening.'

'You don't have the original Headstrong Book?' asked Morley.

'Alas, no,' said Michael.

'That's a shame,' said Morley. 'I know just the person we might award it to.'

'Very funny, Father,' said Miriam.

'Paine's home is just off the High Street,' said Michael. 'Almost opposite St Michael's, if you want to visit. You can't miss it.'

'Oh, we shall definitely visit Paine's house,' said Morley.

'We shall definitely not,' said Miriam to me quietly.

'Now Paine I am familiar with,' said Morley. 'But these other Lewesians?'

'Oh gosh, yes, we have a tremendous radical history here in Lewes. Home to Dissenters, obviously, Quakers and Baptists, Unitarians. And Lewes Prison once housed Eamon de Valera, after the Easter Rising.'

'I did not know that,' said Morley.

'We don't have a photograph, I'm afraid,' said Michael. 'But you'll have heard perhaps of Reverend T.W. Horsfield, the historian?' He pointed at an engraving of a man who looked very much like a Reverend T.W. Horsfield.

'Ah yes, Horsfield, of course,' said Morley.

'And Gideon Mantell, the great Sussex geologist.' He pointed at another engraving.

'Discoverer of the bones of the iguanodon,' said Morley. 'Now him I do know about.'

'Yes. Born in Lewes, and made his discoveries in Cuckfield. Many of his finds are now in the British Museum.'

'How fascinating.'

'Miriam, radical Sussex,' said Morley. 'Your sort of thing, eh?'

'No women, I suppose?' said Miriam.

'I'm afraid not, no,' said Michael.

'Hmm,' said Miriam, wandering off to sulk and enjoy her cigarette in peace.

'So you're here to write one of your county books, I understand,' said Michael to Morley.

'Yes, that's correct. We are hoping to be able to travel across the county a little.'

'Well, the greatest journey across Sussex, as you know, was that taken by Charles II in 1651, escaping with Thomas and George Gunter of Racton.' Michael led us towards another green baize table, with another deadly dull display – this time of stuff vaguely relating to Charles II. 'He first crossed the Broadhalfpenny Down, Catherington Down, Charlton Down, Idsworth Down, until reaching Compton Down, and then finally through Houghton Forest and so to Amberley and eventually to Brighton.'

'Yes, an extraordinary journey,' said Morley. 'The definitive Sussex journey, one might say.'

'Or one might not,' said Miriam, who had wandered back, bored. 'Depending on one's point of view.'

Miriam looked at me and indicated that we should try to move things along.

'Mr Anderson—' I began.

'Where else would you recommend we visit in the county, while we're here?' asked Morley.

Miriam shook her head at me in disgust.

'Oh, there are so many wonderful places, and always new places to discover. I was visiting recently at a clergy house at Alfriston – I'd never been before – and which turned out to be a rare example of a fourteenth-century Wealden hall house.'

'Really?' said Miriam. 'A fourteenth-century Wealden hall house?'

'Yes, and the churches at—'

'We don't do churches,' said Miriam firmly.

'Well, Selmeston,' said Michael, 'pronounced by the locals Simson. That's rather lovely. Firle, pronounced Furrel. Alciston, which is Ahlstone. The pronunciation takes a bit of getting used to, I'm afraid.'

'Lewes almost sounds like Lose,' said Morley.

'I suppose it does,' said Michael. 'I'd never thought of that.'

'And how do you find living in Lewes?' asked Morley.

'Oh, I adore it,' said Michael. 'I rather think of Lewes as like the nation in miniature, actually. You've got the Medieval alongside the Georgian alongside the Tudor alongside the—'

'Knee bone connected to the thigh bone?' said Miriam.

'We've got the river and the racecourse, and it's an assize town, of course. I think I like it because it seems . . . untainted.'

'Really?' said Miriam, her interest piqued. 'Untainted in what sense, Mr Anderson?'

'It's a place where perhaps some of the problems and pressures brought by outsiders to the country have not reached.'

'And the sorts of problems and pressures you have in mind are?' asked Miriam.

'Well, undesirables, really, you know, the Jews and their—'

One had begun to hear a certain amount of this sort of talk. One didn't necessarily expect to hear it under the ancient tie-beams of the Barbican House in Lewes.

'Oh dear,' said Miriam, wagging her finger at Michael. 'No, no, no. I didn't realise you held such objectionable views, sir.'

'Everyone is entitled to their opinion, miss, are they not?'

'If their opinion is based on facts,' said Miriam.

'I think you'll find if you look at what's happening in London, miss—'

'Do you know the play *Sir Thomas More*?' asked Morley, who had been unusually silent for a moment, clearly gathering his thoughts.

'I can't say I do, sir—'

'It's about—'

'Sir Thomas More?' said Miriam.

'Precisely,' said Morley.

'Relevance, Father?'

'Bit of an Elizabethan obscurity, admittedly, but in the play – which I saw performed by students in London a few years ago, a really remarkable production—'

'Anyway, Father.'

[244]

'Anyway, in the play, More asks Londoners to imagine the plight of the "wretched strangers" – something like that – arriving with their children and their worldly goods at the port of London and he asks them – I'm paraphrasing here, obviously – what would you think, if *you* were the wretched stranger? To ignore the plight of the stranger, in More's words, is to display "mountainish inhumanity". It would not do for us English to be mountainish inhumane, would it?'

'It rather depends, I think, Mr Morley, if one thinks that one does more good by encouraging people to come to this country, leaving behind their own culture and ways, or whether one might do better to encourage them to remain in their own countries and work for the good of their own people.'

'And if the latter is not possible?'

'Well, I'm afraid I'm an Englishman, Mr Morley, and for me, my nation and my people will always come first. Britain first.'

'And last, with that sort of attitude,' said Miriam.

A silence descended upon the great room of the ancient Sussex Archaeological Society, as the great irreconcilable differences between us became apparent.

Morley glanced up at one of the maps on the wall.

'Regnum, I believe the Romans called it,' he said, attempting to restart and redirect the conversation. Michael, in fairness, played along, through gritted teeth.

'Chichester? Yes, Regnum, the great rural capital of England,' he said.

'And the southern terminal of Stane Street, I believe, which was one of the great ancient Roman roads, was it not?'

'That's right,' said Michael.

'The others being, Sefton?'

'The other?'

'Great Roman roads in Britain?'

'Erm . . .'

'Never mind. Romans. Anglo-Saxons. Vikings. Normans. Huguenots. Have all trod those roads, and doubtless made their homes here in Lewes, over many generations.'

'All the more reason for us to protect the place now,' said Michael.

'Again, we shall have to agree to disagree,' said Morley. He pointed to an area on the map.

'Do you know, Mr Anderson, I've always wanted to have a look at Manhood,' he said.

'I think we've all wanted to have a look at manhood, Father,' said Miriam.

'Manhood, the name of the West Sussex peninsula,' said Morley. 'Just here.'

'Lovely spot,' said Michael.

'Your West Sussex of course is never to be confused with your East Sussex.'

'Certainly not,' said Michael.

'The West with its Chichester,' said Morley, 'its Crawley, its Horsham. The East with its Lewes, its Brighton and its Eastbourne. Anyway. Speaking of manhood.' He was always liable to such unexpected swerves in conversation. 'I hope you don't mind if I ask you a personal question, Mr Anderson.'

'A personal question?'

'It's just, with the terrible tragedy of the death of Lizzie

Walter I wanted to check something. Someone mentioned that the two of you were . . .'

'Engaged,' said Miriam.

You will doubtless have heard before the expression that a person's face 'drained of colour'. Until one sees it for oneself, it's hard to believe that a face can *actually* drain of colour, but that's exactly what Michael Anderson's face did at this point in our conversation.

'Well,' he said, his face drained. 'Engaged? No. Well, I mean . . .'

'Not engaged then?' said Miriam.

'We had been stepping out together for a while, but . . .'

'Engaged or not engaged, then?' said Miriam. 'There's a simple answer.'

'We are – we were – very close,' said Michael, choosing his words carefully and speaking slowly. 'But we – drifted apart – recently.' The colour had now not only returned to his face, he had started to turn a shade of puce that would have suited a spluttering colonel in a children's comic.

'Because?' asked Miriam.

'If you don't mind my saying so, miss, I don't think that's any of your business,' said Michael.

'Perhaps the two of you disagreed on the future of fascism in this country, did you?' said Miriam.

'You've got a damned cheek, miss!'

'That's quite enough, Miriam, thank you,' said Morley, first laying a hand upon her arm and then stepping towards Michael. 'Apologies, Mr Anderson. I'm sure there was no intention to offend on my daughter's part.'

'It's absolutely disgraceful,' said Michael.

'Now. Calm, please, Mr Anderson. Can I just ask—'

'Can *I* just ask that you leave,' said Michael, squaring up to Morley.

I stepped forward and between the two men, gently pushing them apart.

'We are leaving, Mr Anderson,' said Morley, perfectly calm. 'But before we leave – we are dealing with a serious matter here – I wonder if you could tell me if you think you would recognise Lizzie's handwriting, if you saw it?'

'Again, I don't think that's any of your damned business,' said Michael. 'I have asked you to leave.'

'We are simply doing our best to establish the facts of the matter,' said Morley, 'about Lizzie's tragic death.'

'I think you'll find that's the police's job,' said Michael. 'Not some crowd of . . . outsiders.'

'We are doing our best to assist the police,' said Morley.

'I'll call them then, shall I, and they'll confirm that?'

'I am simply asking, Mr Anderson, if you think you would recognise Lizzie's handwriting.'

'Of course I would. We frequently corresponded.'

Morley produced the handwritten list of names.

'And does this look like her handwriting?'

Michael looked at the list, looked at Miriam, looked at me.

'No,' he said. 'Definitely not.'

CHAPTER 27

'WELL, I don't quite see where all that's got us,' said Miriam. 'Apart from annoying the hell out of that awful little man.'

We were back at the White Hart.

'Oh, I think it's got us quite far, actually,' said Morley.

But before he was able to explain exactly how far our unpleasant confrontation in the Lewes Museum had got us, the cook Bevis appeared at the door of the residents' lounge, where we were about to enjoy afternoon tea. He was vast and resplendent in his chef's whites.

'Sorry to interrupt,' he said, without sounding at all sorry.

'That's perfectly all right, sir,' said Morley.

'There's a bit of a problem,' he said to me.

'With the tea?'

'Have you met Bevis, Father?' asked Miriam.

'Bevis, as in the giant of Sussex legend?' asked Morley.

'We've already established that, Father. He was named after an uncle, isn't that right?'

'That's right, miss.'

'And the problem?' asked Miriam.

'You might need to come and see for yourself,' he said, again looking at me, lowering his voice, though there was no one else in the residents' lounge and so there was really no need. 'It's not the sort of thing we can talk about in here.'

'Very well,' I said, getting up.

'Right-o,' said Miriam, also getting up.

'You don't need to come, miss.'

'If you get one of us, you get all of us, I'm afraid,' said Morley, also getting up. Our encounter with Anderson in the museum had clearly put us on our guard, and forged a bond between us – a bond that was about to be tested. 'And if there's a problem to be solved, sir, the more the merrier.'

∽ ∾

'So?' said Morley, as the four of us stood out the back of the hotel in the afternoon sunlight.

'Someone's complained about a smell,' said Bevis.

'Right,' I said. 'I don't know how I can—'

'Plumbing?' said Morley. 'Super! If I'd known there were so many sewage problems in Sussex I'd have brought my equipment. Have you got a set of rods? I'm assuming you're not on a septic tank here, are you?'

'I think it's the dog, sir,' he said to me, nodding towards the Lagonda.

In the turmoil of what had been happening we'd all forgotten about Pablo.

'Ah,' I said.

'Where is he?' asked Miriam.

'I'm afraid the only place we could find to put him was . . .'

'Oh, Sefton! No! Tell me you didn't.'

'You put him in the back of the Lagonda?' said Morley.

'I'm afraid so, Mr Morley.'

'What were you thinking, Sefton?'

Morley was something of a car fanatic, a collector indeed, and a member of the esteemed RAC Club on Pall Mall, where he had only recently given a talk entitled 'Everyman's Castle: The Motor Car'. (The talk was published in the *Practical Motorist*, September 1937. His idea of Utopia, Morley writes, is 'Motopia', with everyone having the freedom to travel by car. 'God Bless Karl Benz!' he concludes. 'The People's Liberator!') Storing a dead dog in the boot of the Lagonda was clearly not his idea of how to treat a vehicle. I could see he was having to contain himself.

'In the back of a Morris maybe,' said Miriam, 'but in the Lagonda, Sefton!'

'We didn't know what else to do with him,' I said.

'We couldn't have him in the kitchen,' said Bevis.

'I thought it would be cool enough to keep him outside and . . .'

Morley and Miriam had gone over to the Lagonda. Morley indicated for me to open the boot, which I did. Miriam gasped.

Pablo in his winding sheet made for a pathetic sight, though the smell wasn't actually too bad. I think the smell was really from the hotel's bins, or its plumbing.

'Oh dear,' said Morley. 'What are we going to do with the poor fellow?'

'Can we not take him home?' said Miriam.

'Not in this state, Miriam. We'd have to get him into ice.'

'Which would melt,' I said.

'Yes, well done, Sefton,' said Miriam. 'Thank you for that. You're an expert in preservation, all of a sudden? It's you who caused this problem.'

'I'm sure he was acting out of the best of intentions, Miriam,' said Morley, who had already put his emotions aside and was busy working on the problem at hand. 'We could take him to George Bristow, in St Leonards, on the way home. If we could get him into ice. Specialises in birds, Bristow.'

'Birds?' said Miriam.

'Yes, rarities mostly. Not sure if he's much of a dog man. The black lark, the masked shrike, the olivaceous warbler. That's more his sort of line.'

'What? He breeds them, Father?'

'Breeds them?'

'The birds?'

'My goodness, no, Miriam! He stuffs them.'

'We're not having Pablo stuffed, Father.'

'Why not?'

'We have quite enough at home,' said Miriam.

(St George's did indeed boast the most extraordinary range of animals both stuffed and unstuffed: the diorama in the entrance hall would have happily graced the Natural History Museum.)

Morley was staring at the mummified Pablo.

'The problem is always decay,' he said.

'Indeed, Mr Morley,' I said, in my gravest undertaker tones.

'Dogs, birds. Cultures. I mean, even a decomposing dodo's not a lot of good to anyone, is it?'

'I suppose it's not, Mr Morley, no.'

'Certainly not to the Ashmolean, eh?'

'They had a dodo?'

'Everyone knows they had a dodo, Sefton,' said Miriam.

'Up until 1755,' said Morley, 'when they were clearing their collection of poorly preserved specimens, and out went the old thing.'

'Yes, of course.'

'You know, we could probably do him ourselves,' said Morley. 'If we got him home.'

'What, stuff him?' said Miriam.

'Yes.'

'Don't be ridiculous, Father. You're not a taxidermist.'

'I've done a mouse,' said Morley. 'I wrote an article about it, for the *Boy's Own Weekly* I think it was.'

'I hardly think that qualifies you as a taxidermist,' said Miriam. 'And it certainly doesn't qualify you to do a dog.'

'But it's the same principle, my dear. Just a matter of scale. Do you know Montagu Browne's *Practical Taxidermy*, Sefton?'

'I can't say I do, Mr Morley, no.'

'Published in numerous editions during the late nineteenth century. Excellent guide. I'm pretty sure he covers dogs. Charles Darwin hired a Guianese slave to give him taxidermy lessons, did you know?'

'I did not, Mr Morley, no.'

'And when his beloved raven, Grip, died, Dickens had it stuffed and mounted.'

'Well, you're not Dickens and you're definitely not Darwin,' said Miriam.

'You must admit Pablo would make an interesting addition to the collection, though,' said Morley.

'We are not having him stuffed, Father. And that's final.'

'We used to have everything done at Rowland Ward's. Do you remember my taking you there when you were a child, Miriam? Do you know them, Sefton, Rowland Ward's?'

'I fear not, sir.'

'One of the greats of Victorian taxidermy, Rowland Ward. Premises on Piccadilly. Specialises in big game—'

'Vile,' said Miriam.

'Not to my taste, certainly,' said Morley. 'They don't so much stuff animals as upholster them. Also, they have a terrible habit of turning things into ornaments—'

'Vile, vile. Utterly vile,' said Miriam.

'And items of household furniture: rhino-foot doorstops, zebra-legged tables, paperweight hooves and what have you.'

'Sounds . . . charming,' I said.

'Revolting and repulsive,' said Miriam.

'Any more revolting and repulsive than the plight of the poor chicken in the pot?' said Morley.

'I am not going to dignify your question with an answer, Father,' said Miriam. 'If you cannot see the difference between an animal killed for sustenance and an animal killed to become a table lamp, then really . . .'

'What about an animal killed for sustenance *and* to become a table lamp?'

'I refer you to my previous non-answer, Father. So. Anyway?'

'Yes, Mr Bristow produced a catalogue recently that included the white-winged snowfinch – difficult to believe it was found in Sussex. And the grey-tailed tattler.'

'The grey-haired warbler,' said Miriam.

'Anyway,' said Morley, 'we *could* visit Mr Bristow on our

way home and try to persuade him to do a dog. But we'd need to get this poor fellow into ice.'

Bevis was still awkwardly hanging around, clearly regretting ever having got involved with me, Morley, Miriam and the dog, but keen to help us resolve the problem.

'There's an iceman in town, but he won't be delivering till morning.'

'No,' said Morley.

'But there's always Potter's Museum, in Bramber, sir,' he said.

'Of course!' said Morley, with a sudden burst of glee. 'Good thinking, man! Potter's Museum!'

'The what?' said Miriam.

'How far's Bramber from here?' Morley asked Bevis.

'It'd be twenty miles, sir.'

'The Whatter Museum?' said Miriam.

'Closer than St Leonards?'

'Definitely closer, sir,' said Bevis.

'That's it then,' said Morley. 'Bit of a run out there, but I'm sure they'll be able to help us. And we get to include Potter's Museum in *The County Guides*. Two birds with one stone, as it were, *uno in saltu lepide apros capiam duos.*'

'What is Potter's Museum? Father?' asked Miriam.

'Wait and see,' said Morley.

CHAPTER 28

ON THE WAY to Bramber and the mysterious Potter's Museum, Miriam and Morley slipped into a game of Greece or Rome, which was one of their favourite car games, in which participants take it in turns to argue for the merits of one or other classical civilisation. ('Greece!' proposed Miriam. 'Athenian democracy!' 'Which was a very limited form of democracy,' countered Morley, 'while the Romans handed out citizenship to millions.' Etc.) It was not the sort of thing that would have made the pages of the *Journal of Hellenic Studies*, but it passed the time and got us – at least momentarily – off the subject of Lizzie Walter and Pablo, though alas Morley soon drifted back, inevitably, to the question of taxidermy.

'"I do remember an apothecary,"' he said, launching into a quote, '"and hereabouts he dwells . . . and in his needy shop a tortoise hung, an alligator stuff'd and other skins of ill-shaped fishes."'

'*Romeo and Juliet*?' said Miriam.

'Correct!' said Morley. 'Act?'

'Five,' said Miriam.

'Scene?'

'No one remembers the scene, Father.'

'Scene one,' said Morley. 'You know, the history of the hanging of stuffed alligators and crocodiles is rather fascinating.'

'Is it, Father?'

'It is if you're a herpetologist,' said Morley.

'Which you are not,' said Miriam.

'An amateur herpetologist,' said Morley. 'The symbolic meaning of the hung crocodile I think is generally believed to have been a sign and a warning about the presence of evil, and God's power to overcome it.'

'We could do with our own stuffed crocodile then, couldn't we?' said Miriam.

'Indeed. Do you know, Miriam, when we get home I think perhaps I might consider a little book on the history of taxidermy.'

'No, Father. No more plans for books.'

'We would start with the history of the preservation of animals and animal parts from the – what? – sixteenth century, I suppose, when explorers and adventurers began hauling home their souvenirs and specimens from their trips all over the world, through the history of the *Wunderkammaren* . . . The word of course derives from?'

'*Wunderkammaren*?' said Miriam. 'German? Just a guess.'

'Sorry, no, the word "taxidermy", I mean,' said Morley.

'From the Greek *taxis*?' said Miriam.

'Obviously,' said Morley. 'Meaning?'

'Arrangement?' said Miriam.

'Correct,' said Morley. 'Arrangement, and *derma* – meaning?'

'Skin?' I offered.

'All that expensive education not entirely to waste then, Sefton,' said Miriam.

We arrived eventually at what appeared to be an insignificant roadside village, which Morley claimed was Bramber, but which showed absolutely no signs of being such.

'Alas,' said Morley, as Miriam pulled over, 'I see that the villa- and the bungalow-builder has been let loose upon Sussex, as in so many other parts of the country.'

As soon as we had stopped, pretty much immediately, a deeply scowling local emerged from his bungalow on the main – the only – street.

'Is this Bramber?' asked Morley.

'You'll be looking for the museum?'

'Yes, we are indeed, sir, how did you guess?' said Morley.

'Drackly up the road, by the station and the pub.' The man pointed further up the street and then went back inside his house.

'Marvellously friendly in Bramber, aren't they,' said Morley, entirely seriously.

Potter's Museum, suffice it to say, is pretty much the opposite of the Lewes Museum. It is a small building that rather resembles a Nonconformist chapel but which announces itself with an enormous sign saying simply 'MUSEUM' and two other only slightly smaller signs, stating 'OPEN' and 'DAILY'. You approach it through a gate into a garden

The Potter Museum, Bramber

with a small fountain, some flowerbeds and some benches. The price of admission is a penny for a child, twopence for adults, and for 'ladies and gentlemen' it is 'what they please'. But what's really remarkable about the place, and what distinguishes it from the Sussex Archaeological Society's Lewes Museum, is that it is extremely popular with visitors. We had arrived late afternoon and the place was still thronged, packed with children, adults, ladies and gentlemen, locals, tourists and people who had come to Bramber on the train, all of them paying what they pleased, or what was required, with the sole purpose of visiting Potter's Museum.

The place is 'an absolute must-see', according to Morley in *The County Guides: Sussex* and as its name perhaps suggests, it features the work of a Mr Potter, Walter Potter, born in Bramber, son of the owner of the White Lion pub – and a keen amateur taxidermist. Where others may have used their skills in the art and craft of preserving animals for educational purposes, to create zoological specimens and museum displays, or to make hunting trophies, or indeed merely for ornaments, Mr Potter used his skills to make dead animals into incredible stories. The museum – a couple of rooms really – features the occasional pathetic display of some freakish two-headed lamb, and a four-legged chicken, a three-legged pig, but mostly the animals are arranged together in mahogany display cases, in tableaux depicting scenes or episodes, or illustrations of stories and tales. Thus, there is 'Monkey Riding a Goat', which features a monkey riding a goat, 'Kittens' Wedding', featuring kittens at a wedding, 'Rabbits' Village School', 'Guinea Pigs' Cricket Match', and so on, which are all self-explanatory. There are cigar-smoking, card-playing squirrels. There are rats getting drunk. There are kittens playing croquet, and a guinea pig brass band. The true Potter masterpiece, however, around which the crowds were gathered on that cool dark autumn afternoon, is undoubtedly 'The Death and Burial of Cock Robin'.

According to *A Guide to the Chief Objects in the Bramber Museum*, an excellent little guide – indeed, 'one of the finest museum guidebooks in the country' according to Morley, outdoing, in his opinion, the official guides to the Victoria and Albert Museum, the National Museum of Antiquities of Scotland, and the National Museum in Cardiff – this thing, 'The Death and Burial of Cock Robin', this piece, this artwork, whatever one might want to call it, took Walter Potter seven years to complete. The story goes that when he was a young man, reading his sister's book of nursery rhymes, he came across the famous rhyme about Cock Robin and decided to illustrate the tale. Thus, into a small mahogany display he crammed almost a hundred British birds, depicting Cock Robin's funeral cortège making its way through a graveyard. There is a parson rook, there are robin pallbearers, there is the sparrow with his bow and arrow, and of course poor Cock Robin himself in his coffin. I have never seen – you have never seen, no one has ever seen – anything quite like it.

'Marvellous,' said Morley.

'Ghastly,' said Miriam. 'Animals are not objects, Father, and should not be treated as such.'

'But these are tableaux, Miriam. They are tales. They are—'

'Frankly as repulsive, if not more so, than the display of animals as hunting trophies or examples of extinct species.'

'Are you not fascinated with the taxidermist's craft, Sefton?'

'I can't say I am, Mr Morley, no.'

'An endless source of fascination,' said Morley to himself.

'Ghoulish, odd and unpleasant is what it is,' said Miriam.

'Hardly,' said Morley.

'Pursued by the ghoulish, the odd and unpleasant.'

'I think it's rather like our own enterprise, in some ways, actually,' said Morley.

'I don't quite see how, Father.'

'Well, I wonder if what we're embarked upon is in fact a sort of taxidermy project: the preservation of a nation.'

'The what?'

'Are we not, like Mr Potter, up to our armpits, as it were, in arsenical soap, scrubbing up and scrubbing down this poor dying creature for the purposes of deconstruction and display?'

'No,' said Miriam.

'Attempting to capture the vital flame that once animated this land, to fan the vivifying sparks that remain, to bring light again to eyes grown dark, to tongues become mute—'

'Not sure about this, Father.'

'To encourage our readers to an encounter that can never quite take place, to inhabit the great historical diorama that is England . . .'

As Morley spoke, and despite Miriam's objections, I suddenly realised the horrible truth of what he was saying: that we were indeed embarked upon such a task, that England was dead and was dying, that Morley was a kind of Walter Potter, and that *The County Guides* were nothing more than a set of elaborate mahogany display cases.

The crowd who had been looking at Cock Robin had now turned and were looking at us.

'The Potter style, while certainly extreme and unusual, is not entirely original,' said Morley, to himself, to Miriam and me, and to everyone else who was now listening. 'There was a chap called Hermann Ploucquet, I believe, who was the taxidermist at the Royal Museum of Natural History in Stuttgart, who designed displays of frogs shaving frogs, and piano-playing cats, and ice-skating hedgehogs, and so on. Mid-nineteenth century, Ploucquet. So there are precedents. I think what's truly remarkable about Potter is the sheer range, is it not? The sheer audacity of his imagination, and the way in which he is clearly using these dead animals, posed as men, women and children, to remind us what we all have in common.'

'Which is what?' asked a woman standing with her young child.

'That we are all going to die,' said Morley.

'Father,' said Miriam. 'The children.'

'And so when beholding these stuffed animals what we are in fact staring at is our own inevitable fate.'

There was a moment of silence in Potter's Museum, and then there could be heard the terrible sound of crying children.

'Excuse me, sir,' said a man who came striding into the room, who had clearly been alerted to our presence, presumably by a concerned parent. 'I'm Mr Potter.'

'The son?' asked Morley.

'The grandson, actually.'

'It's very nice to meet you, Mr Potter,' said Morley. 'Your grandfather was clearly a brilliant individual.'

'We like to think so, sir, yes. Now—'

Mr Potter had obviously been intending to strong-arm us out of the museum. He was braced to usher us out – you could tell. But he suddenly did a double-take. This happened often with Morley: just as we were about to get into serious trouble, or arrested or apprehended, someone would recognise him and we would escape with a chastisement or a scolding; it was like being associated with some gangland godfather.

'Is it Mr Swanton Morley? The People's Professor?'

'It is, sir. At your service.'

'Well, we are honoured to have you here at Potter's Museum,' said Mr Potter.

'We were just passing,' said Morley.

'If there is anything we can do while you're here, sir, anything at all, just let me know.'

'There might be something, actually,' said Morley.

We wandered back out of the museum, accompanied by Mr Potter, to the great relief, no doubt, of the many weeping children and the other visitors.

'Where on earth did your grandfather manage to obtain the large number of animals he used in the displays?' asked Morley. 'It really is quite remarkable, simply in terms of volume.'

'My understanding is that he had arrangements with some local farms, Mr Morley,' said Mr Potter. 'There's a farm up near Henfield which supplied a lot of the cats, and the rabbits, I think, came from a breeder who lived up the road in a place called Beeding. But also the public brought him various items of interest.'

'Not what you know, but who you know,' said Morley.

'Precisely,' said Mr Potter.

'Speaking of which . . .' said Morley, as we reached the Lagonda, and I opened up the boot.

'Ah,' said Mr Potter.

'So, we have this poor fellow,' said Morley, unwrapping Pablo a little from his winding sheet, 'and we were wondering if you might at least be able to store him for us, until we are able to make arrangements for his . . . disposal.'

Mr Potter examined the dog.

'We wouldn't normally, Mr Morley.'

'No, of course not.'

'But since it's you, sir, that's not a problem.'

'Thank you, Mr Potter! That is really very much appreciated.'

'In fact, if you would like,' said Mr Potter, 'we would probably be able to work on him for you.'

'You mean you would . . . ?'

'I don't have all the necessary skills myself, sir, but there are people in the village who knew my grandfather and who assisted him, and who help us maintain the collection. It requires a very unusual set of skills, you see. One has to be something of a craftsman as well as a scientist.'

'And an artist, of course,' said Morley.

'Exactly, sir. In terms of how to paint the inside of a nose, or to colour a tongue.'

'Ugh,' said Miriam.

'People often don't realise, miss, but beyond the simple art of preservation, taxidermists also need to be barbers and woodworkers, all sorts. I'm sure everyone in the village would be honoured to work on a project for you, Mr Morley.'

'Well, it is my daughter's dog, actually, and I don't think she's keen, I'm afraid.'

Miriam was looking sadly at poor Pablo and his strange Bedlington features.

'Father was thinking of doing it himself,' she said.

'I wouldn't necessarily advise that,' said Mr Potter. 'Though of course it is growing in popularity as a hobby. Ladies are becoming particularly keen to master the art. Feminine taste and skill can be brought very effectively into play when it comes to taxidermy.'

'Is that right?'

'I think so, miss. Certainly, from our experience here, it seems women as much as men love to collect and mount their own specimens.'

'That makes sense,' said Miriam.

'A buck's head in the dining room, say,' said Mr Potter. 'Or a pretty bird in the parlour.'

'Mmm.'

'We'd take good care of the dog, miss.'

'I'm sure you would,' said Miriam. 'It's very kind of you. Perhaps I'll think about it.'

'Very good, miss.'

'And in the meantime . . .' said Morley.

'We can take care of the dog in the meantime, Mr Morley, yes.'

'I do appreciate that,' said Mr Morley. 'Very much.'

I assisted Mr Potter in unloading Pablo, and then we were ready to depart.

'Well, an amazing place,' said Morley, shaking hands with Mr Potter. 'I'm so glad we could make it. We shall certainly tell all our friends.'

'Very good, sir.'

'Do you happen to know Herbert Wells?' said Morley.

'Herbert Wells? No, I don't think so,' said Mr Potter.

'H.G.,' said Miriam wearily. 'H.G. Wells, he means.'

'The writer?' said Mr Potter.

'Yes, writer, socialist, futurist, amateur historian, amateur scientist—'

'Amateur everything,' said Miriam, making a face in my general direction. 'Sound familiar?'

'A man of insatiable curiosity,' said Morley.

'I don't know H.G. Wells, no, Mr Morley,' said Mr Potter.

'Well, anyway, I think Herbert would absolutely love it here.'

'He's quite odd,' Miriam whispered to me.

'I'll definitely tell him to look you up. He published a short story a few years ago, in the *Pall Mall Gazette*, I think it was. "The Triumphs of a Taxidermist". You didn't happen to come across it?'

'I don't think so, no, Mr Morley,' said Mr Potter.

'In the story, there's this taxidermist, who is sitting up late at night – somewhere between his first glass of whisky and his fourth – when a man, in Wells's memorable words, "is no longer cautious and yet not drunk".'

'I am certainly familiar with that state, Mr Morley,' said Mr Potter. 'Our family being publicans.'

'Ah yes, very good. Anyway, in the story, Wells's taxidermist muses upon his craft. He boasts that there is no man who can stuff like him: elephants, moths, everything. He also claims to have stuffed human beings – chiefly amateur ornithologists – though of course this is merely Wells being witty.'

'Hilarious,' said Miriam.

'I believe there are examples of stuffed humans in museums,' said Mr Potter.

'Really?' said Morley.

'Though the museums in which they reside are not anxious to exhibit them or publicise their existence,' said Mr Potter. 'As you can imagine.'

'Indeed. The preparation would be exactly the same as for a gorilla, though,' said Morley, 'would it not?'

'Yes, or a large antelope,' said Mr Potter.

'Gentlemen, please!' said Miriam. 'The thought is quite horrid.'

'I don't know about that,' said Morley. 'I wonder in fact if it might ever become a viable alternative to burial. Stuffing one's relatives?'

'Father! That's disgusting.'

'Is it though, Miriam? I can't see the problem, in many ways. In fact, wouldn't it be rather wonderful if you could keep all your dear ones by you once they're dead and gone? You might even have them fitted up with clockwork, in order for them to be able to do things. Couple of coats of varnish and they'd last for years.'

Morley was someone who was always prepared to allow his imagination to roam where others might not dare to go. It was a part of the secret of his success. He simply allowed himself to dream and his thoughts to roam.

'Father!' said Miriam. But Morley was now too far gone in his musing.

'The human body is a paradox, you see, reminding us both of the presence and the absence of the self, reminding us that we wander through our lives untouched and untouchable, as through a habitat diorama, or perhaps as the figures on Keats's Grecian urn. "Bold Lover, never, never canst thou kiss,/ Though winning near the goal – yet, do not grieve;/ She cannot fade, though thou hast not thy bliss,/ For ever wilt thou love, and she be fair!'"

'Not following you there, Father.'

'No,' said Morley, who had a far-off look in his eye.

On the way back we took a short detour via somewhere called Chanctonbury Ring, where the view was, admittedly, remarkable. Down below us was the village of Washington, and Arundel Castle, and the spire of Chichester Cathedral. To the north, Box Hill, Leith Hill and the Hog's Back, to the east the Devil's Dyke, and Wolstonbury and Poynings. To the south, Cissbury and the sea.

Morley was unusually quiet.

'Everything all right, Father?' asked Miriam.

'Not really, Miriam. I think I may have worked out what happened to poor Lizzie Walter.'

'Really?' said Miriam. 'How? What? When?'

'There are just one or two more things I need to check,' he said.

CHAPTER 29

ON MY TRAVELS with Morley I often found myself in towns and in cities late at night or early in the morning and rather at a loss. What does one do in a town like Lewes when you can't sleep? It was a problem I never seemed to face in London: then again, it was the sort of problem that made for fewer problems.

I found myself in the cool of that morning, standing smoking in the churchyard behind St Michael's Church on the High Street. It was a rather lovely spot: a weeping willow, a nice view of the Castle Keep, Tom Paine's house. You get to appreciate a place early in the morning, even in the cold and the dark: Lewes, I realised, sits in a kind of shallow hollow, surrounded by hills: Firle Beacon, Mount Caburn, Mount Harry. It feels secure and permanent.

Early mornings are deceptive.

Morley came striding past.

'Good morning, Mr Morley,' I called to him.

He seemed neither startled nor surprised.

'Good morning, Sefton!'

'Early start?'

'I have been for a walk, Sefton, a good long walk, to mull

things over. Up and over Mount Caburn to Glynde, from Glynde to Ringmer and then from Ringmer over the hills to Lewes again.'

'That sounds like quite a walk.'

'There was a lot of mulling to be done, Sefton. But yes, it was a super route. You should try it.'

'Perhaps I shall.'

A milkman came rattling past, three bottles in each hand, cigarette clamped in his mouth. Miriam's milkman. Morley whistled a cheery hello in greeting. The milkman whistled back and carried on his way.

'Come on,' said Morley. 'Let's walk together. I have done my thinking and have reached my conclusion.'

'Your conclusion?'

'About Lizzie's death.'

'Right,' I said.

'There's good news and there's bad news, I'm afraid.'

'Well, shall we start with the good news?'

'I say good news . . .' Morley tutted, as if scolding himself. 'I was on the telephone last night to an old friend, Bernard Spilsbury. Do you know him?'

'I can't say I do, Mr Morley.'

The iceman was unloading ice outside the fishmonger's.

'Good morning!' said Morley.

'Good morning, gents.'

'Pathologist – the Brighton trunk murder cases? The blazing car murder? Brides in the bath? Dr Crippen?'

'They certainly ring a bell,' I said.

'He's the best in the country, Bernard. I wanted to check something with him. It was something you said.'

'Something I said?'

'You said that when you pulled the poor girl from the swimming pool there was a something around her neck?'

'Yes. It looked like a shoelace.'

We passed the baker, the butcher, the window cleaner, and greeted them all.

'The shoelace,' continued Morley, 'is what made everyone think it was murder. Yet the doctor assigned to the case here – I spoke to him yesterday evening – told me that if the girl had been strangled he would have expected a deep groove in the neck.'

'A deep groove?'

'Precisely. Dreadful, I know. But they found no indications of such a groove, or indeed of asphyxia. Which rather casts doubt upon the possibility that she died by strangulation. Nor was there evidence that she had been subjected to forceful sexual intercourse.'

'Thank goodness,' I said.

'But . . .' Morley paused and stopped walking.

When out in the country he could not spot a bird's nest, a squirrel, a mouse or indeed almost anything else without commenting upon it. There was not a ditch he would not pause to examine, forever seeking frogs and tadpoles and admiring every variety of fern and grass. But when in town, if anything, it was worse. He liked to stop at every shop. He had paused now outside a shop selling basketware.

'They also sell dog leads,' he said. 'Look. And paraffin, for stoves.'

'Very good, Mr Morley,' I said.

'Hooks, chains, ropes. I wonder if it was at one time a chandler's?'

'I don't know. You were saying?'

'I was?'

'About Lizzie?'

'Oh, yes. Lizzie.'

Lewes's high-class greengrocer drove past in his van, bringing his provisions, ready to serve Virginia Woolf and the rest of Sussex's artistic crème de la crème.

'She was pregnant,' said Morley.

'Lizzie?'

'That's correct.'

'Oh God.'

'Indeed.'

'So, you think . . . ?'

'I rather fear Henry will be charged with her murder, yes. On the assumption that the child was his and they argued and . . . A shoelace has been found in his possession that matches the shoelace around her neck.'

'Dear me,' I said. 'So you think he killed her when he learned that she was pregnant?'

'Oh no. I don't think for a moment that Henry killed her, Sefton. It's just proving that he didn't that's the problem.'

I knew exactly how to prove that Henry didn't kill Lizzie – to get Miriam to confess that she had spent the night with him. But I had given my word.

'It's hardly our problem, though, Mr Morley, is it? That's a matter for the—'

'I promised Molly I would do anything I could to assist her in proving her son's innocence before leaving Sussex. Anything.' He looked quite forlorn. 'There's one last thing left I can try, Sefton, if you'd like to accompany me. I may need your support.'

CHAPTER 30

WHAT YOU FORGET is the smell of the houses back then: the smell of coal, and the smell of paraffin, the all-pervasive smell of damp, from the cold and from the condensation. And you forget about the sheer endless drudgery of household chores, the clothes boiled in a copper, the food cooked on the old ranges that had to be constantly blackleaded, and the mangles, the oil lamps, the hearths, the doorsteps forever to be whitened. The old feather beds, even, that you had to retick, rubbing soap inside to stop the feathers coming through. It was never-ending, and it was awful. The good old days weren't just times of great hardship. They were appalling. Years after the completion of *The County Guides*, I would receive letters from people harking back to the good old days, recalling their memories and praising the England that we knew then and we wrote about, and how things were no longer the same. And I would always think, do you really want to go back in time?

The front door of Lizzie's parents' house opened to the red brick-floored living room, the kind of red brick floor that people used to rub with another brick to clean. There was a rag rug, a big old black coal range on which the cooking was done, and opposite, against the wall, a long black settle. And that was it. Leading out back you could see a tiny larder, with a little stone slab on which the milk was kept, something wrapped in brown paper. There were also a couple of earthenware crocks and the remains of something hanging on a hook in the ceiling.

Mrs Walter, Lizzie's mother, was doing the ironing by the range on a worn wooden board. She took up her iron, spat on it to check the heat and then proceeded.

'We won't disturb you for long, Mrs Walter. I can see that you're busy.'

'That I am,' said Mrs Walter.

'Shall we?' Morley nodded towards the settle.

Mrs Walter nodded and continued with her chores.

Morley had very little grasp, to be honest, of the working and domestic lives of ordinary people. Though from the very humblest of beginnings, at St George's he now enjoyed the assistance of a housemaid, a cook, a gardener and a gardener's boy. At one time he also employed a gamekeeper and a chauffeur. The cook was up to light the kitchen range at five every morning. The housemaid would set the fires and lay breakfast and bring water to the bathrooms for the washbasins. The laundry was taken once a week in its wicker hamper to the washerwoman in town, and there was always someone available to clean the lamps, and the cutlery, and the shoes, and to generally sweep and polish and dust. Having come from nowhere, he had successfully created for himself the life of an Edwardian country gent. Mrs Walter's life was the opposite. You could certainly understand why Morley was a classical liberal. And you could certainly understand why Mrs Walter and her daughter might have turned to fascism, communism, or any other -ism.

We had introduced ourselves as school inspectors.

'But we're not school inspectors,' I'd said to Morley.

'Did we or did we not inspect Lizzie's school when we were there?'

'In a sense,' I said. 'Insofar as we ransacked her desk.'

'There we are then,' said Morley.

'I cannot begin to imagine your grief, Mrs Walter,' he said.

Mrs Walter spat on her iron and said nothing.

'I wonder if you might be able to help us with something.' Nothing.

'We came across this note, Mrs Walter, in your daughter's desk drawer at school.' Morley produced the note with its list of names.

Mrs Walter appeared entirely uninterested.

'I believe this note, Mrs Walter, may have been responsible for driving your daughter to the most extreme of measures.'

'What sort of a note?' said Mrs Walter.

'It is a note containing a list of women's names.'

'And what's that got to do with Lizzie's death?'

'We think it might be a list of Henry Harper's lovers.'

I looked at Morley, startled. This, presumably, was one of the things he'd concluded on his long morning walk.

Mrs Walter carried on ironing.

'We wonder, Mrs Walter, if perhaps Lizzie felt she had no one to turn to, that she was sent this note, that she felt she was being mocked and that she therefore . . . But we would only be able to prove that if, for example, she had left a note.'

Another note? The note listing Henry's lovers and—

'You mean a suicide note,' said Mrs Walter.

'That's right,' said Morley.

'I told the police, there was no note.'

'I know what you told the police, Mrs Walter. But I wonder if perhaps you might have misplaced it or overlooked it?'

'I told the police there was no note.'

'If there were a note,' said Morley. 'If it were to find its way into our hands it would be possible for us to present it to the police, along with this note, and no questions would be asked.'

'What difference would it make?'

'Well, if it were the case, Mrs Walter, that your daughter had . . . was . . . a suicide, then an innocent man would be going to prison – and indeed in all likelihood would be facing the death sentence – for a murder he did not commit.'

'An innocent man?' she said.

'That's right. Henry Harper.'

Mrs Walter had finished her ironing, which she piled up next to us on the settle. She wandered out back into her larder, took a rough-looking biscuit from the earthenware jar and poured herself a cup of milk – breakfast, presumably – and stood looking at us. She offered us nothing. She looked at us as if we were her sworn enemies.

'You people have no idea.'

'I don't know which sort of people you mean by that, Mrs Walter.'

'You people.'

'Which people?'

'Educated people, with your operas and your theatres, coming into town. There's nothing in it for any of us, is there?'

'But Lizzie was involved in the staging of the opera at the Hudsons',' said Morley.

'She had ideas above her station,' said Mrs Walter. 'And look where it got her.'

'Mrs Walter,' said Morley, 'do you know—'

'Do you know how long my family has been in Lewes?'

'I don't, Mrs Walter.'

'Four hundred years. How long have you been here?'

'A couple of days,' said Morley.

She snorted in derision. 'Well, you've had your fill. I think it's time you went.'

Morley and I got up to leave.

'We know that Lizzie was pregnant, Mrs Walter,' said Morley.

'You do, do you? You think you know everything, don't you?'

'No,' said Morley, 'but—'

'And what does it matter to you, that she was pregnant?'

'It . . . I—'

'Do you know what it would have meant to her?'

'Being pregnant?' said Morley. 'Bringing a new life into the world and—'

'It would have meant she'd have lost her job. After all those years of study. And what would he have done, do you think? Stood by her?'

'I'm sure Henry Harper is a man of honour, Mrs Walter.'

'Ha!' Mrs Walter spat out a bitter laugh. 'He's a rich American is what he is. Drifted in here, working on some . . . thing for a couple of months. Lizzie meant nothing to him. She was just a bit of fun for him.'

'I'm not sure that's true, Mrs Walter.'

'Are you married?'

'I was . . .'

'I've been married twenty years. I know what you're like. You're all the same. You're worse than dogs.'

'I do not know what happened between Henry and Lizzie, Mrs Walter,' said Morley. 'But I do know that whatever happened, Lizzie was terribly disappointed with Henry and that her . . . actions may have been intended to punish him, but I'm not sure that she would have wanted him to go to prison, and possibly hang.'

'And you'd know her mind, would you?'

'I know that in order for justice to be seen to be done, justice must be done, Mrs Walter – not injustice.'

'And I know that oftentimes people like you get away with murder.'

'Even if it wasn't murder?' said Morley.

A boy came clattering down the stairs. He was perhaps six or seven years old. He was dressed in a thin woollen jersey and a pair of ill-fitting shorts. He looked vaguely familiar.

'Good morning, Sidney,' said Morley.

It was the boy from King's Road School. Lizzie's little brother?

'Good morning, sir,' said Sidney.

'How do you know this man, Sidney?' asked Mrs Walter, furious.

'He was at school.'

'And Sidney did himself proud, Mrs Walter,' said Morley. 'Everyone deserves a chance. Isn't that what your daughter had devoted her life to?'

'Goodbye,' said Mrs Walter, indicating the door.

We lifted up the latch – by means of an old shoelace – and stepped outside.

Morley took a deep sigh as we set off down the street.

'Well, we did our best, Sefton.'

As we were about to turn onto the main street, Sidney ran up to us and gave us an envelope.

'Here,' he said. 'From Mother.'

And then he ran off happily down the street, kicking a stone as he went.

CHAPTER 31

HENRY WAS RELEASED from police custody after the unexpected emergence of Lizzie Walter's suicide note. According to a report in the local newspaper, Lizzie had attempted to asphyxiate herself before drowning in Pells Pool. There was no mention of the anonymous note listing Henry's lovers, or of the shoelace found in Henry's pocket, or indeed of Lizzie's having been pregnant.

There was much jubilation at Henry's release. He made it to the Hudsons' just in time for the first night of *Don Giovanni*, which was considered by all to be an absolute triumph.

After the show, back up at the Hudson house, where there was a grand celebratory party, at which wine and good humour were flowing, the cast were surrounded by well-wishers and admirers. Molly was signing programmes. I thought I'd get mine signed, as a sort of souvenir of our time in Sussex. She was still in her Donna Anna costume and wearing her stage make-up, which gave her a bawdy, mutinous sort of a look. Her manager, Giacomo, was standing close by. The Hudsons, proud patrons of the arts, were hovering, laughing, chatting. Everybody was there.

Everyone was having a good time. I joined the throng swirling around Molly and she happily, absentmindedly signed my programme with her loopy handwriting, quite unEnglish. I recognised it instantly.

She said nothing to me, and turned immediately towards another young man waiting to meet her in the crowd.

Morley didn't come to the performance.

'What happened to your father?' I asked Miriam. 'He's not here to support Molly?'

'No,' said Miriam. 'It's rather odd, given their great – or should I say terrible – friendship. What do you think's happened, Sefton?'

'I don't know,' I said, which was not true. 'But I think I'm going to head back to the hotel. I'm tired. Shall I leave you the Lagonda?'

'No,' said Miriam. 'You take it, I'm sure I'll persuade someone to drop me back, Sefton.'

'I'm sure you will,' I said.

Out the back of the Hudson house, where the cars were parked, I found Henry smoking and laughing and talking with a young woman – she was perhaps eighteen. Local. One of the other stagehands.

'Sefton!' he said, calling me over.

The girl said something out of my hearing, and hurried back inside.

He ground out his cigarette as I approached.

'I hear from Mother that we owe you and your boss a debt of gratitude.'

'Hardly,' I said.

'Come on,' he said, lighting another cigarette and patting me on the back. 'English modesty.'

'Not really.'

'Buddy, look. I do appreciate what you did. If there's anything I can ever—'

'I'm not your buddy,' I said.

'Hey,' said Henry. 'Just trying to be friendly.'

'But I'll tell you what you can do: you can be a little less friendly in future.'

'What?'

'You know what I mean,' I said.

'I'm not sure I do.'

'You had Lizzie,' I said. 'You had Miriam. And I see you've already got yourself another lined up.'

'Oh, right!' he said, laughing. 'All's fair in love and war, yeah? We are staging *Don Giovanni*, after all.' He thought it was hilarious.

I could feel my fists clenching.

'First, I doubt you've been to war,' I said. 'Second, you clearly have no idea of the meaning of love. And third, if you're really so fucking stupid you can't tell the difference between life and art, then you're even more stupid than you look.'

'I don't know what's wrong with you,' he said, 'but I'll tell you what, buddy, you really need to cool it.'

I could imagine him saying exactly the same to Lizzie, her confronting him in the heat and excitement on Bonfire Night, finding herself powerless in the face of his cool American superiority, and her rushing away to Pells Pool, perhaps having planted the shoelace in his pocket, and then tying the other around her neck as a kind of token, and abandoning herself to her fate.

'I'll tell you what, *buddy*,' I said. 'Why don't you fuck off back to where you came from.'

He grabbed me by the lapel.

'Easy,' I said.

'Don't you ever talk to me like that again,' he said. 'You cheap piece of English shit. I do what I want, with whoever I want, whenever I want.'

'The American Dream, eh?' I said.

As his grip tightened and his face contorted I reached into my jacket pocket, found exactly what I was looking for, and thrust my right arm up, swift and hard.

You'd be amazed at the damage you can inflict with a stick of Brighton rock.

Back at the hotel I was surprised to find Morley in the bar, nursing a glass of water with ice and listening disconsolately to a swing band who called themselves the Meteor Quartet.

'Not bad,' he said, 'but alas not quite as meteoric as their name perhaps suggests.'

They were playing what Morley referred to, disapprovingly, as 'gutbucket' blues, meaning, I think, that they were making a particularly sorry sort of sound; which indeed they were, but which seemed appropriate, Morley being in an uncharacteristically sombre sort of a mood. He said very little while I made my way through a couple of consolatory glasses of whisky, except to complain that the band were 'barrel-housing', which was again something of which he heartily disapproved. Exactly where he acquired these sorts of terms I wasn't sure; although I recall that in one of his most extraordinary articles, in something called *Upbeat* magazine, in March 1934, 'Why They Call Him Satchmo', he describes how he had met Louis Armstrong on a number of occasions, and that they had discussed Debussy, race and laxatives.

'Rather limited, xylophonically speaking,' he said, as the band struck up another tune.

'Pardon?'

'Xylophonically speaking, not the best,' he said. 'If you listen.'

I listened to whatever it was, which sounded to me like any other jazz standard, though perhaps with a little bit of added jingle.

'It's supposed to be "Dance of the Octopus", by Red Norvo,' said Morley. 'A xylophone classic. Not so much dance as a bit of a lumber.'

'How did you know?' I asked, on my third whisky.

'How did I know what, Sefton? About Red Norvo and the "Dance of the Octopus"? It's a very popular tune.'

'How did you know that Lizzie had killed herself?'

As he spoke, Morley kept his gaze upon the Meteor Quartet.

'The list of names that we found, Sefton, since we established it was not written by Lizzie, was clearly written by someone wishing to cause her pain and humiliation, in an attempt to warn her off.'

'But that wouldn't necessarily have led her to kill herself.'

'No, but she was a young woman, Sefton, who had lived here all her life, who had worked hard to become a teacher

– an example to young people – and who clearly held herself to the highest standards of personal conduct and public duty. She had been abandoned by her fiancé.'

'Michael Anderson.'

'Correct. And had fled into the arms of an unsuitable lover.'

'Henry.'

'That's right. Who, I assume, also rejected her on learning of her pregnancy.'

'And so she—'

'I think she used her body, Sefton, as a final reminder to the men in her life that she was not to be forgotten or underestimated. It came to me at Potter's Museum, that grim tourist destination *memento mori* . . .'

'I think I know who sent the note to her, Mr Morley,' I said.

Morley held up his hand, as Miriam approached our table and the strains of 'Dance of the Octopus' faded away.

'No more, thank you, Sefton.'

Miriam, fresh from the Hudsons', proceeded to cheer Morley with a discussion of the work of Mr Red Norvo, compared to the work of Teddy Brown, Lionel Hampton, Rudy Starita, Sid Plummer and Chick Webb, all xylophonists of note, apparently, about whom I knew little, if anything. (At St George's Morley had a vast collection of musical instruments, including a collection of xylophone-type instruments, not one of which I could tell apart from another, but which were apparently as different as, say, a trumpet from a cornet from a flugelhorn. God save a man who visited the music room at St George's and mistook a vibraphone for an octarimba.)

At the end of this discussion – to the accompaniment of the band's version of 'Star Dust' – Morley made a surprise announcement.

'We're leaving tomorrow,' he said.

'But are there not lots of other places on our Sussex itinerary?' asked Miriam, who was drinking a cocktail, and who was clearly settling in for the night.

'I'm tired of Sussex,' said Morley.

Miriam looked at me and raised her eyebrows triumphantly.

We sat in silence through 'Bugle Call Rag' and 'Lady Be Good' and then the xylophonist left the stage, presumably for refreshments. Banging sticks on sticks is no doubt thirsty business.

'Come on, Father,' said Miriam, taking Morley's hand.

'Miriam!' protested Morley.

'It's our big chance,' she insisted. 'Our big break into the world of showbiz. We're going tomorrow. Let's show these boys really how to kick out, shall we?'

The two of them got up onstage. Morley spoke to the bandleader, and promptly stationed himself behind the xylophone: he looked bizarrely businesslike, like a priest preparing to celebrate Mass. I had heard his xylophone playing before: after his morning exercises he often liked to limber up with a few scales and hymns. If you've never been woken to the sound of 'Will Your Anchor Hold in the Storms of Life', then don't.

I thought for a terrible moment that Miriam was going to start singing. Miriam's talents were almost but not *quite* endless, ending exactly at around the point at which she would occasionally break into some Gilbert and Sullivan, or some weird *chanson française* she'd managed to pick up on her foreign travels, and at which sound even the cats and dogs at St George's would flee. In fact, to my great relief, rather than starting to sing, she leaned over and spoke a few words to one of the band members, who, grinning, and to my horror, handed her his – I think I am right in saying that the right word is – banjolele. The only banjolele tune anyone knows – apart from 'My Little Stick of Blackpool Rock' – is 'The Window Cleaner', with its lyrics chronicling exactly what a window cleaner gets to see on his window-cleaning rounds, and it occurred to me that Miriam might indeed launch into the song, perhaps encoring with some other bawdy celebrations of what Morley liked to refer to as the body's 'lower stratum'. I wouldn't have been at all surprised if she had, but I was completely and utterly astonished at what in fact followed.

The bandleader counted in, the band struck up, and Miriam went scorching through a set of three or four numbers, soloing on 'It Don't Mean a Thing (If It Ain't Got That Swing)' and ending with a barnstorming performance on 'Sophisticated Lady'. She seemed almost possessed, her fingers moving at a speed and with a rhythm and fluency I had never seen.

'My God, Miriam!' I said when she came offstage, and had made her way back to our table, amid the cheers and applause of the audience.

'I had no idea you could—'

'No,' she said. 'You didn't. Please do not underestimate me, Sefton. It really doesn't suit you. I saw Henry, by the by, on the way out of the Hudsons'.'

'How was he?'

'Not the best, actually,' said Miriam.

'Oh dear.'

She leaned close to me and whispered in my ear. 'If you ever do anything like that again, Sefton, you'll have me to answer to. Do you understand? And if you think that by that sort of show of bravado you were defending poor Lizzie Walter's honour, I have to tell you, you were far too late.'

It wasn't Lizzie's honour I was defending.

The Martyr's Monument

CHAPTER 32

LEAVING LEWES, we made a brief detour to the Martyrs'
Memorial, a granite obelisk that stands in a garden on
the Cuilfail Estate, upon which the following words are
inscribed:

IN LOVING MEMORY OF THE UNDERNAMED
SEVENTEEN PROTESTANT MARTYRS, WHO, FOR
THEIR FAITHFUL TESTIMONY TO GOD'S TRUTH, WERE,
DURING THE REIGN OF QUEEN MARY, BURNED TO DEATH
IN FRONT OF THE THEN STAR INN – NOW THE TOWN
HALL – LEWES, THIS OBELISK, PROVIDED BY PUBLIC
SUBSCRIPTIONS, WAS ERECTED A.D. 1901

DIRICK CARVER, OF BRIGHTON.

THOMAS HARLAND, AND JOHN OSWALD,
BOTH OF WOODMANCOTE.

THOMAS AVINGTON, AND THOMAS REED,
BOTH OF ARDINGLY.

THOMAS WOOD (A MINISTER OF THE GOSPEL)
OF LEWES.

THOMAS MYLES, OF HELLIGLY.

RICHARD WOODMAN, AND GEORGE STEVENS,
BOTH OF WARBLETON.

ALEXANDER HOSMAN, WILLIAM MAINARD, AND
THOMASINA WOOD, ALL OF MAYFIELD.

MARCERY MORRIS, AND JAMES MORRIS (HER SON)
BOTH OF HEATHFIELD.

DENIS BURCIS, OF BUXTED.

ANN ASHDON, OF ROTHERFIELD.

MARY GROVES, OF LEWES.

'AND THEY OVERCAME,
BECAUSE OF THE BLOOD OF THE LAMB, AND
BECAUSE OF THE WORD OF THEIR TESTIMONY, AND
THEY LOVED NOT THEIR LIFE EVEN UNTO DEATH'
REV. XII. II (R.V.)

We took the road from Lewes to the sea, through
Kingston, Ilford, Rodmell, Southease, Piddinghoe and on to
Newhaven.

Morley was subdued. He seemed exhausted.

Whenever we left a county, there was for him always a
sense of grief, of loss, that we had not encountered all we
could have encountered, or discovered all we could have
discovered. This time, as we drove through Sussex, the
sense of loss was overwhelming.

'We never made it to Hurstmonceux, then,' he said.

'Well, never mind, Father,' said Miriam.

'Or Battle.'

'Where did the Battle of Hastings take place, Sefton?'
asked Miriam.

'Hastings?'

'Sefton!' cried Miriam. 'That hoary old chestnut. The Battle of Hastings occurred on a ridge several miles to the north-east, in the place we now call . . .'

'Battle?' I said.

'Correct.'

'No matter,' said Morley. 'We'll not now see Battle.'

'As it were,' said Miriam. 'Or perhaps we have already seen it, Father.'

'Or Rye,' said Morley.

'Ditto,' said Miriam. 'And home to?'

'Lots of people,' I said.

'Come on, Father. Rye? Home to, most notably?'

'Henry James,' said Morley.

'A very large head, Henry James,' said Miriam. 'I think I would have preferred William, on the whole. Or Alice.'

'Pevensey Castle,' continued Morley, in his mournful listing of the many good things of Sussex that had gone unseen. 'The birds' egg collection at Hastings Museum.'

'The birds' egg collection at Hastings Museum, Father?'

'One of the great birds' egg collections in the world.'

'I'm sure it is.'

'Tarring,' said Morley.

'Tarring?'

'Famous for its figs.'

'Famous, Father?'

'Commonly believed that Thomas Becket planted the first fig trees there. Perfect climate.'

'Oh well, next time,' said Miriam.

'And Worthing, of course, the centre of the country's tomato-growing industry – we never made it to Worthing.'

'Too late in the season now anyway.'

'But it would have been nice to have seen the tomato fields.'

'Well, we may have missed the fallow tomato fields and the figless fig trees of Sussex, Father, but I think we got a pretty good sense of the place, don't you?'

Morley gazed out at the countryside and was silent.

It meant nothing to me at the time, but over the years I have come to recognise Morley's sense of grief and of missed opportunity as we toured the English counties. All those places. All those people. It seems more than likely that I too shall never now make it to Tarring, or to Rye, or to Hurstmonceux, or to Pyecombe, home of the finest shepherd's crooks in the country, or the village of Robertsbridge, home of Gray-Nicolls cricket bats. Or indeed East Grinstead, the home of Sackville College, haunt of ancient peace. I know them only through the pages of *The County Guides: Sussex*, composed and written by our divers hands, in libraries, in grief and in shame, and elsewhere.

'Do you know, Sefton,' said Morley, as we approached Brighton, 'if I could live anywhere in the world I think I might live in Sussex.' (For the record, he also told me during our years together that if he could live anywhere in the world he would live in Bedfordshire, Berkshire, Buckinghamshire, Cambridgeshire, Cheshire, Cornwall and etcetera, all the way through to Wiltshire, Worcestershire and Yorkshire in all its Ridings. And this doesn't include all the places in Scotland, Ireland and Wales where he would have wished to live. I think Dumfries and Galloway came out top, overall, over all the years.) 'Withyham,' he said, 'near Crowborough. If I could live anywhere in the world it might be Withyham. A nice church, a good inn, close to Buckhurst Park.'

Again we drove in silence under darkening skies.

'Sussex light,' said Morley after a while, staring at the far horizon. 'Might make an interesting little book.'

'I'm sure it would, Mr Morley,' I said.

'Sussex light. Quite exceptional,' he said. 'It's to do with the chalk. Very interesting, chalk.'

'Is it, Father?' said Miriam.

'There's an artist, Ravilious,' he said. 'Do you know him, Sefton?'

'I can't say I do, Mr Morley, no.'

'We have a couple of his at home. He captures that chalky underlay of the light,' said Morley, 'that light that lies between things.'

Brighton appeared up ahead. Morley continued staring out towards the sea.

'During the thirteenth and fourteenth centuries the sea inundated large areas of the Sussex coastland,' he said. 'And then of course other areas silted up, leaving us with what dear old Kipling calls "Our ports of stranded pride". Rye. Old Winchelsea, disappeared. Even Pevensey Castle was once surrounded by the sea.' He sighed. 'Nothing lasts, Sefton, is perhaps what shapeshifting Sussex reminds us. Nothing – and no one.'

In all our years together I don't think I ever heard him come quite so close to admitting to personal feelings for someone.

Miriam dropped me on the seafront. The pair of them were going to motor back to London and then up to Norfolk. I'd decided to spend a day or two in Brighton before heading back up to meet them and to start work on *The County Guides: Sussex*, which would largely be a cut and paste job from other sources: each book had its own unique process of composition; each its own sad story.

I went down to the beach. The blue-green swells were heaving against the pebbled shore, just as in Arnold's poem, making a noise very much like the long withdrawing of a weary army. In the distance white sails leaned against the horizon. It was far too cold to consider swimming, except at the risk of one's life.

I took off my clothes and plunged into the water.

I swam out for perhaps a hundred yards and then turned and looked. From this distance, I was surprised to say, England looked pure and untainted. You could almost imagine that all was not lost.

ACKNOWLEDGEMENTS

For previous acknowledgements see *The Truth About Babies* (Granta Books, 2002), *Ring Road* (Fourth Estate, 2004), *The Mobile Library: The Case of the Missing Books* (Harper Perennial, 2006), *The Mobile Library: Mr Dixon Disappears* (Harper Perennial, 2007), *The Mobile Library: The Delegates' Choice* (Harper Perennial, 2008), *The Mobile Library: The Bad Book Affair* (Harper Perennial, 2010), *Paper: An Elegy* (Fourth Estate, 2012), *The Norfolk Mystery* (Fourth Estate, 2013), *Death in Devon* (Fourth Estate, 2015), *Westmorland Alone* (Fourth Estate, 2016), *Essex Poison* (Fourth Estate, 2017) and *December Stories I* (No Alibis Press, 2018). These stand, with exceptions. In addition I would like to thank the following. (The previous terms and conditions apply: some of them are dead; most of them are strangers; the famous are not friends; none of them bears any responsibility.)

50 Watts, Kobo Abe, Giorgio Agamben, Brian Aldiss, Ali al-Du'aji, Haifaa al-Mansour, Wes Anderson, A-WA, Richard Ayoade, Jean-Michel Basquiat, the Blind Boys of Alabama, Michael Bond, the Bookshop Band, Owen Booth, Anthony Bourdain, Lili Brik, Jean-Anthelme Brillat-Savarin, the Bris-

ley Bell, Build an Ark, Cabinet Magazine, Orly Castel-Bloom, CB Editions, Aimé Césaire, Beth Chatto, Jeremy Clarke, Joshua Cohen, Stephen Connolly, Mike Coupe, Dalkey Archive Press, Frédéric Dard, Liz Dawn, Mary Denvir, the Dial House, The Dø, the Doobie Brothers, Danny Dreyer, Ross Edgley, Charles W. Eliot, Elmham Surgery, Equiknoxx, Mohammed Fairouz, Chet Faker, *Fauda*, John-Paul Flintoff, Floating Points, Nils Frahm, Simone Giertz, Natalia Ginzburg, Emma Goldman, Michel Gondry, Gramatik, Ayelet Gundar-Goshen, Ed Hands, Nick Harkaway, Jim Harrison, Charlotte Higgins, HM Tower of London, Chas Hodges, Michael Hofman, Hooverphonic, Michael Hughes, Sean Hughes, Shabaka Hutchings, the Institute of Economic Affairs, Shirley Jackson, Astrid Jaekel, Alejandro Jodorowsky, Velly Joonas, the Joubert Singers, Kersti Kaljulaid, Laura Kampf, Mark Kermode, Sam Leith, Larry Levan, The Lifeboat, Little Georgia, Michael Luck, David Markson, the Vladimir Mayakovsky Museum, Samar Samir Mezghani, Ferdinand Mount, Ben Myers, Mike Nichols, Larry Norman, Martha Nussbaum, Iona Opie, Shelly Oria, Lawrence Osborne, Peter Osborne, Over the Rhine, Nick Parker, Mark Pawson, Tom Petty, Zbigniew Preisner, Quantic, Dorit Rabinyan, the Railway Tavern, Randomer, Rabbi Danny Rich, Shan Sa, Ryuichi Sakamoto, Peter Sallis, Dominic Sandbrook, Luc Sante, Habib Selmi, Tony Servillo, Anoushka Shankar, Michael Shannon, Simon Shaps, Viktor Shklovsky, Nikesh Shukla, Christopher Skaife, Jaz Skaife, Edward Soja, Son Lux, Sons of Kemet, Paolo Sorrentino, Harry Dean Stanton, *Swagger*, The Tangerine, Ayelet Tsabari, Robert Twigger, the Ulster Independent Clinic, the University of Reading, the University of Westminster, Emma Warnock, Jocko Willink, A Winged Victory for the Sullen, Heinz Wolff, the Wolseley, Woodkid, Evie Wyld, Shifu Yan Lei, Howard Zinn.

PICTURE CREDITS

THE NORFOLK MYSTERY

IAN SANSOM

The first of

THE COUNTY GUIDES

Quaint villages, eccentric locals – and murder!

Professor Swanton Morley needs help writing a
history of England, county by county. His assistant
must be able to tolerate his eccentricities – and
withstand the attentions of his beguiling daughter,
Miriam. Stephen Sefton is broke and looking
for an adventure.

The trio begin the project in Norfolk, but when
a vicar is found hanging from Blakeney church's bell
rope, they find themselves drawn into a fiendish plot.
Did the Reverend really take his own life,
or was it . . . murder?

DEATH IN DEVON

IAN SANSOM

The second of

THE COUNTY GUIDES

Cream teas, school dinners and satanic surfers!

When Swanton Morley is invited to give a speech
at Rousdon school, he, his daughter and his assistant
pack up the Lagonda for a trip to the English Riviera.
But when the trio arrive they discover that a boy
has died in mysterious circumstances . . .

Join Morley, Sefton and Miriam on another
adventure into the dark heart of 1930s England,
as they follow up a Norfolk mystery with a
bad case of . . . death in Devon.

WESTMORLAND ALONE

IAN SANSOM

The third of

THE COUNTY GUIDES

**Great lakes, dead poets and a
mysterious crime!**

Swanton Morley sets off to continue his history of
England, accompanied by his daughter and assistant.
But when the gang are stranded in Appleby after a tragic
rail crash, they find themselves drawn into a wild world
of country fairs, gypsy lore and wrestling. And then
a woman's corpse is discovered at an
archaeological dig . . .

Catch up with Morley, Miriam and Sefton as
they journey along the Great North Road and the
Settle–Carlisle Line into the dark heart
of 1930s England.

ESSEX POISON

IAN SANSOM

The fourth of

THE COUNTY GUIDES

**Pipers, gangsters and a fishy case of
food poisoning!**

October 1937. Swanton Morley, the People's Professor,
sets off to Essex to continue his history of England, *The
County Guides*. Morley's daughter Miriam continues
to cause chaos and his assistant Stephen Sefton
continues to slide deeper into depression
and despair.

Morley is an honorary guest at the Colchester
Oyster Festival. But when the mayor dies suddenly
at the civic reception, suspicion falls on his fellow
councillors. Is it a case of food poisoning?
Or could it be something far more sinister?